Praise for ...
Chr...

"Christmas in Silver ... plex mystery to be so... ...d of story!!!"
—*Night ... Reviews*, Reviewer Top Pick!

"Fun, flirty, a little spooky, and super sexy... Terry Spear strikes exactly the right balance between sexiness and emotional resonance."
—*Fresh Fiction*

"A wonderful story that illustrates the best of holiday romances...a howling good time."
—*Long and Short Reviews*

"Spear's wonderful gifts as a writer [are] on clear display... The story is thrilling, containing edge-of-your-seat action."
—*RT Book Reviews*

"Delicious, intense, and charming...a wonderful holiday read."
—*Anna's Book Blog*

"'Tis the season werewolf style...a fun blend of warm fuzzy with romantic suspense."
—*Delighted Reader*

"Terry Spear once again delivers... Well-written, entertaining, and all around an incredible read."
—*BTS Reviews*

"A nonstop action-adventure story that will keep readers turning the pages till the final Christmas surprise is revealed."

— *CK2S Kwips and Kritiques*

"A roller-coaster ride of mystery, intrigue, and wolfy love… Terry Spear is a masterful storyteller."

— *HEAs Are Us*

"The characters are well developed, charismatic, and colorful; the premise is evenly paced with interesting twists; the romance is sexy and cute."

— *The Reading Cafe*

"Spectacular… I loved the story line and how Terry was able to write a story based during the holidays."

— *Book Lovin' Mamas*

"A complete, adventure-filled romance overflowing with the best of what keeps me addicted to books by Ms. Spear."

— *Long and Short Reviews*

Also by Terry Spear

Heart of the Wolf

Heart of the Wolf
To Tempt the Wolf
Legend of the White Wolf
Seduced by the Wolf

Silver Town Wolf

Destiny of the Wolf
Wolf Fever
Dreaming of the Wolf
Silence of the Wolf
A Silver Wolf Christmas
Alpha Wolf Need Not Apply

Highland Wolf

Heart of the Highland Wolf
A Howl for a Highlander
A Highland Werewolf Wedding
Hero of a Highland Wolf
A Highland Wolf Christmas

SEAL Wolf

A SEAL in Wolf's Clothing
A SEAL Wolf Christmas
SEAL Wolf Hunting
SEAL Wolf in Too Deep

Heart of the Jaguar

Savage Hunger
Jaguar Fever
Jaguar Hunt
Jaguar Pride

A *Very* JAGUAR CHRISTMAS

TERRY SPEAR

sourcebooks
casablanca

Published by Sourcebooks Casablanca, an imprint of Sourcebooks, Inc.
P.O. Box 4410, Naperville, Illinois 60567-4410
(630) 961-3900
Fax: (630) 961-2168
www.sourcebooks.com

Printed and bound in Canada.
MBP 10 9 8 7 6 5 4 3 2 1

I've written over sixty novels, and yet, sometimes I get so stuck on a story that I wonder why my muse has abandoned me. Thanks to Donna Fournier for pulling me out of the dark abyss this time! What did I need? Snow for Christmas! And the perfect place for snow is Minnesota!

Prologue

Costa Rican rain forest

EVERETT ANDERSON COULDN'T GET A BREAK DURING this mission, no matter how hard he and his fellow JAG agent tried. He and Matt Bruskrud were pinned down yet again while attempting to reach five-year-old Lacy Heartwood, one of the girls who regularly stayed at Everett's mother's day care. Before the Christmas holidays, Lacy had been stolen from her parents' cabana in a rain forest resort in Costa Rica.

Since Everett and Matt were already nearby in Costa Rica after completing another JAG mission, they got the emergency call from headquarters. They'd quickly located Lacy's father, Ted, who'd pursued the kidnappers, and sent him back to the resort to protect his wife and other children. Because Everett and Matt knew the family, *this* was personal.

The smallest of the triplets, Lacy had been carried ten miles into the rain forest. Since she was a jaguar shifter like they were, they'd given strict orders to her distraught mother not to shift, or Lacy would too while she was with the kidnappers.

"Can you see them?" Matt whispered as they finally caught up to the kidnappers and crouched behind ferns and a fallen tree.

"Twelve o'clock. Three of them. I'm going to the right."

"As a jaguar?"

"Yeah. They won't see me and won't be expecting it."

"I've got your back."

Of the two men, Everett was the faster runner, both as a human and as a jaguar, and Matt was the better shot, so they always worked missions like this.

"If anything happens to me, take care of Demetria for me, will you?" Matt said.

"If I don't make it out in one piece, tell my family I love them," Everett said, then stripped.

They said the same farewell message before every high-risk operation. It was as much a good luck charm as anything. Everett stripped and called on the ability to shift, his body warming throughout, and then he was standing on all four paws, claws retracted until he needed them. He circled around the kidnappers like a jaguar on a hunt, silent in the noisy rain forest. The birds and monkeys warned each other of the jaguar stalking his prey.

Everett glided through the rain forest in stealth mode, powerful muscles rippling, golden fur covered with black rosettes that made his whole body blend in with the fluttering, leafy shadows.

His body brushed against the raindrop-covered plants, the steamy air filled with the scent of water and the intoxicatingly rich floral fragrances of plumeria and the ylang-ylang tree as he made his way to where three men were lying in wait. He saw another man deeper in the rain forest, holding on to Lacy. She was tiny for her age, a wisp of a strawberry blond, wearing a flowery pink-and-orange shirt and pink shorts and sandals. The only thing missing was the set of fairy wings she nearly always wore.

Everett's jaguar coat gave him the advantage of the element of surprise. Jaguars were known to avoid people, and no human would suspect a shifter rescue. The disadvantage? All four men were armed with guns, so trying to kill them as a jaguar would be nearly impossible. If he leaped at one of the men, all four would no doubt jump up to protect themselves, and Matt would get the two Everett didn't take out. At least that was the plan.

Everett lined himself up, judging the distance and calculating the strength he needed to reach his target. He smelled the air, locating each of the four men and Lacy, and not finding any other scents of man in the area. He crouched, preparing himself mentally, and sprang through the air, lunging for the nearest bearded man. The kidnappers didn't react until the man holding Lacy shouted a warning—but the man's partner was too late. Everett slammed into his target, taking him to the forest floor, and swiped at his head to break the man's neck with one powerful swing of his jaguar foreleg and paw.

Another of the kidnappers jumped up and readied his rifle to shoot Everett, but a single shot rang out from Matt's direction, and his target collapsed to the ground a few feet from Everett. The other ambusher turned his rifle on Matt, while the man holding Lacy fired several rounds at Everett. Unable to fight the man, Everett couldn't do anything but leap into a tree, then jump to another and another until he was well out of sight of the shooter. But he had to come back for Lacy and take out the man holding her. With all the gunfire coming from Matt's direction, and none from the kidnappers', Everett suspected that Matt had gone after the other man.

Everett made his way back to Lacy as silently as before. She watched the trees like a good little jaguar would, knowing he'd return for her. She'd seen him and recognized him. But she knew not to alert the man holding her hostage. Glad to witness the other man dead on the ground, Everett reached a tree close enough to jump from. He leaped through the air and onto the hostage taker's back, his wicked claws digging in for purchase. Crying out in terror, the man instantly released Lacy, and she darted out of the way. The man collapsed to the ground and Everett struck him with his paw, killing him instantly.

Lacy was crying when Everett nuzzled her, hating that anyone would scare her like this. She threw her arms around his neck and sobbed. Everett purred softly, soothing her, until she released his neck and he licked her salty tears away. He lay on his stomach and growled softly. She climbed onto his back, and he carried her to where he'd left Matt, her arms wrapped tightly around his neck. He was worried that Matt hadn't come to their aid. But maybe he'd remained quiet, not calling out, in case more kidnappers were around.

The adrenaline was still pumping through Everett's blood and his heart was beating hard, anxiety washing over him in waves as he ran to Matt's location. His face pale, Matt was lying on his back, blood pouring out of his side, his fingers pressed hard against his wound, and he was groaning in pain.

Sick with concern, Everett lay on his belly and Lacy climbed off. Then he shifted, threw on his boxers, and seized the medical pack lying on the ground near his clothes.

"Matt." Everett yanked out bandages, trying not to fumble with them, as anxious as he was.

"Don't bother," Matt gritted out. "I'm not going to make it. Get Lacy out of here."

"I'm not leaving without you." Everett tore open Matt's shirt. It was bad. As much as he hated to admit it, Matt was right. He wouldn't make it.

"Get her home, Everett. I–I should have told Demetria I was going to marry her. I was going to for New Year's. I know you've had your differences. But…" Matt coughed up blood and took in several shallow breaths. "I want you to take care of her. Tell her I love her. Tell her I wanted to stay here in the end. This is home for me, much more so than Dallas. She knows it. Tell her no regrets."

"Hell, man. Demetria would kill me if I left you here."

Matt seized Everett's arm with what little strength remained. "Get. Lacy. Home."

With tears in his eyes, Everett nodded. He'd never thought he'd consider leaving a man behind on a mission.

"I mean it, Everett." Matt glanced at Lacy. "You have to get her back to her parents safe and sound."

Everett knew he did. Matt didn't have any family of his own back home. Everett's family had been Matt's, and then there was Demetria MacFarlane. But despite Matt's request, Everett couldn't leave him behind.

He quickly dressed, fixed a harness for Lacy in front, and packed Matt's wounds the best he could. Then he carried Lacy against his chest and Matt in a fireman's carry, determined to get his partner to the extraction point and back home again. Everett couldn't live with the notion that not only had his friend died, but Everett had left him alone in the jungle.

Matt died an hour later. Five hours after that, Everett reached the extraction point, although he'd never thought they'd make it out alive. It was bad enough that he'd lost a friend who had been like a brother to him growing up, but now he'd have to tell Demetria—the woman Everett loved but had no claim to—that her best friend and lover was dead. He didn't think anything could be worse than that.

Chapter 1

A year later—Dallas, Texas

EVERETT ANDERSON TOOK A SEAT IN THE JAG GOLDEN
Claws' large training hall where Martin Sullivan, director for the special forces group, was meeting with his
agents to discuss a new training mission.

The hall was decorated for Christmas, the tree standing in one corner decorated with jaguar angels, each with
a name inscribed, that represented their fallen agents
from years past to the present. It brought home the fact
that for the past two Christmas parties, Matt hadn't
been there to celebrate the holidays with Everett and
their fellow agents. Looking at the tree, Everett felt the
loss all over again.

Martin lifted the mike off its stand, though he didn't
need to use it, as commanding as his voice was. "Some
of our agents are currently out on operations, so we'll
have to rotate them through this new training when
they return. But we've had some tasks lately that have
required mixed teams from the Enforcer, Guardian,
and Golden Claws branches of the Service, which has
resulted in some difficulties.

"Because we've had a few incidents of 'them against
us' between branches, we're going to pair agents from
our branch with those from other branches on these
training missions to ensure that our teams function

better together. That way, we can get along when future needs arise that require a mixed team. Some paired-team missions have done just fine. Golden Claws Everett and Huntley Anderson and Melissa Overton teamed up with two Enforcer agents and briefly had met with two Guardians to deal with abandoned jaguar shifter cubs and their parents who had been taken hostage in the rain forests of Costa Rica. That's the kind of teamwork we want to see."

Everett Anderson knew which two teams Martin was talking about when he referred to the ones that hadn't worked out. In one case, an Enforcer had been paired with a Guardian who demanded that the Enforcer take kidnappers to be tried instead of killing them on sight. The Enforcer wasn't about to do that because the kidnappers had tried to kill him and the Guardian several times during their pursuit. The disagreement nearly got both agents killed. In another case, on a mission in Belize, a JAG agent had fought with an Enforcer about who should be in charge, wholly compromising the job and nearly ending their lives. The ability to work together was a serious concern for the branches.

No matter which branch they served in, all agents had the same basic training in weapons, combat maneuvers, martial arts, and survival, but then each branch had specialized training. For some, loyalty to their own branches became deeply ingrained.

They had to learn to compromise to get the job done in the best way possible, keeping team members and those they were rescuing safe while taking down the rogues.

"I've set up a roster, pairing each of you with your teammates for the next assignment. These are real case files, and your actions will be tested and graded. In addition to this, each of the branches is creating mixed teams that will teach all of our agents how to work well with other branch agents. We already have one team so far—Guardian Tammy Anderson, now married to JAG David Patterson. They worked so well together that they've joined forces to train our people. The other branches are getting their assignments as I speak and should be on their way to join us. We start first thing this morning. If you have any questions or problems with your new mission, come talk to me in my office."

The Service needed its agents and worked hard to train them properly for assignments, so Everett knew just firing agents who didn't work well with other branches wasn't the solution.

Most everyone in the meeting room nodded in assent. A few grumbled. There were always those who didn't like change.

Everett was eager to see who he was paired with. He was hoping it was the two Enforcer brothers he'd worked with on the abandoned cubs assignment in Costa Rica. He liked the way the brothers thought and believed he could learn more from them. But he suspected the boss wouldn't want him paired with someone he'd worked well with before. He'd never worked closely with a Guardian, so maybe he would be teamed with one of them this time. He just hoped it *wouldn't* be Demetria MacFarlane. Not that he didn't *want* to be hooked up with her—in a lot more ways than on training missions—but he was conscious of her need for space after what had happened to Matt.

Hell, speak of the devil. Demetria entered the training

hall with her best friend—his sister, Tammy. Demetria looked as hot as ever in a black suit, the jacket cut smartly but unable to hide her curves, and high-heeled boots that looked like lethal weapons.

She looked totally professional on any job she did, but he'd seen her around his sister enough to know how amazing Demetria looked when she was wearing a lot less clothing. Like the red bikini she'd worn in the hot Texas sun while playing with his sister in his parents' swimming pool. That had made him wish he was playing right along with them. But she'd been dating his best friend, Matt, and Everett knew he would have embarrassed himself if he had gotten anywhere near her, as strong as his attraction for her was. He swore that if he and Matt had been pure jaguars rather than shifters, he would have fought for the right to have her as his mate. But his human side had dictated common sense.

Martin cleared his throat, and Everett turned his attention to the task at hand.

"I want this to work, folks. We need it to work. Us against the bad guys. Not agents against agents."

Though each agent freely chose his or her branch of assignment, some took the aptitude testing to heart and went to work with the branch they felt they were best suited to. Enforcers took out the trash, permanently. JAG agents did everything, but most of them preferred going after the bad guys. Guardians removed jaguars and shifters from bad situations and provided them with a safe haven.

When Everett looked up the roster on the computer at his training desk, he saw his partner was Howard Sternum, a badass Enforcer. So much for getting to work with a Guardian this time. Everett caught the boss's eye. He nodded once, and Everett knew that he'd been assigned a teammate who *wasn't* a team player with other branches because of Everett's own reputation for working well with others.

Everett rose from his chair and saw his new partner heading his way across the training hall. Howard was muscular, with black hair and blue eyes, a square jaw, and a brooding expression. The man's chilly eyes caught Everett's gaze and held, challenging him. Everett figured the guy had deep-seated issues about something, but he wasn't going to let Howard's attitude get in the way of the mission.

Tammy, an instructor and one of the graders for this mission, cast a dark look at Howard. He smirked at her, appearing just as ominous.

"Good luck, Everett," Tammy said as she handed him the assignment. She gave Howard another scathing look, then stalked off to hand out more assignments.

"Your sister's hot," Howard said.

"She's mated." Everett opened the envelope containing their instructions.

"Doesn't make her any less hot."

Everett ignored Howard, realizing the guy was already itching to start a fight. He knew enough to drop the subject, even though he wanted to slug the Enforcer. He read the instructions to himself and knew why Tammy had given him this job. Brayden Covington, stepson of Lucian Covington, was a teen headed for trouble. They'd been called to step in before, but the director of the Guardian branch had agreed the stepdad could take his son back—with the provision that he took care of the boy like he was supposed to. But this was the third call, and at this point, Lucian didn't have any recourse.

One of the agencies had to take the boy in. Usually the Guardian branch would, but even the JAGs had been known to take in wayward shifter teens and turn them into shifter agents with a real cause. He knew because his half sister, Maya, was married to one. And Wade Patterson's brother, David, had been taken in at the same time.

Everett read the note out loud. "We have to take a teen, Brayden Covington, into custody and—"

"Like they need anyone from the Enforcer branch to deal with a teen issue?"

True, Howard probably wasn't needed. But that was the point of the mission—to teach agents from the various branches different techniques in handling different kinds of cases.

"His stepdad, Lucian Covington, hasn't been taking care of the boy. Financially, yes. But no discipline at all. Kind of hard to do when Lucian's out drinking and gambling all night. So Brayden's been running with a group of human teens who are juvenile delinquents. His biological dad died ten years ago. Brayden's mom died the first of the year in a hit-and-run accident, so Brayden's been on his own since then, and he's not making the right choices."

"Great."

A man raised his voice several feet away, and Everett and Howard turned to see what the matter was. Everett didn't recognize the redhead, but Demetria was facing him down, hands on her hips and frowning at the guy.

No matter how many times he observed her, Everett still saw her as an incredibly sexy brunette, curvy, with killer moves and a quick temper, but with a loving heart for kids of all ages. She hadn't dated since Matt died in the Costa Rican rain forest, and Everett didn't think she'd ever get over Matt's death.

With her long hair pulled back into a ponytail, she focused her dark-brown eyes on the man in front of her, her body posture balanced. She looked ready for action.

Everett wanted to help if she needed his assistance, but he knew that stance. She was a wild cat, ready to take down the big male who was giving her grief. All the agents were highly trained, so no advantage to Demetria there. And the redhead was ready for her reaction, so she couldn't surprise him. Because of his size and weight, he most likely would have the upper hand. That meant Everett was tensing and getting ready to charge in and protect her—regardless of whether she needed him or wanted him to. Who would know until after the altercation ended? Everett didn't want to see her hurt.

Hell, a dozen guys were probably just as ready to protect her, but he didn't have eyes on anyone else—just Demetria and the redhead.

"Now, that's a woman I'd love to team up with." Howard folded his arms across his chest, looking on with admiration.

"Her bite is a *lot* worse than her growl." Everett knew because he'd tried to break up a fight between her and her hotheaded cousin while the two women were wearing their jaguar coats—and Demetria had bitten him! On purpose too. Even though his kind healed faster than humans, he'd still had to get ten stitches.

Not that it kept him from being interested in her. Once he'd learned Matt was dating her, Everett had only wished he had a girl like her. No, not *like* her. Her.

No one was quite like her.

"Listen, Bruce, go find your teammate and play nice," Demetria growled.

She was a contradiction in terms—a Guardian who was all business and strictly professional; yet around his sister, she was fun-loving and quirky.

Demetria also had a rough side that didn't fit with her Guardian job—so many of them were pacifists, avoiding violence if they could. He'd heard Tammy talking to his brother-in-law about how she wished Demetria would find someone she really cared for like she had Matt. Tammy was always trying to set her friend up with JAG agents to date, but she'd never asked Everett. He suspected it didn't seem right. Sure, Matt had been dead for more than a year, and sure, he'd had Everett promise to look after Demetria. And he had, but from afar. He had casually asked Tammy how her friend was doing, trying to give Demetria space but also keep his promise.

The redheaded man jabbed his finger at Demetria. "You're the one—"

Everett lunged forward to take the man down. No one threatened her physically without paying the consequences. He bumped into Demetria while trying to get to Bruce, then grabbed Bruce's arm and flipped him onto his back on the linoleum floor so swiftly that Bruce's mouth hung agape, his eyes wide as he looked up at Everett. If he hadn't used the element of surprise, he probably would have had a lot harder time tackling the big guy. But as angry as Everett was, he would've gotten the best of him eventually, guaranteed.

Bruce glanced around at the audience they had. A few men snickered.

He didn't seem embarrassed or angry. He only raised his brows at Everett a little as if surprised he would intervene, and then he held his hand out to show there were no hard feelings.

Demetria's mouth hung open too. Everett was still breathing hard, still angry at the guy.

He hesitated, knowing Demetria was probably totally pissed off at him. Bruce's smile broadened, his eyes darkening. Everett wondered if the man meant to get him back, but they had to learn to trust each other, which was the whole point of the new training in teamwork protocol. He offered his hand to the redhead, and the guy pulled himself up and turned to Demetria.

"Way to go, Bruce," one of the Enforcers said, making Everett assume that Bruce was an Enforcer too. "I can't believe you let a Golden Claw take you down when you just wanted a little action with the Guardian."

Howard laughed. "You'll never be able to live that down, Bruce."

"I may be with the Guardians, but I'm no softie, Bruce. Stay out of my space," Demetria said. But she turned her scowl on Everett, telling him in no uncertain terms that he had blown it where she was concerned.

Everett would react the same way again in a heartbeat. That's what teaming up with different agents was all about, as far as *he* was concerned. Teamwork. Even if he wasn't officially on her team.

Bruce ignored Everett as if he hadn't just thrown him.

He smiled at Demetria. "Want to make it two out of three? Only this time it will be just between you and me?"

"Give it up, Bruce," Everett said, not caring if she needed his interference again. When it came to Demetria, he just couldn't let it go.

She narrowed her eyes at Everett, then turned and stalked off, heading for Tammy, who gave her an envelope.

"Hey, man, so what's the deal with you and the Guardian?" Howard asked Everett, grinning.

Everett might have lost points with Demetria, but apparently he'd made them big time with Howard. Not what he had expected. "She's my sister's best friend, and I promised Matt before he died that I'd look out for her."

"Is that what they call it now? So where are we going?" Howard asked.

"The briefing note says Brayden normally hangs around Ruby's Burgers this time of day."

"Okay, let's go get this over with."

They headed outside, deciding to take Everett's Land Rover Discovery, the steel-gray color sparkling in the Texas sun. Nearly a week before Christmas, the air was cold and crisp.

"How are they going to grade us?" Howard asked.

"If we bring in the boy without having to kill anyone and keep him safe in the meantime, we should be good." Everett smiled a little.

Howard laughed. "I didn't know anyone in the JAG had a dark sense of humor."

"With the kind of work we do, sometimes it's necessary just to get through the mission. In any event, we have to evaluate each other on strengths and weaknesses."

Howard slipped into the passenger seat. "I can tell

you what your weakness is already. That hot little number who was about to take Bruce to the floor before you took over and pissed her off."

Everett hadn't thought his feelings for Demetria were so noticeable. He figured he'd explained his reaction well enough, though he suspected Howard was just spouting off. "I thought she was *your* weakness."

"Me? Nah. I like the kind of women who *want* me in their space."

"You seem to know this Bruce guy. He's an Enforcer? What was all that about with Demetria?"

"Not certain, though I've heard rumors. He's got a huge hard-on for her. He learned she was single, not dating anyone, and he's tried other approaches to get her attention, but she's turned him down cold. Anyway, I heard he hoped to catch up to her at the gathering this morning and try again. I didn't have any idea what he planned to do."

Everett couldn't believe it. He wasn't surprised other men were attracted to Demetria, but pulling a stunt like that in the training room in front of all the other agents was sheer stupidity. If that was the case, Everett was even happier that he'd taken care of Bruce.

"He couldn't get her attention any other way. That's like getting to first base. Only you sort of screwed up the mission. He's an Enforcer. What can I say?"

Glad he didn't have that kind of Enforcer mentality, Everett shook his head.

"So what if this kid doesn't want to come with us?" Howard asked.

Everett glanced at Howard to see if he was being serious, surprised he'd ask. He figured that as an Enforcer,

Howard's way of doing business would be to knock the teen out and haul him back to headquarters. Maybe Everett had him figured all wrong.

Howard shrugged. "I don't usually deal with mixed-up teens. I go after the real scum and take them down. Jaguar shifters, of course. Humans, I turn over to the police. So taking care of teens who aren't in any real trouble is new to me."

Everett explained how most JAG agents would handle it. "We talk to Brayden. If he doesn't willingly come with us, we arrest him. He doesn't have a choice in this. He's going to get himself into serious trouble if he doesn't have someone from our jaguar kind looking out for him. We'll secure a foster home for him with shifters who work with at-risk kids."

"All right. Sounds good to me. What about the kids he's hanging with? Or his old man?"

"*They* could be trouble."

Because they couldn't just arrest the kids since they were human. Brayden's stepdad? He was a jaguar shifter. He was fair game.

Demetria couldn't believe Enforcer Bruce Meyers wanted her to throw him in a mock confrontation in front of all the other people at the JAG training hall. He had assured her that it was part of a test to see how everyone else would react. She'd been getting ready to take him down when Everett Anderson intervened.

She wished Everett hadn't seen her in the confrontation. She regretted biting him a couple of years ago when he tried to break up a fight between her and her rotten cousin, especially when she learned how many stitches he'd needed. But his sister had warned her never to tell him she was sorry for what she had done, that he'd worn that bite as a badge of honor until it healed and faded away. Demetria couldn't believe it.

He was still devastatingly handsome, his dark frown and tense posture indicating he had been poised to lunge at Bruce if necessary. He must have thought she was a wild, cantankerous she-cat.

But then Bruce had poked at her, and his aggressive action had spurred Everett on. When he'd bumped into her to get to Bruce, he'd brushed his delicious jaguar and hotly aggravated male scent on her, and she'd enjoyed it as if he'd rubbed her with his body in courtship. Maybe this was supposed to have been part of the training plan.

Knowing her history with Everett, she didn't think so. She'd been so ready to prove she could handle Bruce, but Everett's reaction had startled her. That rarely happened to her. She was quick and usually focused when anyone threatened her.

Was Everett's reaction to Bruce's posturing just because he was keeping his promise to Matt to protect her?

She growled a little. Tammy had told her that Everett had promised Matt he'd keep an eye on her, and she didn't want Everett feeling like he had to keep that promise. Demetria could protect herself.

Even so, when Everett had finished tossing Bruce to the floor, she had met Everett's gaze. A queer little flutter had ruffled through her belly. She swore Everett was looking at her with interest, and not just regret that their mutual friend had died.

Then she saw the man Everett was teamed up with.

Howard Sternum was casting her a sardonic smile. He had earned the reputation of being the hardest man to deal with on a mixed team. He really needed this training, but she wouldn't have wished him on anyone.

She went up to the board and saw the name of the Enforcer she was to work with. But his name had been crossed out, and no one else had been added to take his place. She read the instructions Tammy had given her. "No," she said in a frustrated way. She didn't need a teammate for this, but she was totally irked that Brayden Covington needed their intervention again. He was most likely at Ruby's Burgers, and she had to pick him up before he got himself into trouble.

Demetria had hoped Brayden's stepdad would step up to be the father the boy needed. She hated that Brayden would not be able to stay with family and in his own home, but if his stepdad wasn't going to watch over him like a good jaguar dad should, foster care was for the best.

She was used to dealing with teens who weren't getting along at home. She'd been glad when her dad left for good so she wasn't put in a similar circumstance when she was a kid, though his leaving had been hard financially on her and her mother. Unfortunately, she had her dad's short fuse, and if someone was hurting a kid, she'd be right there to protect the child and take the adult down. That made her somewhat of an anomaly within her branch. Other Guardians would just talk their way out of the confrontation with a difficult parent or guardian. She didn't have any qualms about getting physical to get her point across.

She jumped into her Jeep Renegade and headed

downtown, ready to handle the case, though she wondered how she was going to be graded if she didn't have a teammate from another branch. She sighed. She was ready for a break for the holidays—doing some shopping for her mom for Christmas, taking in the lights at night, and enjoying Christmas carols at one of the local theaters. Maybe even watching some Christmas stories on TV.

That's what she was thinking of when she pulled into the Ruby's Burgers parking lot and saw Everett and Howard getting out of Everett's vehicle. She frowned. Had they been given the same assignment? Another test to see how they handled a situation like this where they didn't know she was going to be on their team? Or maybe she was supposed to manage this on her own before they had a chance.

Everett's eyes widened a bit. He appeared totally surprised. She hoped she hid her surprise better.

After Everett had given her the awful news that Matt had died in the jungle, she'd learned from his sister how he'd risked his life and Lacy's to bring Matt's body home. She'd been so broken up at the time that she hadn't ever thanked Everett properly. He had seemed just as upset and uncomfortable about bringing her the news. Matt and Everett had been like brothers, and Matt's death had been just as hard on him. So Demetria and Everett had continued to avoid each other, though she'd run into him a number of times when he'd gone home to see his family and she was visiting Tammy there.

She took a deep breath and stalked toward Brayden, ready to take care of this business on her own like a Guardian normally would.

Chapter 2

DEMETRIA'S DARK-BROWN EYES STARED RIGHT BACK AT Everett, ready to challenge him. Or maybe she was angry that he had taken Bruce down instead of letting her have the honors.

Why had she been given the same assignment, but hadn't been assigned to their team? Knowing Martin, it was his way of throwing a wrench into the works by creating more of a challenge and forcing the agents to deal with it to prove they could handle another branch's unforeseen involvement.

"Hell," Howard said. "What's *she* doing here? Did you know she broke an Enforcer's nose on her last mission? That's probably why she's here without a partner."

Everett hadn't heard that story. But that was the point of this training, to team up with someone from another branch and learn how to get along. "How did it happen?"

"She's quick and accurate."

Everett got that. He frowned at Howard. "*Why* did it happen?"

"Now that's what we're all dying to know." Howard laughed. "But Petrov isn't telling, and no one has had any luck getting the truth out of her."

Everett still wondered why Demetria had been fighting her cousin, both of them in their jaguar coats, that time he'd tried to break up the fight. And he *had* broken it up, although not exactly as planned—the fight had stopped when Demetria injured him.

She was a beautiful black jaguar, a rarer variety than the usual beige or brown, and her coloration appealed to him. Maybe because his brother and mother were black jaguars, and he loved how sleek they were, how beautifully they blended in with the night.

Demetria and her cousin, Taramae, had been snarling and biting, and he had only wanted to stop the fighting before either of the women got hurt. He'd dated Taramae once after he'd learned Matt was seeing Demetria, mistakenly thinking she might be like her cousin. Everett soon learned she wasn't. All she could do was put Demetria down, and Everett hadn't liked it one bit.

Brayden watched all three of them approach, Demetria from the south and Everett and Howard from the east, but he stood his ground, looking wary, with his hands shoved in jeans pockets and his unkempt curly, blond hair hanging down to his shirt collar.

Two of the boys with him had shaggy brown hair and their arms folded across their chests. One of them was wearing black jeans and a light jacket; the other, blue jeans and a heavy sweater. They sized up Everett and Howard. The other two boys were clean-cut, nicely dressed, and didn't seem to fit in with the rest. Sometimes teens like that could be the worst—kids with money had dads with lawyers to get them off the hook if they got into trouble.

Demetria quickly identified herself and showed her badge. "Brayden, I need you to come with me." Her voice was no-nonsense and authoritative, yet softer than Everett's would have been.

Everett and Howard moved toward the other boys in case anyone tried to stop Demetria from taking Brayden into custody.

The boy wearing the black jeans narrowed his blue eyes at them. "You cops?"

Demetria flashed her badge at him. "We are."

"So what's he done?" the other one in jeans asked.

"Come on, Brayden." Demetria was still letting the choice be his, for the moment.

"What if I don't want to go with you?" Brayden seemed to be trying to act tough around his friends.

"I'd have to tell you that you have no choice. But you'll be better off if you come with me and don't give me any grief." Her tone was hard-core now. She was ready to use force if necessary.

"He didn't do nothing," the boy wearing black jeans said.

The clean-cut kids just stayed out of the confrontation, which Everett was glad for.

"Brayden?" Demetria waited for his compliance.

Brayden had to smell she was a jaguar shifter, and he surely knew they meant business since he'd been through the drill before. He might have even dealt with Demetria before.

He glanced back at the other kids, but Everett noted that Brayden looked longer at the one with the stained black jeans. Everett suspected he was the leader of the little gang.

"Are you going to send me to foster care? I'm seventeen. I can manage on my own." Brayden smiled a little, but his smile was shadowed with sarcasm. "Unless *you* want to foster me."

Wrong thing to say. Everett knew Demetria would react to his taunt in a heartbeat.

In a flash, she seized Brayden's arm and hauled him to her Jeep. "We'll talk about the arrangements later, but you're not going to have to deal with your stepdad any longer." She cast a glance in the direction of the other teens, but then directed her comment to Brayden. "And you'll get your education, training, and some perks, I suspect, when you work with us."

"A cop?" The leader of the boys sounded incredulous.

"And you'll thank us for it," she said to Brayden, ignoring the other boy's comment. Then she left Brayden at the passenger's door and waited for him to get in. Again, giving him the choice, for the moment.

"If it doesn't work out?" Brayden's voice wasn't as deep as a man's and a little anxious, his bravado slipping a bit.

"It will. I guarantee it."

"My stepdad will be pissed off when he learns you've taken me into custody again."

"Then he should have been providing better guidance at home."

Looking disgruntled, Brayden climbed in and closed the door.

Everett and Howard watched while she drove off, then headed back to Everett's car.

"I'd say we work well together as a team, even if we didn't do anything," Howard said, surprising Everett.

"Sometimes having a good mission doesn't mean you have to do anything but be backup for another team member, even if she wasn't exactly on our team. She's one of us, and we're in this together, fighting the bad guys."

"Hell, you sound like you should be teaching that 'love one, love all' crap."

"Not me. Like you, I like to take down the bad guys, not just talk about it. I want to run by Brayden's house and see if we can have a word with his stepdad."

"You said his mom died?"

"Yeah, at the beginning of this year. Brayden's biological father died when he was seven, and his mom remarried a year later. I'm not sure how his stepfather, Lucian, felt about the boy initially, but we started getting calls like this a few weeks after he had the funeral for Brayden's mother. This is the final straw though. Hanging out with human delinquents is just asking for trouble. We had to take him in."

"So you've been involved in this before."

"Not directly. My sister checked on him when she was doing only Guardian work. Lucian supposedly straightened out and began watching the boy. I suspect that's why I got the case this time. And Demetria might have worked with him before. Tammy just wanted to make sure someone she knew well took care of Brayden this time. I'd never met the boy, but his mother's death seems to coincide with the boy's neglect. So what do you say? Shall we see the stepdad?"

"Hell, we're teamed up on this one. If it means we're going to get any action, I'm in."

Everett smiled a little at Howard. So the big bad ass who couldn't work with any other branch agents wasn't so bad to work with after all. Maybe it had all been for show.

When Everett and Howard arrived at the well-kept French provincial–style home, Everett thought it was a shame the situation with Brayden couldn't have been resolved with his stepdad. But there was more to raising a kid than providing a nice home and other amenities. The boy needed a family to help him grow up, whether he was shifter or human.

No one answered the door, not surprisingly. Everett got back into the car with Howard and checked with his office to see where Lucian worked.

"Where to now?" Howard asked.

"Lucian works for a painting contractor, and there's no telling where he is currently. But I would like to tell him personally that his son has been taken into protective custody and will be living with another family."

They got the information from Lucian's boss and headed to the newspaper office where he was supposed to be painting the outside of the building. But when they arrived, he wasn't there.

"Guess text messages and emails will have to do," Everett said. "Lucian has a hot temper. Even though he doesn't take care of the boy, he doesn't want anyone inferring that he can't handle it."

Howard shook his head. "Sounds like a hard case to me. Glad the boy will be helped though. I never thought a case like this would be that important. But I can see that it is. If we don't catch teens when they're at risk, we'll have to track them down later."

"Agreed."

When they arrived back at the branch, Howard and Everett got out of the car. Everett offered to shake his hand, but Howard declined. "Don't want to ruin my reputation." Then he gave him a maniacal smirk and headed across the parking lot.

Everett wondered if Howard was going to write a scathing review of working with him, just to maintain his reputation. Everett's review of Howard would be glowing, and he was glad he'd had a chance to work with the agent. He saw Demetria walking Brayden into the building, so he followed them in to get a word with her and Brayden.

———

Demetria saw Everett closing in on her and Brayden, and she waited for him to catch up, expecting him to be annoyed that she'd taken over his and Howard's case. But she'd been given the case too.

Everett appeared as tense as he had when she was having issues with Bruce earlier, only this time he had a different mission in mind. "Do you mind if I have a word with Brayden for a minute?" he asked.

"No, go ahead." She waited.

When Everett didn't say anything for a moment, she thought he expected her to leave him alone with the kid. But Brayden was her charge now. She wasn't about to give him up to anyone except the jaguar family who would foster him.

"Brayden, I tried to get ahold of your stepdad, but he wasn't at work or at home. We'll keep trying."

"I've asked several agents to help contact him. We don't want his stepdad to believe Brayden's in trouble," Demetria assured Everett.

"Like he even cares. All he cares about are his poker games and drinking. That's all he cares about," Brayden said, his face flushed.

"How did he act toward you when you were growing up? Was he a good stepdad then?" Everett asked.

Demetria rephrased the question for Brayden. "What he means is, did your stepdad treat you like you were his son?" Lucian could have provided a roof over Brayden's head and food and such, but if he hadn't wanted the boy and had only been interested in the mother, then it was a different situation. Though in that case, Demetria couldn't imagine why Lucian wanted the boy home now. If he didn't really care about his stepson, why not let him be raised by someone else? Was it guilt? A promise to his mother to take care of him? An alpha male need to prove he was in charge, even if technically he didn't want to be?

Brayden shrugged. "He paid for things." Tears filled his eyes. "He just didn't want to see me around."

"Why?" Demetria hated this part of the mission, hearing about the emotional and sometimes physical trauma these kids faced.

Brayden swallowed hard and angrily swiped away tears suddenly running down his cheeks. "I reminded him of Mom."

Demetria gave him a hug. "It's not your fault. None of it is."

"Was he a good father to you before your mother died?" Everett asked.

Demetria rolled her eyes at Everett.

He raised his brows at her in a question that said, "*What* did I say wrong?"

"Did he play with you, have father-son talks, take you places like a father might?" Demetria asked. How would Brayden know what a good father was? A man could be a good father while he took his son on all kinds of father-son excursions, but another who did none of that could be just as decent. What was a "good" father supposed to be like?

Brayden looked at the floor and shoved his hands in his pockets.

"What, Brayden?" Demetria asked.

"He tried to lose me in the Amazon once. That was his idea of a father-son outing. I was eight, and my mom had just married him. It was kind of a honeymoon with the kid. Okay? Lucian wanted to take me on a jungle hike while Mom was cooking catfish. I saw a baby caiman and I wanted to check it out. The next thing I knew, Lucian was gone. I wasn't scared at first. I knew I could just follow his scent and find him. But I lost his scent at a river. I–I felt panicked. Like I couldn't breathe. I called out for my mom and stepdad. No one answered. They couldn't hear me. My jaguar roar wasn't that loud back then.

"I was scared. Then I finally figured I had to find my way back to the campsite. I was worried they'd think I was lost for good and go home without me. I didn't know for sure, you know. I was only a kid. I thought I was being stupid and got distracted. My stepdad said that afterward. He was furious with me. And I felt guilty for ruining everyone's vacation. And I was mad at myself for not paying better attention."

"Ohmigod, Brayden. Why didn't you tell anyone? Any of the Guardians that took you in before." Demetria couldn't believe he hadn't told anyone how he'd felt all these years.

He shrugged, his eyes glistening with fresh tears. "Mom was searching for me, calling, and I finally heard her and called back. We found each other, and she told me that I shouldn't have wandered off. That Lucian was beside himself with worry and couldn't find me anywhere. He was afraid a caiman had gotten me when he crossed the river."

Demetria wanted to kill Lucian. If he had truly done that to his stepson, he deserved the strongest punishment they could mete out. "But you suspect he left you behind on purpose?"

Brayden nodded. "At first, I believed Mom and I believed him. He said he was angry I hadn't stayed with him and went off exploring on my own, as if he was upset he'd nearly lost me too. I thought it was all my fault. He and Mom had a fight over it. He said if he was going to help raise me, I had to mind him. Mom wouldn't even let me leave the house for weeks once we returned home. Not for punishment, but because she was so upset she might have lost me. But a few days ago, I was in my bedroom, and I overheard him talking to a friend on the phone about the trip we'd taken in the jungle. He said the jungle was the perfect place to lose a kid you didn't want, if it worked out right and the damn kid didn't find his way back. And then he laughed and went outside. I left the house after that and stayed away."

"Why wouldn't he have tried to get rid of you later after that incident?" Everett asked.

Everett had a valid point. If more incidents had occurred, it would seem more likely that his stepfather had truly tried to leave Brayden to perish in the jungle. Then again, Lucian and Nina had been newly married. Perfect opportunity, perfect motive.

"Mom watched over me like an anxious mother

jaguar would. I just thought she was being overly protective after she nearly lost me. We fought about it because I wanted some freedom, and I thought she was going overboard with all the restrictions. She was so upset that we never returned to the jungle. But I think she must have suspected something. Maybe she warned him that she had told others about what he had done. I don't know. All I know is once Mom died, he didn't care what I did."

"Yet every time we've taken you in, he wants you back." Demetria couldn't understand that part of the equation. If Lucian didn't want the responsibility for the kid, why not let him be fostered by a Guardian family who really wanted to raise him?

Brayden shrugged. "I don't know. Maybe he's afraid I'd tell you what happened and maybe you'd believe he hadn't been looking for me in the jungle. Or maybe he's just controlling that way."

Demetria wasn't sure. It sounded to her like an easy remedy. His wife was no longer around to take care of Brayden, and the Guardians were willing to take him in, so why not let him go? Unless he was managing a trust fund for Brayden.

"Do you have a trust fund?" Demetria asked.

"Yeah. Mom set it up for me when Dad died. She said it was mine when I reached twenty-one, because I'd be responsible enough to manage it then."

"How much?" Everett asked.

"Around a hundred and twenty thousand when Mom died."

"So Lucian's in charge of it until you come of age," Demetria said.

"Yeah. Mom was until she died."

"Whose idea was it to go to the jungle on the honey-moon?" Demetria asked.

"Lucian's."

"Okay. Well, it's not an unusual place to go for vaca-tions. We all prefer the jungle because of our jaguar nature, and he wasn't used to being responsible for a cub. Men, even real dads, can get distracted and forget to watch younger ones," Demetria said. "But we'll sure look into it." Not that they might ever be able to deter-mine the truth, but they would try. And they'd check into the management of the trust fund too.

Everett handed him a business card. "If you need anything from me or just want to talk or anything, give me a call."

Demetria was grateful Everett had offered to talk with Brayden. He might feel more comfortable speak-ing with a male.

"Demetria said I'd be working with the Guardians when I wasn't doing school lessons with the family I'm moving in with. But I'd rather work with the JAG. You get to do really cool things." Brayden glanced back at Demetria as if he suddenly was worried that she wouldn't like to hear how he felt about her job.

She got that all of the time. Most guys thought they were too macho to be Guardians, but the ones who joined her branch turned out to be great at the job. Taking down bad guys wasn't the only worthwhile job. Sometimes they just needed to be there for the good guys.

"We do things for the good of our kind too." Demetria wanted Brayden to know that her work was important, but most of all, she wanted the best for him—whatever would keep him out of trouble and allow him to become another jaguar model citizen. "You can take the aptitude testing and see where you might best be suited."

"Yeah, I'd like that. Can I work with you on a case?" Brayden asked Everett.

He smiled. "I'm off for a couple of weeks, playing video games and chilling out during my vacation time. Your foster family will want you to enjoy the holidays."

"Demetria said I had to work to keep myself out of trouble and learn to help others of our kind," Brayden said.

Everett was surprised she was such a taskmaster, though he had to agree with her on how to handle at-risk jaguar teens. "After the holidays, if it's a local case and not too dangerous, we can see."

"I don't mind going to the jungle. Really. And I promise to stick close by you at all times."

Everett smiled. "You would need a lot of training before you could go on a mission south of the border."

Demetria felt bad for the boy and realized he probably needed closure about visiting the jungle. Not a mission down there though. Something fun. A good experience. She would talk to the foster parents, and if they had no plans to visit an area south of the border, she would find a family that would be willing to take Brayden with them. "It's all right by me if you can use him on a local case after the holidays. It doesn't really matter, as long as Brayden wants to do the job and can help out. That really is the sole purpose of the program anyway—to give teens some focus that would aid our kind."

"Can I stay with you too?" Brayden eagerly asked Everett.

Demetria gave Everett a look that told him no. Everett curbed the inclination to smile at her. He knew Brayden needed to be with a family for Christmas and beyond until he was able to be on his own, not staying with a footloose, jaguar bachelor. Besides, she had to have figured that Everett wouldn't want to be saddled with the teen either.

But really, he wouldn't mind for a day. "We could do that for a day or so."

"Cool," Brayden said. "Today?"

"Uh, no. I've got work to do. After the holidays, but we need to make sure it's all right with your foster parents and coordinate a time."

"Okay." Brayden sounded glum.

"Come on, Brayden. Let's get you settled. You'll love the family. They have a twin boy and girl your age, and they're excited to take you in." Demetria stalked down the hall with her charge as Everett watched.

Then he pulled out his cell phone and called her.

She answered her phone and glanced back at him, her brows raised in question, and she mouthed the word, "What?"

Everett smiled. "Want to have dinner with me tonight? And discuss this issue concerning Brayden's stepdad?"

"What?" she said into the phone, sounding thoroughly confused.

"I could call Howard, and we could get the truth out of Lucian that way. Or...you and I can come up with another plan."

Demetria sighed audibly over the phone, continuing down the hall with Brayden until she was out of

Everett's sight. "If we're discussing this issue, we can't do it out in public."

"My place? We could get some takeout. Your choice." He thought if nothing else, they could discuss if they believed that Lucian had truly intended to leave the young boy in the jungle to fend for himself, maybe with the notion the trust would no longer be needed for the boy. They had to eat anyway. Might as well team up and try to decide how to deal with Brayden's stepdad in the best way possible for everyone concerned.

"Do you want Chinese? I can be over in a couple hours after I visit with Brayden's foster parents and him and make sure everything's going to be fine. I just need your address. I like anything, so feel free to order whatever you'd like."

"Beef? Shrimp? Hot and spicy?"

"Anything sounds good to me."

Everett gave her his address and told her he'd see her in a couple of hours, and they ended the call. He felt like he was on top of the world, even though this wasn't really a date. He thought about calling Howard, but he decided he'd check in with him later. For now, he wanted to visit with Demetria alone, which told him he was already ditching his real teammate in this case for the woman of his dreams.

He hoped the visit wouldn't turn into a nightmare. It could if she took him to task for throwing Bruce earlier today, and she probably had every intention of doing so. But if that happened, he was ready to deal with the consequences of his actions.

Everett was failing on his mission with a mixed team if he didn't let Howard know what had possibly happened to Brayden in the jungle. But Everett wanted to hear Demetria's thoughts on it first. Hell, he could lie to himself all he wanted, but the truth was, he could invite them both over to discuss the issue.

No. Way.

He was glad they had taken Brayden in so he'd have a temporary home with a foster family. If he hit it off well with the foster parents and their twin teen boy and girl, he would be a welcome member of the family forever.

Everett went to his boss's office to let him know about the mission and to tell him what Brayden had said concerning the jungle incident.

"Hell, we terminate jaguar shifters for less. Trying to kill a shifter child he's supposed to be protecting? Doesn't matter if he's his biological father or not." As director of the JAG Golden Claws branch, Martin had a plush office furnished with leather couches and chairs, an oak table and desk, and a view of a parklike setting outside his window. "I can't believe it. I damn well wish we'd known about this beforehand," he said as he sat in his desk chair.

Everett sat on one of the chairs facing the desk. "No more surprised than I was, and I agree. I mean, it's possible that the boy misunderstood the situation. That it actually was his fault he became separated from Lucian, and the stepdad wasn't responsible. But if Brayden is right about his mother keeping a close eye on him afterward? I'm wondering if she confided in family or friends. I'll check into it, besides interrogating Lucian. But if Brayden's mother told anyone, I'd think that person would have come forth a long time ago. At least I would hope so."

"I wholeheartedly agree. I'm taking you off leave since you have this case to work. I can't believe Demetria is helping you too. With Howard serving from the Enforcer branch, that makes for the perfect mixed team."

Everett felt another pang of guilt about not telling Howard about the jungle story. Yet, he fully intended to talk further to Howard about the case. Just not until after he had dinner with Demetria tonight.

"I'd like for you to head a mixed team for future assignments that require one. I had planned on asking you before this training mission because of your previous work with mixed teams, but I didn't get the chance. As usual, you've proven you have what it takes to work well with others. You can decide after the holidays and choose who you'd like to have on the team."

Well, hell. It wasn't too late to ask Howard to join them for dinner, as much as Everett hated the notion. He loved working for Martin. Even though the final decision was Everett's, the way his boss made the "offer" meant Martin expected Everett to accept it. Everett didn't mind. If he could work with Howard and Demetria, he figured he could work with just about anyone.

"As soon as you're done with whatever you are doing today, take the rest of the day off. You've earned it."

"Thanks, Martin. I'll get back with you on your offer first thing after the holidays."

"Good show. And about Brayden's case, good luck."

As soon as Everett left the director's office, Tammy hurried to catch up with him. "Hey, how'd it go with Howard?"

"Good."

"You're kidding."

His sister looked so astonished that he smiled. "Nope. I'll be working with him on Brayden's case over the holidays, it looks like."

"You're *really* kidding."

"Nope. And Demetria too."

Tammy closed her gaping mouth.

"Want to have coffee in the lunchroom, and we'll talk during your break?"

"Yeah, sure. Listen, I was supposed to help Mom set up a stage for the Christmas play she's working on with the children at her day care, but Martin asked me to work this afternoon instead. Is there any way you can drop by and help her?"

"Yeah, sure. I'm off the rest of the day."

"Oh, thank you so much. Did Demetria *really* say she'd help you with the job?" Tammy sounded shocked.

"Yeah, but I agreed, as long as she doesn't shift." Not that he'd actually said so. He had been thinking it though.

Tammy laughed.

"You were handing out assignments. Did you know we would all end up on the same job?"

Tammy worried her lip for a moment, then sighed. "It was Martin's idea."

Everett arched a brow in question.

Tammy shrugged. "You know him. He does things in his own way, but he's the boss, so he doesn't have to explain his reasoning."

Everett wondered if it had to do with seeing how well he handled the case when another agent showed up for the job. One last test to see if he could handle the position that Martin wanted him to fill.

"Okay, so what's going on with Brayden? I thought

Demetria would fix him up with a family, and that would be the end of that." Tammy added sugar and a ton of cream to her coffee.

"Yeah, but there's an issue we need to look into." He explained to his sister about the jungle incident.

"Ohmigod, I'll kill the bastard myself."

"We don't know that it's anything more than Brayden getting separated from his stepdad in the jungle. Kids do that all the time when they're out shopping with parents, or otherwise. In a jungle, it would be easy to do."

"Bull."

"Okay, I agree. It sounds damn suspicious. Especially when there's a trust fund involved. But we don't know for sure whether it was an honest mistake. So until we learn the truth, mum's the word. I just thought you should know because you've worked with Brayden before and Demetria will probably share with you anyway. So what was the deal with Demetria and her cousin that day?" He'd asked his sister before, but she wouldn't say. Maybe she would talk about it now since he was going to be working with Demetria.

"I have no idea, but it will teach you to try to break up a fight between two snarling jaguars when you don't have your own jaguar teeth to protect you."

"Amen to that."

"Thanks for telling me about Brayden. If it turns out Lucian did abandon him… Well, damn it. I wish I'd kept him out of the stepdad's home the first time, but Brayden was willing to return, so I agreed to it."

"It's hard not to do it. Why did he want to return?"

"Lucian either has the best intentions but doesn't stick with them, or he is a master manipulator."

Everett nodded. "We'll learn which once we locate him." He drank some of his coffee, pondering what Howard had said to him earlier about Demetria and her last assignment. If anyone would know what really had happened, Tammy would. "I heard Demetria broke someone's nose on her last mission."

Tammy smiled. "Okay, Petrov's version: he spouted off about wanting to see her moves, and I don't mean her combat arm maneuvers. Her version: she swung a lamp at a perp when she lost her gun in a struggle to take the guy in, and her Enforcer teammate got in the way."

Everett smiled. He suspected Demetria's version was closer to the truth, and the Enforcer didn't want to let on he'd made the mistake of getting in her way. "What about the Enforcer she had trouble with in the training room?"

"I have no idea what that was about. As soon as we both have some free time, I'm finding out. I know you think she's a wild cat, but really, there's usually a reasonable explanation." Tammy sipped her coffee. "Speaking of wild cats, I saw one raring-to-go, alpha-male jaguar jump to her aid."

"Yeah, I'm sure she wasn't really happy I did."

Tammy shook her head. "As well as I know Demetria, even I'm not sure. I was afraid she would do something about it—sock you, tell you off, or something—but instead she's working with you on this case. I know how much she loves to help kids in need, but…maybe I've been trying to hook her up with the wrong guys." Tammy finished her coffee.

Everett could have told his sister that all along. Then he got a call, saw it was their mom, and answered it. "Yeah, Mom?"

"Tammy said she couldn't make it to help me set up the stage this afternoon, and I know you're busy, but…"

"Already on it. Just having a coffee break with Tammy, and then I'll head over there." Everett ended the call and finished his coffee.

"My break is over. Tell me what happens on the case, will you? Even though I love training everyone, I miss being out in the field sometimes. Besides, Brayden is a sweet kid. I want to see this resolved in the best way possible."

"I sure will."

Tammy returned to work, and Everett headed out to help his mom set up the stage in one of the larger rooms at the day care. After that, as soon as he got home, he turned on all his Christmas lights, looked over the town house to see what needed to be done, and realized what a mess the place was. Damn good thing Demetria wasn't arriving for another hour. He began a cleaning frenzy, not believing his town house was so dusty, or that he had so much stuff scattered around the place—boots, tennis shoes, socks, a pair of boxer briefs, slippers.

He grabbed all his stuff and hurried to shove it in the closet, then seized a roll of paper towels and the dust remover and began to squirt away. When he finally finished, he realized he hadn't even ordered the food!

Chapter 3

EVERETT'S DOORBELL RANG. HE HAD BEEN AFRAID IT would be Demetria, so he was glad to see the Chinese food delivery instead. After paying for the meal, he hurried to set the table.

He told himself it was like getting together with any other teammate working on a mission, discussing the issues over a meal. But spending time with Demetria would be a nice way to wrap up the day's work.

Yet, Everett couldn't help but feel somewhat apprehensive that he still held a torch for her, while she was holding one for his dead best friend. It felt wrong. He reminded himself again that this was nothing more than working and sharing a meal. So why did he comb his hair again? Shave off his five-o'clock shadow? Throw on a green cashmere sweater that his sister had bought for him last Christmas because she said it brought out the green in his eyes and was so soft it made him huggable?

He'd ordered a full spread of Chinese dishes too—beef and broccoli, pork with pea pods, cashew chicken, sesame shrimp, wonton soup, egg rolls, white rice, fortune cookies—to make sure he got everything she might like.

The lights on the Christmas tree and patio sparkled, offering a cheerful, festive welcome to his dinner guest. Even though he lived alone, Everett had always decorated for Christmas because family invariably stopped by and the decorations put everyone in a good mood.

The doorbell rang and he took a deep, steadying breath, then stalked to the door and opened it.

"Hey," Demetria said in greeting. She entered the town house looking like a million bucks in a soft, red sweater, black pants, and killer high-heeled boots, with her hair in silky curls around her shoulders. She smiled at the decorations and all the food set out in bowls. "We could have had Brayden and his foster family and Howard over to eat all this."

Everett laughed. "I just wanted to make sure I got what you'd like."

"Really, when it comes to Chinese food, I like everything. I talked to Fabian and Corinne Stone about Brayden's story privately, so if they have a chance to talk to him about his home life over the next several weeks, maybe he'll open up or remember things he couldn't before." Demetria set out glasses of ice water.

"Okay, good. He was stressed out, and I can imagine telling us what he did was hard to do. He probably was afraid we wouldn't believe him or would make things worse with his stepdad." Everett set out the silverware, and they took their seats and began passing the dishes around.

Demetria poured some soy sauce on her food. "True. About…something else." She poked her spoon into her wonton soup and stirred it.

"Yeah?"

"I want…I want to apologize for biting you when you got in my way when I was fighting Taramae."

"My mistake. I shouldn't have interfered. It wasn't

any of my business." Everett was glad she wanted to apologize. He'd felt bad about that situation ever since it occurred and had blamed himself for getting in her space.

"Your sister said you were proud of that bite. She wouldn't let me apologize to you, but I just couldn't let it go."

He raised a brow. Never in a million years had he thought Tammy would tell Demetria that. Sure, he had shown it off because all the guys wanted to see the bite wound so they could rib him about it. He'd acted like it was no big deal, not wanting to let on that Demetria had upset him, if she had even cared. But he had upset her, and that's what had bothered him the most. "What were you fighting about?"

"My cousin was being a jerk. Not the first time. She said my dad left us for good reason. She was jealous that I got hired as a Guardian when she couldn't pass the physical or aptitude test. It's not that she couldn't have passed; she just didn't want to make the effort. So she got mad and started mouthing off about my dad. She'd done it lots of times to rile me, but my mom overheard that time. She was having a particularly bad week, and Taramae upset her. So I did what any protective jaguar would do—I stripped, shifted, and took my cousin to task. It was way overdue."

He hadn't known that Demetria's father had left her mother, just that she was close to her mother and he'd never seen her dad around. He'd never discussed it with Tammy or Matt. And he hadn't been on really close terms with Demetria, so he would never have asked her. "I'm sorry."

Even sorrier that he had dated Demetria's cousin. He

remembered the day of the fight like it was yesterday. Demetria had invited his sister over to have burgers at her mom's house. Matt had offered to grill them, and Everett had joined in. No one had expected Taramae to show up and start making a scene.

"I'm the one who should be sorry. I was so angry with her that it wouldn't have mattered who stepped into the middle of it. I felt bad when I heard how many stitches you had. I was going to apologize, but Tammy forbade me to. She said you were getting a kick out of all the ribbing your fellow JAG agents were giving you and were handling it on your own."

"It was all in the line of duty."

"But it wasn't."

"Sure it was. Jaguars having a knock-down, drag-out fight, with teeth and claws on full display, made it my business as a Golden Claws agent—especially when one of the she-cats had always interested me."

Her lips parted, and she looked shocked to the core. Her eyes teared up a little, and he wanted to kick himself. He had never intended to reveal his past feelings for her. Ever.

She looked down at her food. "You mean, you were interested in my cousin."

"No, I don't mean I was interested in your cousin. I'm sorry. I shouldn't have mentioned it. So…what do you usually do around the holidays? Anything special?"

She took a deep breath and picked up her egg roll. "I watch Christmas plays, go caroling, and see the lights at night, though I haven't done that in a few years. Watch Christmas stories on TV. The usual. What about you?"

"Same. Except for the Christmas plays and caroling."

Demetria nodded and took a bite of her egg roll. They ate in silence for some time. Everett felt he'd really put his foot in his mouth, sure he had made her uncomfortable with the revelation about his feelings.

She let out her breath on a heavy sigh, looking saddened again, and he figured bringing up the memory of Matt was upsetting her. He missed him too.

They finished dinner and talked about what they were going to do next on the case, and then Demetria said good night. Before she left, she made one more comment. "By the way, just for your information, the issue between me and Bruce at the meeting at your headquarters? That was a staged fight."

Everett couldn't believe it, which must have shown as she turned and headed for the door. "He said it was some kind of test to see if anyone would respond. I was hoping no one would get involved." She eyed Everett as if she meant *him* specifically.

"Hey, I learned my lesson last time." Well, kind of, because he couldn't keep from getting involved this time *either*. He took her hand and squeezed it. "Thanks for having dinner with me. It was a nice way to end the day. I'm glad to know the 'disagreement' between you and Bruce was just staged." Though he couldn't believe Martin would set something like that up between an Enforcer and a Guardian. He wondered if Bruce had made the whole thing up. Everett didn't know the guy, so he wasn't certain one way or another. "Howard thought Bruce had a crush on you and the staged fight was a way to get your attention."

Demetria turned fifty shades of red. "Better not have been."

Everett laughed.

"I enjoyed dinner. I'll see you tomorrow to work on the case some more. Thanks." Then she quickly squeezed his hand back, released him, and said good night.

But he knew he'd regret it forever if he let her go without kissing her good night. Knowing he could get slugged for it, he pulled her close and pressed his lips to her kissable mouth. She was as sweet as he knew she'd be, and he wanted more.

She kissed him back just as sweetly, and that small gesture kindled the slow-burning flame even more. He felt the heat between them, the desire sparking in her dark eyes, the sweet smell of the she-cat and woman teasing him. Before he could do anything more about it, she said good night again, although he hoped this was only the beginning.

He watched as Demetria's car lights disappeared into the night, then cleaned up the kitchen and went to bed. He tried to get to sleep, but couldn't. Thinking of possibilities with her. Coming up with plans to take her out. Hoping he could get to know her like he'd always wanted to. Had he been mistaken all along about her interest in him? He was determined to set things right and hoped he wasn't reading the cues all wrong.

Still unable to sleep, he grabbed his phone off the bedside table, then made the call he needed to make that he should have made earlier.

"Hey, Howard, are you on another case already?"

"Not yet. What's up?"

Everett explained what was going on with Brayden.

"I'll kill the SOB myself if he tried to get rid of the boy like that. Did you tell Demetria?"

"Uh, yeah, a little while ago."

Dead silence ensued.

"So, were you afraid I'd kill Lucian first and ask questions later, and that's why you didn't tell me at the same time?"

Everett laughed. "Nothing that drastic."

"Ah, hell, you had dinner with her, didn't you?"

Everett laughed again.

"You did, didn't you?"

"Yeah. I should have called you and had you come over too." Everett didn't really mean it.

Howard laughed this time. "Right. If I had been in your shoes, hell, I would have done the same thing. Next time I see Bruce, I'll warn him there was more to you taking him down than you were letting on, so don't go there. Though I suspect everyone who saw the action between the two of you already knew it. Okay, so we're meeting tomorrow at the JAG headquarters?"

"Yeah. And don't go killing Lucian before the meeting."

"I can wait…a little while longer. After that, no promises."

Chapter 4

DEMETRIA WAS GLAD TO BE WORKING THE CASE WITH Everett. He'd said ten, but she had been ready—well, almost ready—since four this morning. Way too early, but she couldn't help herself. She wanted to resolve Brayden's case before she started her vacation.

Despite telling herself her eagerness was because she wanted to learn the truth about Brayden, she knew it wasn't just about that. She'd messed with her hair and makeup way more than she ever did when she was getting ready to go on an assignment. She'd changed her clothes several times this morning, trying to figure out what would be appropriate for the job. She never changed clothes this much for anything—except when she'd known she'd be seeing Everett at Tammy's mother's home this past year. So what was up with that? She'd never fussed as much when she was going to see Matt.

She scoffed at herself for being so ridiculous.

She'd made three unanswered calls already this morning to Brayden's father, after several last night, but she made one last call to Lucian to tell him where his son was. He hadn't made any effort to connect with anyone concerning Brayden's whereabouts. Still no answer. She left a message again, probably a little terser than the rest. She was tired of not being able to get ahold of him and had even asked someone to check whether he had been injured. But at last report, he was home sleeping off drinking and gambling all night. Though no one had been able to locate him before he got home.

When she arrived half an hour early at the JAG headquarters, Everett had already set out a case file on Brayden's family. She liked how he'd pulled the file and gotten started on it right away.

Everett checked Demetria out as much as she checked him out. She swore he was sporting a brand-new shirt and haircut, the pale-green shirt making his eyes stand out more than usual. His mouth curved a smidgen, as if he was glad she'd noticed.

"Did you learn anything?" She poured a cup of coffee for herself.

"The wife had no family to speak of. Lucian does. A sister. We can question her, but unless she was close to Nina, Brayden's mother, she probably didn't know anything about the jungle trip. I haven't had time, but I thought we could see if Brayden can tell us the names of any of Nina's friends," Everett said. "I received authorization to check out the trust fund and discovered Lucian is paying himself a hefty commission to manage it. Which could be why he's worried about losing control of the boy. If Martin has one of his accountants take charge of the trust, Lucian will lose the commission and that extra spending money. The JAGs will handle the account free of charge for Brayden."

"Okay, that sounds like a good reason why Lucian wants the boy under his thumb and a good way to handle it."

Howard walked into the room carrying a cup of coffee. "Morning. What do you need me to do?"

After that, they all made calls, first to Brayden for a list of his mother's friends, then to the friends. No one knew anything about the jungle incident.

"Do you think Nina didn't tell anyone because she was protecting her mate?" Demetria asked.

"Or the boy really did get lost. It happened to me once." Howard refilled his coffee cup.

Demetria was dying to hear the story. Everett was smiling.

"Hey, it happens. I was off exploring, kind of like what happened to Brayden. Next thing I knew, my mom and dad were somewhere else, and I got scared."

"In the Amazon?"

"A rain forest in Belize. Anyway, I got scolded good. I had to stay in the cabana for a whole day and wasn't allowed to go out and play with my sister and brother. They stuck close to my parents, afraid they'd get in the same hot water as me. But I'd scared the hell out of them. And myself. I heard about that from everyone in the family—Mom, Dad, my sister and brother—for the next twenty-two years."

"How old were you when it happened?" Demetria asked.

"Same age as Brayden. I was fearless until I realized I was out in the rain forest all by myself."

Demetria's phone rang. She picked it up to look at the caller ID. Lucian Covington.

She couldn't believe he'd finally called. She expected he would not be pleasant. "It's Lucian. Putting on speaker," she told everyone. "Yes, Mr. Covington. You must be calling about your son. He's with a foster family and doing great." As if his stepdad really cared.

"You can't do this."

She stiffened. Yeah, they could. "Listen, Mr. Covington—"

"No, damn it. You listen to me. You had no right picking him up and giving him to some other family to raise. I told you people that before! He's my son, and I want him returned to me at once. Do you hear me? Damn it! No one else is raising my son."

As if *he* was raising his son! Someone needed to take the boy in hand because the stepfather sure wasn't doing the job. Demetria and other Guardians had left messages on Lucian's cell phone for hours and also sent emails letting him know his son was in their custody. There hadn't been one peep from Lucian until now.

"When did you learn he wasn't even home?" she asked.

"That's none of your damned business."

Lucian's ugly response prompted Howard to say, "Brayden was telling us about how you lost him in the jungle when he was eight. I want to know exactly how you managed to cross a river without realizing he wasn't following you. Any decent father would have made sure he was right there with him. I also want to know why you didn't immediately retrace your steps or call out to him when you 'noticed' he wasn't with you on the other side or still swimming across to join you."

"Who the hell are you?"

"Howard Sternum, Enforcer Branch, and I take out the trash." Even if Howard's growl hadn't been enough of a threat, just mentioning the Enforcers should have been enough for Lucian to understand the seriousness of the case. Enforcer agents didn't

normally take on cases that didn't require having someone terminated.

"Hell, the kid got lost in the jungle. Kids do stupid
things like that all the time."

"Knowing that, you should have been more responsible, since you were the adult," Demetria said.

"Who do I need to talk to so I can get this straightened
out? I want him home at once," Lucian said, changing
the subject.

No way would she or the director allow Brayden to
return to Lucian. "You'll have to speak to the director of
the Guardian branch concerning Brayden. Once we had
word he was at risk—hanging around with other at-risk
teens and without adult supervision and homeschooling,
which you know is mandatory for our kind—we had to
take him into protective custody. Not only that, but this
isn't the first time we've had issues with you over this."

"Who's the director, and what's his number?" Lucian
growled.

Demetria gave him the director's name and number.
"I'll patch you through to him." Before she could,
Lucian hung up on her. She wasn't totally surprised he
was angry but was a little surprised he'd taken so long
to realize Brayden was in the Guardian's custody. If she
and the other Guardians hadn't left messages, Lucian
would never have known his stepson hadn't been home
all night. Did his stepfather do this all the time?

"Well, what do you think?" Howard asked.

"He didn't deny that he'd lost him in the jungle,
which would have been his word against Brayden's,
and he could be right about just not realizing Brayden
wasn't with him," Everett said. "As a new stepfather,

he might not have realized how important watching out for a young boy in the jungle could be. By the way, nice touch mentioning your branch affiliation to communicate a threat, Howard."

Howard gave him a dark smile. "We don't always terminate the subjects we're pursuing. Most of the time, but not always. So the mention of our branch usually gets a response."

"I agree with Everett. Perfect comment to Lucian, in case he thinks the Guardian agents don't have any backbone. Particularly when his stepson has gone home with him twice before, but that has been Brayden's choice. We always take the kid's wishes under consideration. Without finding someone else to corroborate that Lucian actually planned to leave Brayden in the jungle, we don't really have a case to pursue," Demetria said. "Even so, he's not getting Brayden back, and that's the main thing for now."

"Not even if Brayden decides he wants to return to his stepfather's home?" Howard asked.

"No. It's too late for that. He's an at-risk teen so he belongs with a family who will ensure he has rules to follow and a good home."

Wanting to check on how Brayden was doing, Demetria called and let him know his stepdad had finally gotten ahold of her and wanted Brayden returned home.

He was distressed right away. "He doesn't care what happens to me! He wouldn't have known if I disappeared for days! I know because I've done it before!"

Demetria had been afraid of that. Brayden might have been testing to see just what he could get away with before his stepfather took notice.

"I like staying with the Stone family. They've been really good to me. I don't want to go back this time. Not ever."

Demetria was glad to hear that Brayden was content with the arrangement. "All right, Brayden. Believe me, we have laws to back us up here. You're staying right where you are. I just wanted to let you know your dad isn't happy."

"Stepdad."

"Right. Stepdad. But at least he's well aware you're with a family now. He will most likely call the director and try to convince him to release you into his custody again, but it's not going to happen this time. Your stepdad would have to prove he's going to make some real changes in his life. The Guardian branch would require him to be monitored for a year first. If he even agreed to it, by the time the year passed, you'd be eighteen and could decide for yourself what you wanted to do."

"What if he learns where I'm staying and tries to make me come home?"

"The foster family's name and location are confidential. No one will give out that information. The only way he'd learn of it is if you tell him or he discovers where you've been hanging out and catches you there."

"Okay."

"I need to talk to Mr. or Mrs. Stone for a moment. Because of your interest in returning to the jungle, I want to see if they had any trips scheduled or if I could find another family who does and would be willing to take you with them."

"The Stones are! I can't wait. I mean, it's okay, isn't it? They said I had to check with you in case I had work to do with you or Everett. They're going during the New Year's holiday."

"Oh yes, Brayden. I'm thrilled for you. We'll make sure you're off for your entire vacation. We'll talk later. I just wanted to make sure you'd be able to go there. Also, Tammy wants to show you some of the training they're doing for new JAG agents. She'll tell you the times you'll need to be there."

"Thanks. Do you still want to talk to my foster parents?"

"Yes, please." Demetria spoke with Mrs. Stone again about Brayden's past jungle experience, wanting to make sure that his upcoming trip to South America would be as pleasant as could be.

"Believe me," Mrs. Stone said, "he will have a ball, and all of us stick together at all times."

Relieved that the issue was taken care of, Demetria finished speaking with her, and they said their good-byes.

"Sounds like a good deal for the boy," Howard said.

"I'm thrilled he's going to be able to visit South America again. Hopefully, he will have a much better experience. I've got to call my boss and update him on the case."

Everett nodded. He was reading his emails or texts or something.

Demetria's boss picked up immediately. "I've already gotten a call from Lucian Covington," Ben Knight said. "I'd spoken with Brayden, and I'm completely satisfied he's happy with his foster family. Lucian said we had no business taking his son into custody, and like last time, he wants him returned home at once. I read him the code about unsupervised shifter teens. No way are they allowed to run freely with human teens, who are also at risk, without any kind of adult supervision. Brayden is just asking for serious trouble. Even if he didn't do anything wrong, if the other kids he's running with did, they could all end up in jail together.

"Anyway, Lucian didn't like my response. I believe he thought he could intimidate me into giving up the boy because he felt he had done it successfully before. But I've got our shifter law behind us. There's no going back. He knows the rules: take care of your kids, or we will."

Demetria sighed. "Do you think we'll have any more trouble with Lucian?"

"I wouldn't be surprised."

She frowned. "What's wrong with some people anyway? He doesn't show any interest in his son, but when Brayden finds a lovely family to live with, Lucian all of a sudden wants to what? Protect him? Show some fatherly love? I doubt it. More likely, this is all about the trust fund arrangement."

"Agreed. We need written permission from the beneficiary, Brayden, and Lucian, the current trustee, to change it. We'll ensure that Lucian agrees. If you have any further trouble with him, direct him to me. I'll take care of it. Keep me informed."

"Yes, sir." She figured this was the last she'd get to work with Everett on the mission, and she was really disappointed. But maybe working together wouldn't end there. She smiled a little. No, it could be just the beginning.

When she ended the call, she said to Howard and Everett, "I guess we're done with this case for now, unless something else happens to warrant further investigation."

"I agree," Howard said.

"I'll be on leave for the next two weeks," Everett said.

"Me too. I am so looking forward to just lazing around in my pajamas until I feel the urge to go out and do something fun."

Both Everett and Howard raised their brows and smiled at her.

She felt her face warm. She could say that to her female friends, and they totally understood. Say that to men, and they immediately envisioned something completely different.

"Well, before you go home and do that, do you want to have lunch out?" Everett asked.

She couldn't believe he'd ask.

Howard smiled. "I'd say yes, if you were asking me."

She laughed. "Sure. It's nearly noon."

"Okay, I just made reservations. I can drive," Everett said.

Howard just shook his head. "See you around. If I learn anything more about the jungle incident, I'll let you know."

"Thanks, Howard," Demetria said. When he left the room, she turned to Everett. "You didn't think I had other plans?"

"I considered it, but I figured you would have said you had to run to have lunch with someone."

"Always an agent."

"Got to keep on my toes."

"So where are we going?" she asked.

"Does the Japanese hibachi steak house at the mall appeal?"

"Ohmigod, yes. Really? I never get to go there. It's so expensive. For real? You're paying, right?"

Everett laughed. "Yeah, I'm paying. And if you don't have anything else to do, I thought we could see a matinee movie and do a little Christmas shopping. I usually do it online—fewer crowds and less of a hassle. But I wouldn't mind checking out a few stores if you want."

"Yes, I'd love to. I usually try to run in, grab what I need, and run out—I'm not a window shopper—so that sounds like a great plan. We could even split up if the places I want to go wouldn't interest you, and vice versa."

"It's a deal."

Everett told himself he needed to go slowly to not make Demetria feel as though he was desperate to see her. She was an independent free spirit, and he didn't want her to believe he was planning to monopolize all her time during her vacation. Though when she mentioned staying in her pajamas late into the day during her time off, that sure made him wish he was lounging with her and enjoying the holidays, chilling out, and more. He was trying not to mentally make plans with her for the next two weeks.

It wasn't working. As soon as the night was through, he'd be asking her out for tomorrow.

He'd hoped if he made the reservations for the restaurant, she wouldn't back out or ask Howard to join them. He knew Howard would understand where he was coming from and would butt out. As Plan B, if she had said she had other plans, Everett would have asked

Howard if he wanted to join him. Wouldn't *he* have been surprised? Demetria too, he suspected.

Everett was glad she'd said yes to everything. When they arrived at the mall, he realized he actually hadn't been here during the holidays for a number of years. Online purchasing was just so much less of a hassle. No vying for parking spaces or dealing with all of the crowds.

And yet, he really felt the Christmas spirit at the mall. He enjoyed hearing the Christmas music, seeing Santa and his elves, the kids all lined up eager to sit on Santa's lap, and the shops all decorated in Christmas trees and wreaths or other holiday fare.

Demetria was all smiles, looking at all the decorations and smelling the sweet scents from a candy shop decorated in giant-sized candy canes and lollipops.

"Did you want to go in?" He could probably get some gifts for his family in there.

"Yeah, after we eat. This is where I'll buy us dessert."

He smiled. "Dessert's on me. I need to pick up some gift boxes too."

"Okay, but next time…"

So many people were rushing to do last-minute shopping that it was hard not to bump into someone. Everett took advantage of the situation, wrapping his arm around Demetria's shoulders to pull her close and shield her a little. At least, that's what he told himself.

She smiled up at him. "Crowded, isn't it?"

"Yeah. That's why I normally shop online. But this is fun for a change." Only because he was with Demetria. She made it fun.

"I agree."

Everett swore more people had brushed against him than not when a young boy holding a sticky, red-and-green candy cane nearly ran into him. "Hey, buddy, watch out." He spoke with authority to get the kid's attention, but not in a mean way. Still, wide amber eyes gazed up at him, as if the kid could see Everett was really a jaguar in human disguise and all of Everett's wickedly sharp jaguar teeth were on full display.

A woman with two more children that looked just like the boy—who couldn't have been much older than four—quickly intercepted him, giving Everett an apologetic, frazzled smile. "So sorry. Just saw Santa. I shouldn't have let them have the candy canes Santa gave them until we got home. I usually have more help when I'm at the mall."

"No problem." But when he took a breath as she hurried past him to grab another of her triplets, he smelled wolf. He cast a glance back at the slightly built woman, a brunette with amber eyes, her boys all favoring her. The boys were staring at him as if he were a big, bad wolf, eyes rounded, mouths open wide.

The mom looked back at him as if to see what the matter was, frowned, then hurried her children along again.

"Did you know her?" Demetria asked. "Cute kids. I can't imagine trying to take triplets to the mall during the holiday rush without some help."

"Nah, I didn't know her. She and the boy closest to me just smelled of…" He shook his head.

"Of what?" Demetria slid her arm around his waist.

Everett tightened his arm around her shoulders, glad she was hugging him. "Of wolf. I just can't imagine anyone with young kids, triplets and all male at that, owning a wolf dog."

"Girls can be just as out of control." Demetria glanced back at them. "I missed the scent. Some people like to live dangerously."

"I guess."

After that, they ate at the hibachi restaurant, enjoying the entertainment as the chef tossed a cooked shrimp at Everett and he caught it between his teeth. Demetria smiled and took hold of Everett's arm, leaning close and whispering, "I'd love to see you do that as a jaguar."

"The chef would leave all of it for me and run."

"More for us then," she said, since they had to share a table with six other people.

"You sound hungry."

"I am, but I'm saving room for dessert."

He smiled at her, and she laughed. "Why is it that when I'm saying something perfectly innocent, you don't look as though I am?"

"Hey, I'm the innocent here."

She laughed again. "Somehow I find that hard to swallow." She pulled out her phone to take a picture when the chef created a fiery volcano in the center of the grill. But then another woman offered to take a picture of the two of them sitting together with the fire display in the foreground.

Even better.

After that, they had fun in the candy shop. Everett bought a bunch of boxes of candy for gifts and peppermint fudge for dessert. Demetria eyed it for a long time, then asked the clerk for a sample, though Everett had offered her a bite of his, waggling his brows at her. After that, she chose a piece of it too.

They shopped some more, then went to the theater to choose the movie. The choices were a sci-fi adventure thriller and a Christmas murder mystery. Everett left it up to Demetria. They both read the reviews, but neither of them knew anyone who had seen the new releases yet.

Demetria picked the Christmas murder mystery because it looked like it had a happier ending than the other. Halfway through the movie, Everett was sure the choice had been a mistake. Demetria was tense, wiping away tears trailing down her cheeks and visibly upset. Hell, who would have thought the hero would have flashbacks of fighting terrorists in the jungle now that he was at home during the Christmas holidays. He was trying to solve the murder of his best friend, involving the woman he loved, a woman who hadn't known how the hero felt about her.

Even Everett felt uncomfortable with the similarities in the story to their own true-life situation, as much as they were dissimilar. He tried to see it as just a made-up story, not like their lives in the least, but that didn't help. Not when he was sure Demetria was feeling distressed.

He didn't want to intrude, but he didn't want her to believe she had to see the rest of the movie because he wanted to, that it would be okay if she felt like leaving. Either way was fine with him. Then again, maybe she cried a lot at movies, and if he said anything, he would embarrass her.

Damn, he hated second-guessing the situation. But he didn't want her feeling bad.

"Is the movie all right? Do you want to go?"

She shook her head. "I'm fine. I want to see the happy ending."

They saw the happy ending—boy and girl fell in love, and the murder mystery was solved—but Everett was sure they should have watched anything other than that movie. "Well, that was kind of a downer," he said, walking her to the car and rubbing her back lightly.

"I had a lovely time, Everett. Don't worry about it."

"If you're not doing anything tomorrow…" he said.

"I'm going to just…veg tomorrow. I've really needed this vacation."

"Sure, I understand. Me too." But he still would have loved to spend some time hanging out with her. Maybe he should have started out more slowly. "If you decide you want to do anything, just let me know. I was thinking of going to see that ice sculpture place. They're featuring Christmas around the world. I've never been before, and I thought it would be fun."

She smiled, but her smile was sad. "I haven't been either. Maybe some other time."

"Sure thing." He dropped her at her car parked at the JAG headquarters, but before he could open her door, she hurried to get out of the car, her body language saying she wanted out of there, no kissing, no hugs. He wished the evening had ended a whole lot differently.

Chapter 5

DEMETRIA HAD A WONDERFUL TIME WITH EVERETT, but she wished she hadn't picked that movie to watch. How was either of them to know that it would hit so close to home? She tossed and turned all night, unable to quit envisioning Everett and Matt in the jungle fighting to save Lacy, and Matt losing his life.

She finally managed to sleep in, did her laundry, changed bedsheets, and dusted. She did everything she could think of while trying to get her mind off Everett and how unhappy he'd seemed that she'd so quickly ended the night with him. But she couldn't help it. Everett was the hero in the movie, had the crush on her while she'd been dating his best friend, and yet, she hadn't loved Matt like the woman had loved the man who had died in the story. As a friend, yes, but not as a man Demetria had wanted to promise her love to forever.

How could things get so complicated?

She gave up on trying to sort it out in her own mind and called Tammy. "Hey, girl, need to talk. When is your next break coming up?"

"I work only half a day today. Students are training in combat maneuvers for the rest of the afternoon and through the night so I've got a break. Want to get together?"

"Yeah. I'll fix enchiladas."

"You sound down. You're on your vacation. You're supposed to be happy. Is there something wrong with the case you've been working on? Brayden Covington's case? Don't tell me Lucian's being a total jerk again."

"No. I went and saw *Christmas Trouble*."

"Oh."

"You've seen it?"

"Umm, yeah. I never read reviews or what the movie's about. The title said Christmas, and my mate wanted to go. Believe me, getting him to see a Christmas movie is like pulling jaguar teeth. So we went and we both immediately thought of…" Tammy paused. "Well, anyway, I'll be over in half an hour. Do you want me to bring dessert?"

"Yeah, sure."

Tammy could always cheer her up. The problem was that Demetria had never told Tammy how she had felt about the two men.

Demetria finally threw on jeans, sneakers, and a sweater, brushed her hair and applied a little makeup. Then she turned on her Christmas tree lights before Tammy arrived. She was there in twenty minutes, as if she figured Demetria was about to go off the deep end.

"Hey, Demetria," Tammy said, handing her their favorite chocolate-chip mousse cake from a shop near her and giving her friend a hug.

"Sorry to be so glum."

"No problem. I brought the fixings for Christmas margaritas, perfect to go with your out-of-this-world enchiladas."

Demetria smiled.

"Let me just grab my bag out of the car."

"You're staying the night?" Demetria was thrilled. "What about David?"

"He's got nighttime tactical maneuvers with the students. You and I haven't had a sleepover in eons. Besides, I can't drive after we have a couple of Christmas margaritas and"—Tammy pulled a handful of Christmas movies out of her bag—"I brought a bunch of fun Christmas movies that David prefers I watch by myself. He'll play a shoot-'em-up computer game instead while sitting with me on the couch. It will be fun to watch with someone who really wants to see the movie with me."

Demetria laughed. "Okay, sounds good." She started serving the enchiladas and rice.

Tammy began making the margaritas, adding some cranberry juice to change the lime green color to red and running a wedge of lime around the edge of the glasses, then dipping them into a saucer of sugar and adding thinly sliced limes on top.

Demetria picked one of the Christmas comedies and started it, and then they settled on the couch to eat and drink and be merry. Until she got a call from her mother. "Hey, Mom. Tammy's here to watch Christmas movies with me."

"Oh, okay, dear. I just wanted to let you know your father is back in town."

"I'm coming over."

"I don't need your protection. I'm fine. I'll call the JAG branch if I have any trouble. Have a good time. I just wanted to let you know in case you got word he was back in town."

"Mom—"

"I'll handle it. Okay? I guess I shouldn't have told you."

"Of course you should. I'll let you deal with it then. But you call me too if he's a problem. All right?"

"You know I will. Have fun with Tammy. Night, dear."

"Night, Mom." Ugh. Demetria couldn't believe her dad was back in the area. After leaving them with no word for the last two years?

She was still thinking about that when Tammy took a sip of her margarita, turned to her, frowning, and said, "Wait, you did not go to see that movie all by yourself, did you?"

***

Everett had spent the day playing video games, thinking about Demetria and their time together and wishing things had ended better between them. He was trying to pretend that seeing the movie hadn't happened.

Before he retired to bed, he sat in his boxer briefs fighting the third dragon he had to kill before he could get on with the story on an RPG, a role-playing game, when his cell rang. It was two in the morning. Worried something was wrong, he grabbed the phone off his desk and saw that Demetria was calling. He was both concerned and eager to talk with her.

"Hello, Demetria? Is everything all right?"

"I can't believe you took Demetria to see *that* movie."

"Tammy?" For a moment, he tried to sort out his confusion. His sister was slurring her words, which meant she'd been drinking. Hell. "Where's David?" As if he was supposed to keep Everett's sister in check.

"Out training. Nighttime. Maneuvers."

"Are you home?" She couldn't be. She had called from Demetria's house. "You're at Demetria's place?"

Which was why she knew he and Demetria had gone to see the movie. He was a little slow on the uptake.

"Yes, and she told me you took her to see *that* movie."

"She wanted to see it. It was her choice." Everett took a deep, settling breath. "We didn't know anything about the movie. I asked if she wanted to leave partway through it, but she said no. What did she say to you?" He hadn't meant to sound so defensive, but Tammy was clearly on the offensive.

His sister let out her breath in an exasperated way. "She won't talk to me about it. She always talks to me about everything. What did you do to her?"

"I didn't do anything to her." Except upset her by taking her to see the movie. Everett ran his hands through his hair as he studied the paused game screen, the blue dragon spewing ice instead of fire at his party of highly trained warriors. "Let me talk to Demetria."

"She's sleeping."

"I am not," Demetria said in the background, sounding like she was half-asleep.

"Do you want to talk with him?" Tammy asked, paused, then added, "Demetria shook her head."

"Are you planning on going home tonight? If so, I'm coming to get you." No way was Everett letting his sister drive home, considering how she sounded.

"No, I'm staying with Demetria. She needs me."

"Is she really upset?"

"She looks like a sleepy big cat."

He smiled and wondered what the sleepy big cat was wearing for the slumber party.

"Let him come over. He can wash the dishes." Demetria's words were just as slurred as his sister's.

Everett's smile broadened. If he was getting an invitation, he was on his way. Solely to make sure the ladies didn't get themselves into trouble, of course. But if he could end this on a better note with Demetria, he was all for it. "On my way over."

"She didn't mean it!" Tammy said. "Did you, Demetria?"

Everett was hurrying to dress. "What's her address?"

"This is a Guardian party, no Golden Claws allowed," Tammy said.

"Tammy…" he said in his authoritative Golden Claw voice.

"Oh, all right. Next time you take her to the movies, ask me if it's all right first." Tammy gave him the address. "Do you want a drink too?"

"Don't let her fix one for you," Demetria said. "She broke the glass. I can't afford for her to break any more."

"It slipped. It was the fae's fault."

Smiling, Everett shook his head.

"Slippery fingers, lime, whatever," Tammy said.

"Don't you have to work tomorrow?" Training started at five in the morning, but Tammy usually got off at three in the afternoon. And she needed her sleep.

"Uh-huh."

"It's two in the morning."

"I can't see the clock. Is it really two in the morning? Ohmigod, I have to get to bed. Night, Everett. Night, Demetria." Then Tammy hung up on him.

He wasn't sure what he'd find when he arrived at Demetria's place—probably both women sound asleep. He was glad he didn't have to work tomorrow. He'd stay, make sure Tammy was fit to send in to work and Demetria was okay, then return home to sleep.

When he arrived, he found the door locked, which was good. But no one was answering, which he'd suspected would be the case. He used his lockpicks on the door and entered the condo, closing the door and locking it.

Only the Christmas tree lights were still on.

"Just me," Everett said, well aware both women had guns, though Tammy probably hadn't taken hers with her to see her friend. But Demetria might not be sober enough to realize he was just there to help.

He turned on a light in the dining room and kitchen and saw the mess on the floor: margarita mix, tequila, broken glass, slices of lime—the works. He walked around the mess and headed into the living room, where he found Demetria snuggled up against a couch pillow, her silky, dark hair falling over her neck like a scarf and her feet tucked under another couch cushion. She was wearing a pair of red flannel pajamas decorated in penguins and snowman. He smiled, never having seen her in something so whimsical. Now when he thought of her lying around in her pajamas all day, he'd have a better visual. He pulled a red-and-green afghan off the end of the couch and covered her with it.

Dirty dishes and glasses were sitting on the coffee table. He'd take care of those too.

Then he checked on his sister in the guest room. She was snuggled under the covers.

"Hey, Tammy, I'm here. I'm going to clean up the mess you ladies made and just hang around until you get on your way to work tomorrow. All right?"

Tammy looked up at him with narrowed eyes, as if

she couldn't get them open any wider and wasn't sure who she was seeing. Then she took a deep breath. "Oh... Everett. 'Kay." Then she closed her eyes, covered herself again with the blue comforter, snuggled against her pillow, and fell back to sleep.

He checked again on Demetria, but she hadn't moved, so he went into the kitchen to begin Operation Cleanup.

Even though he would have been at home still playing his game and killing the dragons plaguing their world, he was glad to be here as a brother, a friend, and a Golden Claw agent whose mission was to take care of jaguars in need. Still, he'd never believed he would be serving as a maid.

He was nearly done mopping the floor when he saw something move out of the corner of his eye and turned to look. Demetria was leaning against the wall next to the china cabinet, looking half-asleep, her dark hair in curls around her shoulders.

"Are you okay? Do you need something to help settle a hangover?" he asked, continuing to mop the floor.

She snorted. "What are you doing?" Her words were still fuzzy.

"Cleaning up after the party and ensuring Tammy gets to work tomorrow. You don't want to see Martin when he gets a call that one of his trainers didn't show up first thing in the morning. Or hear how upset David would be if he learned he had to be out training all night and his mate didn't come into work the next morning to teach. If she had just...vanished."

Demetria sighed. "Got it."

"Why don't you get some sleep if you can? I'll leave first thing in the morning."

She nodded and turned, and nearly fell.

He sighed, set the mop against the counter, and stalked toward her. She held up her hand to ward him off. "I can do it."

"Yeah, and you'll make it by the time I leave in the morning." He gently scooped her up in his arms, feeling way too much like he was taking her to his bed, and carried her down the hall to the room she indicated was her bedroom, putting her in her own bed. He covered her up and, well, hell, kissed her cheek. Which is what he had wanted to do before they ended their time together last night. Well, kiss her lips, hug her, more.

Her eyes widened a little. He smiled and said good night. Then he went back to his maid duties.

When he was done, he removed his clothes except for his boxer briefs and stretched out on the couch, covering himself with the afghan, wrapping himself in Demetria's scent, and thinking this was as close as he might ever get to heaven.

Chapter 6

EVERETT GOT HIS SISTER UP AND RUSHED HER OFF AT four in the morning so she could get to work on time. Then he checked on Demetria, but she was still sound asleep. He sighed. He hoped she would feel okay when she got up. He had every intention of making her a concoction to take care of a hangover, but thankfully Tammy didn't have one, so he hoped Demetria would also be fine.

He grabbed a cup of coffee and had just settled back on the couch, closed his eyes, and fallen asleep when he got a call. Hell, had Tammy not made it to work after all? He should have driven her. Then he saw that it was half past five, shortly after his mother opened her day care, and that's who the call was from. Mary Anderson owned and operated the Little Angels Day Care—for jaguar shifters only. If a human family tried to reserve space for a child, she'd quickly tell them she was booked. Jaguar referrals or shifter families she already knew were usually the only ones she signed up to stay at her day care.

Mary took in jaguar-shifter cubs for working parents and watched older kids from time to time so moms could run errands or go to social events without worrying about their kids or finding a sitter. Sometimes moms wanted time to run alone as jaguars and would leave their children off at the day care for a couple of hours, which meant their kiddos would turn into jaguars cubs, so his mom couldn't ever take in a strictly human child.

She loved all the kids like they were her own, but when she called him like this, it had to mean trouble.

Everett didn't mind helping her out when she needed some muscle to put things together or whatever. Though he'd really wanted to sleep in a bit this morning after playing video games so late and then the business with Demetria and Tammy last night. But the thought of actually managing a bunch of pint-size kids? That was better left to others who were into the little tykes. He had no problem with teens.

Even now, he could hear the kids screaming and crying in the background.

"You have to come help me right away." His mother had dealt with a number of crises with kids at the day care over the years, anything from a jaguar cub biting another who was still in his human form and breaking the skin, to a jaguar cub slipping out into the backyard, leaping from a playground castle to the fence, and jumping over it to run free. That escape had caused a massive jaguar hunt for the wayward preschooler for two hours until Everett had heard him snoring, sound asleep underneath an overturned fishing boat in a distant neighbor's yard.

"If it has to do with kid problems at the day care, someone else can take care of it. Maybe Huntley? He and his mate managed jaguar cubs in the jungle and did a great job of it." Everett desperately tried to think of alternatives, but if his mom was calling him, there couldn't be any. He was definitely a last resort.

"You know very well they are away on missions or

teaching new JAG agents. And Maya lives over three hours away. You're not working any cases right now. You told me you were off for the next two weeks. And this is an emergency. I need you now." Then she hung up on him.

So much for getting out of it. He sighed. He knew she had to really need his help, and he was already getting ready to tackle whatever the problem was.

Looking at the cold, wintry day outside, he scribbled a note for Demetria, telling her to call him if she needed anything and that he hoped she was feeling better. He wanted to say he'd planned to fix her breakfast, if she could stomach it. Or whatever else she needed. But she might just sleep half the day anyway, so he only said that he needed to go.

He drove to the day care twenty minutes away and parked, braced himself, and headed inside, the doorbell playing the rendition of cats meowing the tune of "Jingle Bells" instead of the usual "Yellow Rose of Texas" melody. The place was cheerful, perfect for jaguar shifters, the walls painted in vivid jungle motif—green vines and trees, with colorful orchids, monkeys, jaguar cubs, and parrots hiding in the dense foliage. Even the child-sized furniture included chairs and tables hand-carved in the form of zebras, giraffes, and jaguars. A large fish tank sat against one wall, featuring all kinds of colorful fish, and an iguana had his own exhibit nearby.

Tons of children's handmade Christmas decorations hung on a Christmas tree—everything from colorful paper-chain garlands, strings of cranberries, and popcorn garlands to handprint angels in clay molds and reindeer cut out of colored paper with red pom-pom balls for noses, making it appear Santa Claus even made trips to the jungle.

Everett's mother rushed out to greet him, wearing green jeans and a T-shirt with a jungle print featuring a jaguar's portrait, the cat wearing a Santa's hat for Christmas, and the name of her day care written across the top. Her dark-blond hair, streaked with strands of white, had fallen loose from her bun. She looked like she was having a really tough day, even though it had only just begun. She wore a deep frown and was wringing her hands, but she gave him a quick hug. "We have a real crisis on our hands."

Everett noticed that whenever his mother had a real crisis, their father, Roy Anderson, stayed clear of the place. He was an undercover operative of some sort, but being undercover, he'd never told the family the real story of his work.

"One of the kids is deathly sick? Or dead? Wounded? Escaped again?" Everett couldn't imagine anything else that could be that drastic.

"No, no, worse."

"Worse?" What could be worse than any of *those* situations? His mother wasn't given to hysterics without good cause, he reminded himself.

"We were getting ready to practice for the Christmas play when three of the four-year-olds shifted." She headed toward a back room.

"The mom or moms didn't tell you they were going to run as jaguars?" He didn't get what the severity of the problem was. He was certain that had happened at her day care before, and it was no big deal.

Then he heard a growl, a bark, and a small howl

coming from the room. He frowned. They didn't have dogs at the day care.

"Come here, you. Come here!" Lacy said from the back room.

Everett wondered why she was here.

A louder bark and growl, then scratching and more hissing and snarls sounded.

"No, no, no. It's okay, puppy." Lacy's voice was alternately in charge and then coaxing.

"A preschooler was dropped off at the day care," his mom said. "To our shock, the boy turned into a white wolf pup."

"*No way.*"

They reached the room, and his mom pulled the door open. "I couldn't get ahold of the cubs to protect them from the wolf pup, or vice versa. Every time I tried, they leaped out of my reach. And the wolf pup scrambled underneath the furniture. Heidi had to take care of the other children while I called you to help us out. Lacy's been trying to get ahold of him."

Six years old now, Lacy was wearing her angel wings and a white angel's costume, her hands on her hips, but when she saw Everett, she ran to give him a hug. She always did, no matter how much time had passed since he saved her in the Costa Rican rain forest. He found the hugs endearing and was glad she hadn't had nightmares about the experience.

But what really grabbed his attention were three jaguar cubs hissing at a wolf pup—a white Arctic wolf pup. He was running back and forth, looking like he wanted to play with them but wasn't too sure, since he kept trying to approach them and then leaping away.

The jaguar cubs moved toward him too but were clearly unsure how to react, alternately sniffing and jumping and scampering backward.

"He's cute, isn't he?" Lacy looked up at Everett with wide, green eyes.

"He is." But what he was doing here was another story. When the pup saw Everett, he ran to greet him. The jaguars chased after the wolf, and Everett scooped him up in his arms to protect him. The pup licked his face in greeting, his tail wagging a hundred miles a minute in appreciation. Everett smiled. Not that this was anything to smile about, but the pup *was* cute, and he liked Everett. That certainly gave the pup points in his favor.

Two of the jaguar cubs were wearing halos around their necks. The other jaguar had managed to slip out of his. White cotton angel gowns lay scattered on the tile floor, along with a set of pint-size clothes—sneakers, socks, underpants, jeans, a blue sweatshirt, a sweater, and a heavy gray jacket.

Everett didn't believe it. "Mom, werewolves *don't* exist."

"I'm not crazy. He shifted."

"Did you *see* him shift?" Even if she had, he didn't think he'd believe it unless he actually saw it for himself.

"Well, no. I was trying to dress the preschoolers in their angel costumes to make sure they all fit for the play in a week. Heidi was busy with spilled cereal and milk when Tommy accidentally tipped his bowl off the table. Then the baby needed his diaper changed, and another started to throw up. I had to leave the room for a moment when Heidi needed me to take care of the baby who was throwing up while she was changing the other baby's diaper. She quickly finished and was headed to the room to take over for me when the doorbell jingled its tune. We had one toddler who hadn't been dropped off yet, so that's who we expected. Then she called out that it wasn't Sarah. And all the growling and barking and hissing began."

Everett glanced at Lacy. She raised her hands in the air and shrugged. "I was helping Heidi clean up the mess Tommy made so I didn't see the new boy shift."

"Where did you get the pup?" Everett asked his mom.

"A woman dropped him off."

He didn't know how his mother could deal with all of it. He'd rather fight terrorists in the jungle.

"The pup smells like a wolf," Everett said as the pup snuggled against his black sweatshirt, closed his eyes, and went to sleep.

Lacy reached up to pet the puppy.

"Heidi thought his jaguar parents must have owned a wolf dog. We were busy. It's always hectic first thing in the morning when the parents drop off their little ones. Though not usually *this* chaotic. We're trying to get them all fed and start our programs for the day." His mom went to remove the halos from around the jaguar cubs' necks.

"I thought the jaguar moms would tell you if they were going to shift." He knew that wasn't exactly the point, but he was trying to make some sense of the chaos.

"They did, Everett. We were just behind. I was fitting their gowns and halos, and I didn't realize it was getting this late."

"What about the person who brought the boy in?"

"Heidi said she didn't see her. We heard the doorbell kitty-cat 'Jingle Bells' song, but no one was in the outer room. The woman just set the boy over the gate and left a bag."

"Are you sure this isn't someone's idea of a prank? Someone just pulling your leg? They switched out the boy with a wolf pup and left him?"

"No. Heidi was with him the whole time. She asked his name, and he said his mommy told him never to talk to strangers, but he said his mommy and daddy were coming to get him later. He started tugging at his clothes to pull them off and said he had to shift. She didn't know what to think. He didn't smell like a jaguar. But human kids would never say such a thing.

"She tried to help him off with his clothes and called out to me in a panic. When she turned back, he had already shifted, still wearing his clothes, all but his shoes and jacket. 'Ohmigod,' Heidi said. 'Ohmigod. He's... he's a wolf.' Well, of course all the kids wanted to see, and the next thing I knew, some of the ones I had been dressing for the play had shifted into jaguars. And that's what you see now."

"So Heidi saw the boy shift."

"You know how fast we shift. She turned her head, and when she looked back, he was already a wolf."

"I can't believe wolf shifters exist. And they're located here?" Everett wouldn't be able to wrap his mind around it unless he actually saw it happening.

The pup whimpered a little, his foot jerking in sleep.

As soon as Mary removed the two boys' halos, all three jaguar cubs raced over to Everett and began clawing at his jeans to get at the pup.

"No, down," Everett scolded the cubs, not wanting them to tear his jeans or cut his skin as their sharp little fishhook claws dug into his leg.

"Come on." Lacy tried to get ahold of one of the cubs. She was still tiny for her age, but she got one of the cubs and held on, telling her she had to behave.

His mom grabbed up one of the cubs. "No scratching," she scolded the other one.

Before Everett could prepare himself, the wolf pup turned into a blond-haired, naked, approximately four-year-old boy, still sound asleep in his arms. Everett couldn't have been any more speechless. He looked from the boy to his mom to see if she had seen what had happened.

Her jaw had dropped. "Ohmigod, I don't believe it. Werewolves really *do* exist."

Lacy's eyes were saucer-size.

Everett thought of the perfect person to handle this. Demetria was wholly suited for the mission because she loved kids of all ages and she was good at her job. Surely, she would believe him and his mother, since she knew them and wouldn't think they were trying to pull her leg. Even so, he suspected she would not believe it any more than he had. Until she saw it happen right before her eyes.

Then again, she might not be in any shape to deal with a wolf shifter or anything else this morning after the party she and Tammy had last night.

Chapter 7

EARLY THAT MORNING, DEMETRIA GOT AN EMERGENCY call from the director of the Guardian branch. She was feeling better, but she was on vacation, had had to take something for a headache this morning, and fully intended to sleep for a few more hours. It was only six in the morning!

Then her heart thumped wildly, her first thought that something awful had happened with Brayden.

When her boss told her the trouble he was calling about, she immediately believed Ben Knight had gotten an early start on drinking mistletoe martinis in celebration of the holidays.

She put the call on speaker so she could get dressed. "Okay, sir, you're telling me that the jaguar shifter day care has an Arctic wolf shifter pup there. Really? That's like saying they have a Bigfoot baby there. They're trying to pull a prank on us."

"I'm serious, Demetria. I need you to go over there immediately. You might know that a JAG agent's mother owns and operates the day care, so she called her son, Everett Anderson, first to take care of the situation with the little boy. Since Everett was working with you on Brayden Covington's case, he called and highly recommended you handle this one. The JAG agency doesn't normally deal with guardian-type services. That's our job."

Mary Anderson's day care? Demetria couldn't believe it. Mary was great at creating fantastical stories and games for the kids, but Everett's mother didn't seem like the type to come up with a practical joke that involved a policing agency.

Demetria squinted at her reflection in the mirror. Ugh. She brushed her hair and began applying her makeup. "We don't handle anything like that for anyone other than jaguars *either*. This has to be someone's idea of a joke. This year, the different branches pulled all kinds of pranks on each other."

"That was on April Fool's Day."

"So, maybe they're a little early for next year."

Ignoring her comment, Ben said, "I need you to check it out and report back to me ASAP."

"All right, sir." This was nuts. And she hated to be the fall guy.

"Okay, but if this truly is a case involving such a thing as a wolf shifter, I'm canceling your leave and assigning you the job. This case takes priority over anything else."

Demetria wished she hadn't had that third margarita last night.

She grabbed her purse and glanced at the clean kitchen, vaguely recalling that Everett had mopped the floor before...before he carried her off to bed. Now she felt even guiltier that she'd said no to a date with him today. Was this a way for him to get even?

She headed out the door, still on the phone with Ben.

"All right?" Ben said, getting confirmation she was going along with the program.

"Yes, sir." Because she knew this was all a dumb

hoax. Though she couldn't believe Everett or his mother would try to pull a prank on her. She didn't know what to think.

When Demetria arrived at the day-care center, the pretend frost covering the windows made it look like a winter day in Dallas. Twinkling colorful lights hanging from the eaves and lights in the windows gave the center a real holiday look. The sign out front had two little angels holding jaguar cubs, signifying to jaguar shifters that one of their own ran the place. She didn't imagine any human day care would include jaguars in its motif, and she wondered what humans would think of having a wild animal as part of the branding.

Looking totally frazzled with her blond hair slipping from her bun, Mary Anderson met Demetria outside and quickly ushered her into the day care. "Oh, oh, I'm so glad you're here, Demetria. This is just, well…just… unreal. And wonderful. And horrible."

Demetria had never seen Everett's mother so rattled. Well, except for the time she was helping search for the runaway preschooler. "My boss sent me to help take care of the situation. May I see the wolf shifter pup?"

"Yes, yes, this way. Everett has been watching over him. He starts crying and whimpering if we leave him alone for even a minute."

"Wolf pack mentality," Demetria said, as if buying into this. "Unless you mean your son."

Mary smiled a little. "Everett will be thrilled you've arrived to take the pup off his hands. He was the one who called your boss and asked for your help. He was a little worried you might not be feeling well because you were a touch under the weather last night, but he knew you were just the one to handle this. We have a serious problem here."

Demetria hoped Everett hadn't told his mother why she was a "touch under the weather" last night. "Besides the fact werewolves don't exist?"

"We don't know who the mother was."

Demetria frowned at her. "You didn't sign the child in?" Even though she knew this had to be a joke, she still couldn't help treating it like a real case.

"No. Neither did Heidi Johansson, my helper," Mary said. "The woman just dropped the child off, then left. If he had been strictly human and hadn't told Heidi he was going to shift and then shifted, I would have called child protective services."

Demetria did smell the wolf scent, which told her that they'd had a real wolf or wolf dog here at some point.

They both reached the doorway to a room in the back of the building and looked in. Smiling, Everett crouched on the floor, playing tug-of-war with the wolf pup, a silver aluminum halo firmly entrenched between the pup's teeth. Demetria smiled at the sight, then pulled out her cell phone and snapped a shot to send to her boss. Now this was seeing Everett in a new light. Though watching him mop the spilled margarita off her floor and clean up all the glass was something she'd never seen him do either. She had to admit she was grateful he'd cleaned up the floor, the dishes, and everything.

"Oh no, Everett," his mother scolded. "We need those for the Christmas play." Mary took the halo away, looking highly annoyed with him.

Everett appeared properly chastised, while the pup

looked disappointed his favorite toy had been taken away and was still eyeing it in Mary's hand.

Demetria didn't believe for one minute that the wolf was a shifter. But it did look like a wolf pup, not a wolf-dog mix or a dog that just looked like a wolf. Changing her mind about how she'd manage this, she decided to go along for the ride for just a bit. She could handle a joke the same as the next guy, though she did even better when she had more sleep. She had to admit both the pup and Everett *were* cute.

Everett hadn't seen her standing in the doorway yet as his mother set the halo out of the puppy's reach on top of a table.

Demetria had never imagined a big guy like that— whose normal missions entailed taking down ruthless animal exploiters and the like—would be playing on the floor with a small, white wolf pup. Everett suddenly turned his attention to the doorway. Rather than looking a little embarrassed that Demetria had caught him on the floor playing with the puppy, he seemed relieved and glad to see her.

As Everett quickly rose from the floor, the pup saw a new toy—the shoelaces on Everett's right tennis shoe—and began to tug at them, growling ferociously. "I asked your boss if he could send you to investigate this. I wasn't sure how you were feeling and I know you're on vacation, but this case is so unbelievable and important for both our kinds that I thought you'd want to be involved. And…it's your kind of case as a Guardian agent."

Mary motioned to Demetria. "Of course she's the only choice for the job. She's like family so she knows this is for real. Anyone else would probably think it was some kind of silly hoax."

Demetria raised her brows a little.

Everett freed his shoelace from the pup's sharp teeth, lifted him in his arms, and carried him to Demetria. "He's all yours." But he didn't make any attempt to hand the pup over.

"Why don't you keep him?" No way was she going to take hold of the puppy, even though Everett *hadn't* actually offered for her to take him. She still figured it had to be a joke, and relieving him of the puppy would show just how gullible she was. The way she handled this would reflect on her branch. "We have to track down his parents," she said smoothly. "I've been given the assignment of taking care of the pup while you track down the mother. That means we're stuck with each other until we resolve this."

Everett smiled a little. "Nothing would give me more pleasure." He sounded totally sincere.

It was just too preposterous. "Because of the ramifications of what a wolf-shifter population could mean to us, this has the highest priority. My boss is calling your boss as we speak to let him know he wants you on this assignment with me." If the JAG branch wanted to perpetuate the joke, they'd have to give her the JAG agent to help "deal with this." She could imagine taking the pup back to her branch and everyone shaking their heads at her for having been so thoroughly duped.

Everett stroked the pup's head. "I haven't even called Martin about it yet."

Why was she not surprised? "Really?"

"He won't believe it when he gets the call from your director. He'll think Ben is pulling his leg," Everett said.

Demetria's mouth hung agape for a moment. That's just the way she felt about Everett and his mom saying this was for real.

"Do you have security tapes?" Everett asked his mother.

"Yes, set up in the front. We looked at them while we waited for you to arrive."

Photoshopped, no doubt. All planned.

As they walked down the hallway, Everett still didn't offer to hand over the pup. He just cuddled him against his chest as his mother led them to the front. At least Everett loved puppies, which made Demetria remember when he'd rescued a pup from a drainpipe, then washed him and played with him until they could find the owners. She'd forgotten all about that. She thought he had real Guardian qualities, though he probably wouldn't acknowledge it. The puppy genuinely seemed to love him right back, which she had to admit was heartwarming.

"Where are all the other kids?" Demetria considered the bright jungle decor in the front room and thought how lucky the kids were that got to stay here. She wished she'd had a place to play like this when she was little. Her gaze shifted to the tropical fish in the tank. She could just imagine the little jaguars loving those and the bright-green iguana she'd spotted.

"All the children are in the back room with Heidi until we can sort this out. I need to help her though." Mary played the video for them. "Heidi and I both checked the videotapes while we were waiting for Everett to arrive, hoping maybe the woman revealed enough about herself that he could quickly locate her."

In the video, several moms and dads checked in their babies, toddlers, and preschoolers. Lacy was dropped off wearing an angel costume and angel wings, and Demetria wondered why she was here, but not her brother and sister. Then a woman wearing a white winter coat, black suede shoes, and a fluffy white knit hat that hid her hair walked the little boy into the room.

"That's her and that's the boy. The wolf pup," Mary said.

Demetria got a blurry glimpse of the woman's face as she lifted the boy over the children's gate and left a blue bag on the floor beside him, then hurried out of the day care. Not once did the woman speak with the boy. He turned to watch her go, then heard Heidi coming to see who had just entered the day care, and his gaze shifted to the brunette with dark-brown eyes, her mouth parted in surprise. "Where's your mama?" Heidi asked.

"Mommy and Daddy are coming to get me later."

Her eyes widening a bit, Heidi hurried over to the door and peered out the window, but the woman had already left. The boy began pulling at his coat and said, "Gotta shift now."

"What?" Heidi took the boy into the back, and that was the end of the tape of his arrival.

"You don't have any security cameras in the parking lot?" Everett asked.

"No. But I doubt the woman was the child's mother. She wouldn't leave him off here and then shift. She would know her son would shift too then. Well, if they're anything like us," Mary said. "And we would have smelled a different wolf scent on her. She was strictly human. At first, Heidi just thought she'd left a human child off. What else was she to think? Then the business with him trying to shift in the front room? Because the woman didn't sign him in, we figured it was a case of getting rid of him."

Demetria shook her head, but this was why she was a Guardian. Kid issues always concerned her.

Everett ran the video again. But none of them saw anything else to aid them.

Mary said, "Why don't you see Maya and ask her if she knows anything about this."

"Tammy might have told you that Maya is our half sister," Everett explained to Demetria.

"Yes, she spoke about Maya and her brother, Connor." Tammy had been thrilled to learn she had a half sister and brother. Demetria couldn't have been more pleased for her, but since they lived near Houston, Demetria had never met them.

"What would Maya know about this, Mom?" Everett asked.

"She called to tell me when she and her mate were coming for Christmas right before I talked to you. I told her I had a wolf pup shifter fighting with the jaguar cubs, and she asked me who was going to handle it. Like every day a boy turns into a wolf pup at my day care! I told her I was calling you because you weren't on a mission, and you'd be on your way immediately. She told me to have you call her as soon as you could. She didn't tell me why. I had to let her go anyway so I could deal with the fighting cats and wolf and contact you."

The door to the back room opened, and Lacy joined

them. She took Mary's hand. "Heidi says she needs you to help with the other kids."

Demetria looked down at Lacy, her red-blond sausage curls framing her face. She was a pretty little girl. Demetria couldn't imagine how awful it had to have been to be stolen from her parents at the Costa Rican resort. And then to see the kidnappers and Matt die… Lacy must have been scarred emotionally. "Are you going to be in the Christmas play?" Demetria guessed that's why the little girl was here.

"Yeah, my sister and brother didn't want to do it this year. They said they were too old. But I'm a big helper this time." Lacy was still tiny for her age. She looked about the size of the four-year-olds, and she had a heart of gold.

Mary squeezed Lacy's hand. "A real angel. Come on, let's help Heidi. Good luck, and let me know what happens with the boy." Mary gave Everett a hug.

He gave her one back and a kiss on the cheek.

Lacy let go of Mary's hand and gave him a big hug too. He smiled down at her, hugged her back, and since she looked like she was expecting one, he gave her a kiss on the cheek too. Then she appeared to be waiting for Everett to give Demetria a hug and a kiss on the cheek. Demetria felt her cheeks burning, especially when she recalled Everett *had* given her a kiss on her cheek—last night when she was a little bit tipsy. Even his mom waited for a moment to see if he'd do it.

He only smiled at Demetria.

When he didn't give Demetria a hug, his mom said, "Glad you're helping Everett with this, Demetria."

Then Mary took Lacy's hand and hurried back down the hallway to take care of the jaguar kids, the door to the hallway locking behind her.

"Where is Maya's home?" Demetria asked Everett as she rummaged through the bag the woman had left with the boy. "Just a blanket with sheep on it and the boy's clothes. No ID."

"Maya and her husband live near Houston, over a three-hour drive from here. She helps to run a garden shop and nursery with her brother and his mate. Her husband, Wade Patterson, is also a JAG agent." Everett pulled out his cell phone and called his half sister. "Maya, what do you know about the wolf pup at Mom's day care?" He paused and listened, then said "All right" and hung up the phone.

"What did she say?"

"She said it was too risky to talk about this over the phone. Do you want to take my car or yours?"

Not about to go any further with this if it was all a hoax, Demetria crossed her arms over her chest. "Prove to me that the wolf pup is a shifter."

Everett's eyes rounded a bit. "Hell, Demetria. I thought you believed us. I would have immediately shown the video of him shifting to you."

Then she felt a little guilty. Yet, until she saw real proof, she just couldn't envision it was true.

"Here, take my phone and look at the video." He fished his phone out of his pocket while juggling the wolf pup on a hip. "When he shifted the second time in front of me, I had put him on the floor and was taking a picture of him to send to my boss. Then he shifted, so I caught it on video. Or at least the blurring of forms like when we shift. It helped because I have both the boy and the pup in one video while he shifted."

She looked at the video and couldn't believe it. "Unreal." She wanted to say it was an elaborate ruse, that somehow he had Photoshopped it. But she had seen the way artists took animal forms and changed them into other forms, humans even, and it wasn't anything like how the jaguar kind really appeared when they shifted. The boy looked like he shifted just like their kind, except he turned into a wolf.

With Mary Anderson seeming so flustered, the corroborative video, and the fact they had a wolf pup at a jaguar-cub day care, Demetria was coming to believe that the story had to be real. Yet, the notion that other shifters existed was so unreal that it still seemed unimaginable.

"Okay, we'll take my car then. I've got a car seat for emergencies. While he's a wolf pup, you can just hold on to him. He seems to like you anyway, even if you are a big, scary jaguar cat."

Everett chuckled. "He thought I was a safe bet when the jaguar cubs were trying to claw at him. But maybe we should take my car and just transfer the car seat."

"Looks to me like you're doing just fine with him. We'll need a leash, crate, collar, and clothes, snack food, something for him to drink, water bowl, dog bed, puppy food, and more. I've got a few things for jaguar cubs we can use, but not everything we'll need for the wolf pup. I'll leave you off at your place because you won't be able to drive and handle the pup, and then I'll pick up the necessary items. We should each pack a bag in case Maya's information leads anywhere and we have to stay overnight or longer somewhere else. I wasn't…prepared for this. I thought it was a joke."

"I don't blame you. But I really did think you believed us. I thought someone had played a prank on my mom at first too. I still can't believe it. I'll call Maya and tell her we'll be there as soon as we can. I can leave my car at the day care for a day or two. Or my sister and mom can move it back to my town house when they have a moment. Tammy's got a spare key for it."

Demetria reached over and ran her hand over the wolf pup's head. He opened his amber eyes and licked her hand, his tail wagging. "We'll need a name for him."

"White Fang," Everett said without hesitation, then headed outside with the pup.

Demetria unlocked the doors, and Everett climbed into the passenger seat.

Tossing the boy's bag in the back of the car, Demetria rolled her eyes. "He's not a scary wolf. I'll think up a name until he shifts and can tell us his own name." She sighed. "Everett, about last night…"

He smiled. "If I hadn't gotten the frantic call from Mom early this morning, I would have hung around your place and fixed you breakfast. Or something for a hangover if you'd needed it."

She chuckled. "I'm almost glad you got the call so you didn't see me fall out of bed this morning. But thanks for coming over and taking care of the mess. I wanted to say thank you."

"You challenged me to do it."

"I did?"

"Yep, and I always accept a challenge."

She smiled, glad he hadn't been trying to get back

at her with some silly boy-turned-wolf story this morning. "Thanks for thinking of me when you needed help with this."

"You were the only one I knew who could deal with this."

"Howard?"

Everett laughed. "He wasn't interested in handling a teen. A four-year-old? I'm sure he would have begged off on this one."

"I don't know. The wolf pup would probably have softened Howard around the edges a little." Then she got on the phone link in her car and called her boss. "Okay, sir, the boy *is* a wolf shifter. Everett will send you the video of him shifting. After we pick up some things for the boy, we're headed south to Houston to see Everett's half sister who might know something about this. Not sure. We might be staying overnight there. I'll keep you posted."

"I'll let the other directors know what you've discovered, and they can disseminate the information. Has anyone gotten ahold of the boy's mother?" Ben asked.

"No. The woman who dropped him off didn't wait to check him in and didn't leave any name for the boy or any ID for herself. Looks like she was trying to get rid of him, but in a safe place. The boy said his mommy and daddy were coming for him. But the chances that a wolf mother would allow a human to drop off her wolf son at a day care and then shift would be pretty much nil, in my book. No way do we believe the parents were coming to get him."

"I agree. What is the boy's approximate age?"

"About four, sir," Demetria said.

Everett said, "Sir, the boy has shifted a couple of times already. So I would think if they're anything like us, the mom's alive. But don't you think it would be better if someone with the Guardian branch took him in while we search for his family?"

Demetria was surprised Everett would include her in the searching part if the boy wasn't going with them.

"No," Ben said. "You'll need to have him with you so we can make sure he recognizes his family when you locate them, and no telling where this will lead you. If you have the boy with you, they can see you're only trying to return him to the family. If he's with a large wolf pack and you only claim to have him, it could be dangerous."

Everett looked at Demetria. "Then I need another JAG agent or Enforcer with me, not a Guardian."

Demetria appreciated Everett's concern for her welfare, but no way was she being left out of this. Not now that she knew it was for real.

"She's trained in combat for any situation. You can't take care of the boy on your own. And she's good at dealing with families in crisis. Keep me informed." Then her boss ended the call.

"Mission impossible?" Demetria asked.

Everett was frowning. "I really don't like the idea of you getting involved if we have to deal with an angry wolf pack."

"You heard my boss—we're a team. I can't imagine a wolf pack being angry with us when we're trying to return their child to them."

"Unless we have the issue of dogs versus cats when we locate his pack. What if we don't find his parents?"

"Then we might be spending this Christmas opening presents with junior. Two jaguars and a wolf pup. Can you imagine?"

Everett stared at her for a moment. Then he smiled. "Yeah. We can do that."

She smiled back. "But surely we'll locate the parents before then. Besides, it'll be easier passing him off as a puppy than if the roles were reversed and we were wolves suddenly saddled with a jaguar shifter cub. But truly? I wouldn't mind. How about we call him Snowflake?"

"The wolf pup? No way. He's a guy, and you'd emasculate him with a name like that."

"He's a cute little wolf pup. Snowflake is not feminine. It's just…white, like snow."

"He'd be called a flake. How about Junior?"

She laughed. "Okay, we'll call him Junior."

She pulled into Everett's town-house complex and then under his carport. "See you in a couple of hours."

He didn't look panicked, just little unsure of his new Guardian role of being in charge of a wolf pup.

"Uh, yeah. The sooner, the better." Then with the wolf pup under one arm and the boy's bag slung over his other shoulder, he headed for the back gate.

She smiled at the sight of the big jaguar with the little wolf pup, thinking she really wanted to date Everett if he was finally ready to date her. She was sorry about getting so emotional over the movie the night before last. But she'd had fun with Tammy too. She chuckled, hoping Tammy felt okay after drinking and staying up so late. Demetria vaguely remembered Everett warning her what would happen if Tammy didn't made it to work on time in the morning.

That showed what a decent brother he was. She smiled again, backed out of his parking space, and headed for town to do some shopping, hoping they'd find the parents quickly. She worried how that would turn out too. How would the wolf shifters react when they learned that jaguar shifters existed, and that they had one of their own?

For better or worse, this would be one Christmas to remember.

Chapter 8

GLAD DEMETRIA APPEARED TO BE FINE AFTER THE rough night she'd had, Everett was even gladder that she was working with him on this mission. As soon as he was in his tiny backyard, he put the pup down on the grass. The pup lifted his chin and smelled the air, then poked his nose in the grass and breathed in all the scents there. A yellow leaf blowing around on the grass caught his eye, and just like a jaguar cub would, he pounced on it. Then the pup squatted and Everett was glad he was housebroken enough to realize he had to pee outside when he was a wolf pup. At least jaguar cubs could use a litter box indoors if they had to.

Everett unlocked his back door and let the puppy into his town house. He hoped his place was puppy proof enough. He hadn't ever considered the trouble a puppy could get into if he was still teething.

What bothered Everett most about the boy's case was that the mom had shifted back and forth so frequently. He wondered if she was newly turned and didn't have much control over keeping her human form. He glanced up at the morning sky where the full moon was still visible. The phases of the moon didn't affect jaguar shifters, but according to the legends he'd heard, it affected werewolves. Were the tales true then? That would be good. Once the full moon waned, maybe the pup couldn't turn into a wolf again until the next full moon. Surely by then he'd be with his family again.

Everett closed the door and headed for his bedroom. Then he had a brilliant thought. At his age, the boy should be able to tell Everett his name and who his parents were. Maybe even where he lived. The woman had dropped him off here in Dallas, so wasn't the boy likely to be from the area? If so, wouldn't he and Demetria be nearer to the boy's parents here than in Houston? Maybe not, if he'd been stolen from somewhere else and brought here.

Everett hated having to take the boy over three hours south if the trip wasn't necessary. He was getting ready to call his boss to let him know his plans when Martin called him.

"I hear you have taken on a priority mission over the holidays," Martin said.

"Yeah. Talk about a surprise call from my mom. And you got the call from Ben Knight?"

"Yeah, the Guardian director said you have the case of the century to work on. He sent me the video. I suspected you had your hands full and that's why you didn't contact me first. I could put someone else on the case, but because the boy was left off at your mom's day care, you were the first one on the scene. Everyone else has a case or some other important mission anyway, so I know you're the right one for the job. I'm going to need a new team of agents who deal with multiple shifter situations. Forget working strictly with a mixed force of jaguar agents. This will take priority if we end up having more cases like this. Want to head up the team?"

"You're joking."

"You know I never joke. Or…rarely. You would be the first to deal with a case like this. And on-the-job-training like this is invaluable." Martin paused. "So the video looks real."

"It is. No joke about this."

"I'll alert our people. It's bad enough when our own kids go missing, but wolf-shifter kids we didn't even know existed? It puts all of us—them and us—in even more danger."

"Tell me about it."

"Is he still a wolf?"

"Yeah. I think it's because of the full moon."

"Hell, I'll have to read up on werewolf lore so I know more about what we're dealing with. Who would have thought any of it was real! So what's your next move?"

Everett packed a bag while he told the director what he intended to do. "But I keep thinking that the family might be in the area, and I'd hate to take him that far away when we might be better off trying to locate them here. We could possibly locate the woman who had dropped him off at the day care and learn where she picked him up."

"Whatever needs to be done, it's your call. I'm letting everyone in the branch know about your circumstances and telling them to spread the message. If anyone runs across people who smell like wolves, they might be actual shifters, not just someone who owns a wolf or wolf dog or works with them. Maybe we'll get lucky and discover the parents or a wolf pack in the Dallas area who know something about a missing boy."

"Oh hell."

"What?" Martin asked.

"I was at the mall shopping yesterday with Demetria—" As soon as Everett said it, he figured he shouldn't have mentioned shopping with the agent. He didn't want to give the impression he was dating her unless he actually was. "Well, some kid nearly ran into me with a gooey candy cane, and I thought I smelled wolf on him. Same with the mom. She had triplets."

"Can you remember what they looked like?"

"Yeah. I'll give our sketch artist the details when I get back. I just thought the family was raising a wolf dog. But they smelled like wolves and the boys were triplets."

"Sure as hell sounds like we might have a pack of werewolves in Dallas then. Who would have ever thought? Once you get the sketches drawn, we can circulate them and set up surveillance at the mall. If the woman shops there regularly, maybe we can question her in case she knows about a missing Arctic wolf child. Not only that, but we might catch the scent of other wolves at the mall."

"Sounds like a good plan." Everett was feeling better about the case already. Not only because Demetria was working on it, but because they might have found the pack living practically on their doorstep. "I still believe the boy must have been stolen, and then the woman changed her mind about keeping him or selling him or whatever."

"Certainly sounds that way. Good luck, Everett, and keep me posted."

"Thanks, sir. Will do."

Everett had barely gotten off the phone when his sister called. "Ohmigod, this can't be for real. Mom called me and said you have the wolf pup. And Demetria's helping with the case."

"I do. Believe me, it's real. How are you feeling? After last night?"

"Fine. Thanks for waking me this morning. I would never have woken on my own. As soon as I'm off, I'm going to bed. Umm, you might not want to mention to David that I was at Demetria's house partying last night. He doesn't mind that I do. But he would be concerned if he learned my brother had to take care of me this morning. How's Demetria doing?"

"She seems to be fine. It's been kind of hectic since I got the call from Mom about the wolf pup. I wasn't able to stay and fix Demetria breakfast or see her before I left."

"This pup situation is worse than Huntley having to take care of jaguar cubs in the jungle while trying to locate their kidnapped parents. At least with that one, everyone back home was asking around to learn if any family had gone to that part of the world at that time. With wolf shifters that we didn't believe existed? That's going to be impossible. I'm training JAG students right now; just taking a break. But at lunchtime, can I come by and see him?"

"Demetria is picking up some supplies, and then we're taking him down to the Houston area to see Maya."

"Why can't she come here instead? Don't tell me. Between helping out with the twins and working the holiday season at the nursery, they can't break away from the business for that long. But..." Tammy paused.

"What?"

"Umm, nothing. Demetria loves kids. Good luck."

"What, Tammy?"

"Okay, she told me this in secret, but you're my

brother and you wheedled it out of me. Demetria's father's back in town. I thought she'd stay close to make sure her mom was okay."

"Is her father abusive? Threatening her mother in any way?" Hell, what next?

"I don't know. All I know is that despite Demetria working at her job as usual, she's still concerned about her mom. Demetria is really secretive about her family. I've known her and her mother for a couple of years, but in all that time, I've only seen her father once. Demetria was always over at our house, but one time she invited me to her place. Her dad was supposed to be out with his friends.

"When I got there, he was still there. He had a hard, scowling face and didn't like that she was having anyone over. Even though I gave him a hard look right back, I'll admit I felt chilled to the bone. He slammed the door and headed out to the pub to meet up with some friends. Then he split and Demetria didn't see him again. She and her mother were so relieved. So anyway, I just wanted to warn you that if she seems distant or distracted, it might be because her dad's in town and she's worried about her mother."

"Thanks for telling me."

"Yeah, but don't you dare tell her I said anything about this. She won't share anything with me anymore, but I worry about her and her mother."

Hell. No way did he want Demetria to come with him to see Maya if she was worried about her mom. Truth be told, he wanted to take care of her dad for her by chasing him right back out of town.

"So what's the deal with Maya?" Tammy asked.

"She's keeping secrets. Hey, got to let you go. The pup's exploring. Don't want him chewing stuff up or leaving anything behind that I have to clean up. But I'll send you the video of him." The directors would be sharing it with everyone pronto, but Everett knew Tammy would love to see it first.

When she got the video, Tammy laughed. "He's adorable. If I didn't know he had parents who have to be desperate to get him back, I'd want to keep him. This is too unreal. Okay, got to go. Tell me what you learn as soon as you can—and what our sister is keeping from us too."

"Will do." Everett hung up and headed down the hallway calling, "Hey, pup. Come!"

The pup came running out of the bathroom, the end of a roll of toilet paper in his mouth and the rest of the roll trailing back to the bathroom as he greeted Everett.

"No, no." Everett tore off the toilet paper, carried the rest back into the bathroom, and stuffed it on top.

The puppy was right behind him, wagging his tail.

Everett couldn't be annoyed with him, knowing he was just like a curious, playful jaguar cub of that age, so he scooped the puppy up and carried him into the living room. He sat on the couch, making the puppy stay on his lap, and then called Maya. "Listen, I want to know what you wouldn't tell me at the day care. I don't want to make the long trip down there for nothing."

"It's not for nothing, and I'm not sharing over the phone, Everett, so don't ask."

"Does your mate know?"

"No, so don't try to go around me on this. Do you have a picture of the puppy?"

He took a quick picture and sent her that and the one of the boy shifting.

"Aww, he so adorable."

"Yeah, but he'd be a lot cuter if he was with his family. I hate to think what they're going through over this." At least Lacy's parents had known she was with the kidnappers and a jaguar team was tracking them. But the wolf pack? Though Everett imagined they were searching for the boy too, they wouldn't know what had happened to him or that a team like theirs was taking good care of him while searching for them.

"Unless…"

"They're dead," he said. "But the mother can't be. The cub wouldn't be able to shift into his wolf form. That is, if they're like us." He kept thinking the wolves were nearly identical to the jaguars in shifting behavior, but what did they really know about it? Nothing.

"Okay, that's good news. We'll see you in about three and a half hours. Are you staying the night?"

"Might be."

"Are you coming with someone? Who's taking care of the pup?" Maya asked.

"Demetria MacFarlane is coming from the Guardian branch."

"Oh good. Do you need two rooms or one?"

"Two."

"Okay, see you in a little while."

After they said good-bye, Everett carried the pup into his bathroom. Everett packed his shaving kit and put it in his overnight bag with his clothes. Then he found an old, clean rag in his rag box and carried everything into the living room. While he waited for Demetria, he played tug-of-war with the pup. He just hoped the pup wouldn't try this on his clothes later.

An hour later, the doorbell rang and the pup began barking and ran to the back door.

Everett had never owned a dog, so everything the puppy did amused him. Jaguars were so quiet. They'd go to see who had arrived, but they'd do it silently.

Everett let Demetria in. "I just called Maya to let her know we might need to stay the night."

"Two rooms, right?"

"Yeah. You and the pup can have one of them."

She smiled. "The way the two of you are bonding, I thought he'd want to stay with you. I was in such a rush that I didn't have a chance to use the bathroom. Do you mind?"

"No, go ahead."

He grabbed his bag and carried it out to the car, leaving the pup in the yard for a moment to do his business if he needed to again. Then he realized that if the puppy had an accident, they'd need some cleanup supplies.

He glanced at the town house. He wanted in the worst way to ask Demetria about her mother and her father. He wished he could take care of her father himself. In any event, he wanted to have someone look after her mother without upsetting Demetria.

She came out of the house wearing a half-amused expression.

"Did you get paper towels, trash bags, and rug cleaner, or whatever else we might need to clean up accidents?" Everett asked.

She smiled. "Yeah. We're good. I think I thought of

everything. Umm…but…did you have some trouble with the toilet paper?"

For a moment, he didn't know what she was talking about. Then he chuckled. "Was it a little wet? Too many teeth marks in it?"

"The wolf pup?"

"Yeah. I don't usually chew on the paper."

She smiled. "I'm glad that's the only reason it was wet and all bunched up on top of the paper holder."

He laughed and threw his bag in the back of her vehicle. He placed the puppy in the backseat, where he immediately curled up on a blue-and-white dog bed. He seemed to like car travel, something else Everett hadn't considered. He remembered his mother saying that both he and Huntley got carsick when they were really little. Not Tammy though. His mother had teased about how she was so much tougher than the boys when it came to car rides.

"Did you need to check on anything before we leave town?" Everett asked. "Your mom? I forget she's all alone and relies on you for things."

"No. She'll call if she has any trouble."

"We'll be three and a half hours away."

"She'll be fine."

"If you need any help with anything…"

"Like…what?" Demetria sounded annoyed, as if she suspected his sister had said something to him she shouldn't have.

He shrugged. "She can call Tammy, and she can get her help if she needs it."

"Why would she need help, Everett?"

He let out his breath. "Don't get mad at Tammy."

He thought that Demetria was ready to slug him. "She was surprised you would be leaving town. And I asked why, concerned that you would need to be here for some reason. I don't want you to feel obligated—"

"*What* did Tammy say exactly?"

"Only that your dad was back in town, and that's it. I swear it. If you need me to talk to him and tell him to clear out, I'd be happy to do it."

Demetria let out her breath and climbed into the driver's seat of her car.

"I mean it. I'll knock some sense into him, do whatever it takes, if he's causing trouble for you and your mom."

"I shouldn't have mentioned it to Tammy."

"Demetria, I'm serious."

"I am too. Just drop it. Mom will be fine."

But he heard the edge to her voice and suspected she would worry about it until they returned home. "Maybe I should call Howard, and he and some of his Enforcer friends can go talk to your dad."

Demetria gave him a hint of a smile.

He sighed and folded his arms. "But I'd rather take care of it myself."

"You can't take care of the whole world, Everett. Me, my mom, your family, the wolf pup, my dad. You have to draw the line and deal with one issue at a time. Just like I have to. Or it will drive you crazy."

"So what's the deal with your dad?"

Demetria ground her teeth, but she didn't say.

Everett finally changed the subject, but he wanted to know what was going on so he could deal with her dad when he got home. "I was wondering if the full moon dictates when the wolves shift."

Appearing relieved Everett was getting back to wolf-shifter business, Demetria pulled onto the interstate. "And that's why he, or his mother, had to shift."

"But I'm also wondering if the mom is a new shifter. That's why he wasn't staying in his wolf form but switching back and forth a couple of times. Who does that? No one. You strip, shift, and stay like that for a while."

"Wow, so that means once the moon is waning, he'll just stay in his human form. Good. Lots easier for us to take him around to places while we're looking for his parents." Demetria's cell rang and she ignored it. "Just another call asking about the wolf."

Everett shook his head. "I hadn't thought of it, but that will be the next thing." As if on cue, Huntley, Everett's brother, called. "Hell, dude, I hear you've got a case and a half. I thought it was bad enough to take care of two jaguar cubs in the jungle, but this beats that."

"I asked Mom if you could handle it since you had the experience."

Huntley laughed. "I'm in Belize again. I'm sure you can take care of it. I hear you're working with Demetria MacFarlane, and she's good at dealing with kids. Are you getting anywhere on this case?"

"Hope to soon."

"Good luck with that." Gunfire sounded in the background. "Got to go. See you soon, hopefully."

Everett frowned. What kind of a mission was his brother on now? It was too late to ask because the line had gone dead, but he wished he was there helping Huntley out. Demetria was right. He couldn't save the whole world all at once, only one little piece of it at a time.

Maya's mate called next. "Yeah, Wade?" Everett said.

"Maya says we've got a unique guest coming to stay the night. We've had to tell everyone we're meeting you in Dallas because all kinds of people have been calling us, wanting to come and see the wolf pup if you're coming here. Someone must have leaked the news."

"Tammy probably, not thinking it would matter if anyone knew. Thanks for the heads-up, Wade. Do you know what Maya won't talk to me over the phone about?"

"No. I'm guessing it has to do with that man at the Oregon Zoo who was trying to recover his jaguar and thought Maya had something to do with stealing her."

"Henry Thompson?"

"Right."

"What does he have to do with all of this?"

"I don't know. He did have wolves painted on his truck, and wolves were missing from his zoo too. Just like the jaguar we had to rescue. Maybe they were shifters?"

"Hell. Who would have thought they might be? Why wouldn't Maya want to share that with me over the phone?"

"I imagine it's because she's afraid we'd want to kill Henry or turn him. He's married to a human woman named Chrissie, and he's raising her kids. He's protective of the animals and helped Maya out. I suspect Maya doesn't want anyone to know he truly knows about us. She only helps run the garden shop and the nursery. She's not a JAG agent like us. She thinks Big Brother JAG monitors everything we do and say."

"Okay, gotcha."

"Got to go before she misses me. I just wanted to warn you not to tell anyone where you're going to be—if everyone in the world doesn't already know."

"Okay, thanks, bud."

When they ended the call, Everett knew he had to tell his partner about the biologist from the Oregon Zoo. He warned her that the human could help them, and they were not going to reveal the truth about Thompson—that he knew wolf and jaguar shifters existed—unless he gave them no other choice.

"I didn't think that was our policy," Demetria said, her brows raised.

He couldn't tell whether it bothered her or not. She was so serious that he thought it did.

"Henry Thompson is one of the good guys." Everett left it at that. Henry had tried to protect Maya from hunters, and Everett's family owed him big time. "I had another thought. I discussed it with Martin already, but I needed to mention it to you." He reminded her about the mother with the triplets and how they smelled of wolf.

"Ohmigod, what if…?" Then Demetria frowned. "The toddlers looked at you really strangely. What if they were wolves, and the mother of course too, and you smelled like—"

"A cat." He explained about having a sketch artist draw a picture of the family and then having Guardians hit the mall to see if they could locate the woman and her toddlers again. Even see if they could locate their scents.

"We could even take the pup—well, when he shifts back—to the mall and see Santa and watch for signs of the woman and her kids, or maybe others in a pack."

"As long as the boy doesn't shift again after he turns back into a human."

"Agreed."

When they finally arrived at the nursery, they saw several vehicles parked there.

"Looks like they have customers." At least that's what Everett was hoping and that it wasn't a bunch of jaguar shifters coming to check out the wolf pup. The nursery sold poinsettias, live Christmas trees, and wreaths for Christmas, so even in winter they had a brisk business. "Connor, Maya's twin brother and my half brother, and his wife, Kat, will be here too. They help run the place." He wasn't sure how much Demetria knew about his extended family. They were so busy running things down here that they rarely had a chance to visit Dallas. So Demetria might never have met them.

All grins, Maya and Kat hurried out to the car. Wade nodded from the porch, a blond-haired toddler in each arm: Connor and Kat's son, Donovan, dressed in a blue sweatshirt, overalls, and red cowboy boots, and their daughter, Kimmi, wearing a pink sweater, jeans, and pink cowgirl boots. But Connor wasn't there to greet them. Probably helping customers so the ladies and Wade could visit with Everett and Demetria.

Before Everett could take the wolf pup out of the backseat, Maya was opening the door and cooing over him. "He's so adorable. Come on, Pup. Let's take you in the house and get you settled." Then she leaned in to get the puppy and carried him into the house.

Beaming, Kat quickly greeted Everett and Demetria and then chased after Maya.

Demetria laughed. "If we didn't need to take him with us to find his parents, I'd suggest we leave him with Maya and Kat for safekeeping."

Everett smiled. "I wholeheartedly agree. Though

Kat's got two toddlers of her own, so I'm not sure how that would go over, considering how the jaguar cubs reacted to the boy at the day care."

"Territorial," Demetria said. "I bet you anything if they spent some time together, they'd become best friends. Not sure about the adult versions though. We could have some real issues on our hands as soon as they know we exist, and I can see some of our people not liking them either. Change can create real conflict."

Chapter 9

EVERETT, CONNOR, AND WADE COOKED STEAKS AND vegetables over the grill on the back patio, while talking about the impact that learning werewolves existed would have on their world.

The ladies were talking about wolf shifters too, as they set the table and got the kids ready to eat. The aroma of cinnamon filled the house, coming from potpourri filling decorative dishes everywhere. The Christmas tree stood proudly in the living room, decorated in a peacock theme, with faux peacock feathers, bright-green-and-blue ribbons and bows and balls, and white lights. No Christmas presents were under the tree yet, like they would have been before Connor and Kat had kids. Everett realized Santa Claus hadn't come yet. Kids sure changed a couple's way of life.

"So is she single?" Connor asked Everett.

"Who?" Everett wasn't about to mention that he was seeing Demetria in a courtship way until he knew for sure he was. He wondered if she had discussed her father issues with Matt. Probably. He'd never said anything about them to Everett, but then again, Matt hadn't discussed Demetria much when they'd gotten together except to say they were going to various places on dates.

Handing Everett a bottle of beer, Wade chuckled. "She's single. Maya made me look her up in the agent database. Tammy told her Demetria is one of her best

friends and she bit you a couple of years back. So that's
a sure sign of something."

Smiling, Connor began grilling the broccoli and potatoes. "Yeah, when they bite, that can be a good thing.
Or *not*."

"We're just working a mission," Everett said, frowning and thinking how much he would like to be dating
her for real.

"Yeah, well, you know what happened on our missions that began just like this one," Wade joked.

"I don't recall any case where the shifters were
looking for a wolf-shifter pup's family." Everett
wasn't going to buy into their good-natured ribbing.
He figured if he and Demetria ever did start dating, he
wasn't letting the whole world know—at least, not
right away.

"Yeah," Connor agreed. "One minute I was in the
jungle as a cat rescuing a damsel in distress, and the
next thing I knew, we were in more trouble than I ever
bargained for."

"Here I was minding my own business on a mission
when Maya danced into my life," Wade said.

"I warned her you were nothing but trouble. Did she
listen to me? Hell no." Connor cast his brother-in-law a
stern look, but it was all in mock fun. The two were like
brothers now.

Wade shook his head. "Hell, I thought you were going
for a harem with two women at your beck and call."

Connor and Everett laughed. Everett could see how
Wade had thought that too.

Everett knew he'd never get tied up in a marital
arrangement on a mission. He was still laughing about

how it had happened to Connor and Wade. Then his brother, Huntley, had managed to get dragged into something, even though both he and his female partner were in relationships.

"You say 'no way' now," Wade said, "but you just wait. Before long, you'll be begging her to say 'I do.'"

That had Everett thinking again about Matt's final words. He had said he was going to propose to Demetria before New Year's. Everett had waffled about telling her that, not wanting to hurt her any more than she already had been when he broke the news. Everett had finally told her, but he'd felt like hell doing it.

He had often thought, why him? Why had he made it out when Matt had his whole life ahead of him with Demetria? She needed that. A mate. The kids. A real family like she hadn't had growing up. Sure, his own family would have missed him, but there were so many of them that it wasn't the same. He hadn't had a fiancée to come home to. Just an empty apartment.

Matt's death had impacted his life to such an extent that Everett had hated going to his old apartment at night after work. Couldn't stay there on weekends. He'd shared too many fond memories with Matt there, especially once Huntley had found his own mate. So Everett had bought a town house and moved out. Had it been a coward's way out? Or a way to move on? But seeing Demetria like this brought it all back to him.

"Are you all right, Everett?" Connor asked. Both he and Wade were watching him.

Everett swallowed the lump in his throat and nodded. "I didn't realize you were on a break," Everett said to Wade, changing the subject.

"Leaving in a couple of days for Costa Rica, so I'm enjoying the time with Maya," Wade said.

"Will you be home for Christmas?"

"Sure hope so. But you know how these missions go."

"Yeah, sure do. What's your case?"

"That guy you all left alive in the area, the middle man trafficking wild cats? Just dropping down there like you said we would to make sure he's still clean."

"Gotcha. You're not going alone, are you?"

"No, my brother's going along."

"Don't tell me Tammy's going too." Their parents were looking forward to the family being home for Christmas this year.

"No, her boss has her scheduled to do more teaching."

"I bet she's not happy about that."

"She said she'll keep the fires burning."

Everett smiled. "What about you, Connor? How are things going with the nursery business?"

"Things couldn't be better, both financially and emotionally. It's great having a family here now." Connor served the food.

"I'm surprised Dad hasn't tried to convince you to join the JAG force."

Roy Anderson had worked undercover for years, and he had encouraged all his children to join the agents' cause.

"No way. I'm happy to just take Kat south of the border on vacations. So what are you going to do about the boy?"

"Try to locate some wolf packs and stir up some trouble, I'm afraid." Everett helped carry the plates of food inside.

Everyone settled in the dining room to eat as Maya explained about Henry Thompson, the biologist at the Oregon Zoo. Kat's twin toddlers were sitting in booster seats at the dining room table, poking at their mashed potatoes and gravy, while the wolf pup ate chicken strips out of a dog dish near the kitchen.

"I thought Henry's trouble was just with the wolves, but then losing the jaguar cat seemed like too much of a coincidence. He seemed to want to tell me something more about the wolves, but then he clammed up. Like he already knew too much about our kind and didn't want to add to the trouble he could get into if he revealed he knew about wolf shifters too. Or maybe since we didn't know about them, I'd just think he was crazy." Maya cut into her steak.

"I called his number to ask if he knew of any Arctic wolf packs. His wife, Chrissie, answered and said he was out of the country on a safari in Africa. Not to shoot anything; just to take pictures. He's doing a study of the animals there. She said he wouldn't have any cell reception for about a week and then he would be calling her. She'll pass along that I wanted to speak with him."

"We can't wait that long," Everett said.

"I figured that. She said there had been an Arctic wolf sanctuary in Oregon, but the man who ran it died, and his wife couldn't manage it alone. The wolves were taken in by other sanctuaries, including one near us. I ran over there today, but I'm sure the two white wolves I saw are just Arctic wolves, not shifters. On a hunch, I asked Chrissie if Henry had learned anything about the wolf disappearances from their local zoo, if they ever found the wolves. She told me no, that the whole situation was really strange. She asked if I knew about the activists who tried to free a wolf from the zoo. One was her good friend Bella Wilder, though Bella would never confirm it was her. She married Devlyn Greystoke after that. Henry had been investigating the two of them. Chrissie said they are the dearest people, and they love wolves."

"Sounds a whole lot like us when we are trying to free one of our kind from incarceration." Everett hoped they had a real lead. At least to a wolf pack. Maybe the packs networked with each other and he and Demetria would quickly find the pup's parents.

Wade reached over and squeezed his wife's hand. "You ought to be working for the JAG with us, Maya. That's great detective work, honey."

Maya beamed at her mate. "Thank you, Wade. I looked up the information about the zoo and Bella Wilder in news accounts. I found information about how Thompson had rescued a red wolf and placed her in the Oregon Zoo. Then the red wolf disappeared, and all that was left in its place was a naked woman. The police assumed someone stole the wolf and, in a sick way, had left the woman there to freeze to death. She was hospitalized, but then someone came and stole her away from the hospital."

"Wow. If any of us had gotten wind of that, we might have figured that wolf shifters existed a long time ago. She must have shifted while she was locked up at the zoo," Demetria said. "She couldn't hold her wolf form."

"Maybe the full moon had waned? I didn't think to check. I also asked Chrissie if Henry had ever mentioned seeing any Arctic wolves anywhere. She said no. That made me wonder if the boy could be an Arctic wolf with a gray or a red wolf pack," Maya said.

Demetria pulled out her cell phone. "What was the date of the story?"

Maya gave her the date, and then Demetria looked up the lunar schedule for that time period. "Yeah, the moon was waning."

"They might have a mix of wolves in the pack," Everett said. "But the boy would probably have Arctic wolf parents since he looks like a full-blooded Arctic wolf with the shorter legs and ears and the all-white coat."

"You're probably right. Where do Bella and Devlyn live?" Demetria asked.

"Colorado. Chrissie gave me their phone number in case they know about any Arctic wolf packs."

"Okay. Well, this is going to make for a strange call, but because of the distance from here to Colorado, I think we need to risk it, don't you?" Demetria asked.

"Yeah, I do." Everett finished eating and started clearing away the dishes.

"I wish I could stay and listen to more of this." Connor had to leave to take care of more customers, but he kissed his mate and the toddlers' cheeks, and then petted Junior's head before walking outside.

"Even though I hate missing any more details of this fascinating story, I'll take the kids into the gardens so you can continue to discuss it without any interruptions." Kat bundled up her boy and girl and took them outside.

Maya lifted the wolf pup in her arms, and she, Wade, Demetria, and Everett took seats in the living room.

Then Maya began playing tug-of-war with the pup with a red, green, and white braided-rope pull toy Demetria had bought for him.

"Okay, I'm going to make the call and hope these people are truly shifters and don't think we're crank callers," Everett said.

"If they're anything like us, they won't believe you." Wade settled against the couch.

"True." Demetria sat next to Everett on the couch, surprising him...and pleasing him.

Maya and Wade's brows lifted marginally. Wade's mouth curved a bit as if to say, "I told you so."

Demetria was watching Maya pull the pup around the floor with the rope toy, and Everett was glad she seemed to have missed his family's reaction. "If someone called me and told me he was a wolf shifter, had come across a jaguar cub shifter, and needed to find the parent, I wouldn't believe him. I'm sure since we didn't know about them, they wouldn't know about us either," Demetria said.

"Agreed. Which is why it would be better if you could meet them in person." Maya laughed when the pup went for her hand instead of the rope toy. "You're just like jaguar cubs."

Everett called the number for Devlyn, and as soon as he picked up, Everett put the phone on speaker.

"Hello?" Devlyn sounded like he could be a big, growly wolf.

"Hi, I'm Everett Anderson, and I'm going to tell you something that is going to shock you as much as it did me. I'm looking—"

"I don't want any." Devlyn hung up on him.

Everyone laughed out loud except Everett. "What did I say?" He clearly had missed the punch line.

Demetria smiled. "He probably thought you were trying to sell him something. Let me try." She punched in Devlyn's number. "Hi, I'm Demetria MacFarlane, and I'm trying to locate the parents of an Arctic wolf pup shifter who was left off at a day-care center in Dallas, Texas."

Silence. At least Devlyn didn't hang up on her.

"I got your name and number from Chrissie Thompson, whose husband, Henry, is a friend of my law-enforcement partner's half sister."

With civilians, they used the guise of being under-cover federal agents. Until the wolf shifters realized the jaguar shifters existed, that would probably be the best approach to use with them.

When Devlyn didn't respond, she tried again. "We don't have any idea how to get ahold of the parents of the little boy, but we had to start somewhere. We realize you probably live too far away to be the ones we're looking for, but we're trying to find anyone who might know of them."

"Have you got proof that you have a wolf-shifter pup?" Devlyn asked.

Everett was practically holding his breath, but from Devlyn's response, he had to be a wolf shifter. Otherwise, he most likely would have just hung up on Demetria.

"Yeah, sure. Just a sec. My partner took a video of the boy shifting, so it shows what he looks like both as a boy and as a pup." Demetria sent the video to Devlyn, and they all waited for a response.

"Hell, we don't take videos of wolves shifting."

Demetria let out her breath in an annoyed way. "Don't

you think we know that? How dangerous it can be for our kind? Though even so, I doubt anyone would believe it was for real. We need to find the boy's family. Once we locate some packs, we'll need to show them something that proves we're not making a false claim. How else are we going to identify the boy without driving all over the country and running into all kinds of dead ends, just like we have with you? Time is of the essence. His parents have to be frantic. How would you feel if you were him, lost and unable to return to your family? How would you feel if he were one of your own children?"

Everett smiled a little. Demetria wasn't like any Guardian he'd ever known, and he loved the way she handled the growly wolf.

"I don't know the boy. We don't know of any Arctic wolves or packs around here." Devlyn's tone of voice was still gruff, but he didn't sound like he was ready to end the call so quickly now.

Everett noted the look of disappointment on everyone's faces. "We really need to find the boy's parents."

"He looks to be about three and a half or four years of age. You should be able to ask him his name and who his parents are, maybe even his home address."

"We didn't have a chance before he shifted." Everett regretted that he hadn't. He hadn't expected the boy to shift and had been so shocked to learn of the existence of werewolves that he hadn't thought of asking anything.

"You're the guy who just called me?" Devlyn asked.

"Yeah. We're working blind here."

"Wolf packs don't advertise their locations. You ought to know that. How *exactly* did you end up with the boy?" Devlyn sounded more curious now.

Everett realized they were getting further by just showing the video of the boy, even if the wolves might not like it. Everett and the others knew how dangerous it was to have proof that any of them could shift. But under the circumstances, they needed proof that they had a wolf shifter boy.

"He was dropped off at my mother's day care," Everett said. "We couldn't determine the identity of the woman on the security tape, but we assume she stole the boy from a wolf pack, then decided she had made a mistake and left him off at the day care. She left no ID behind. Just a bag and a blanket."

"She must have realized your place was a wolf day-care center. Which means she's one of us. Why else would she have dropped off a wolf child at your particular day-care center?"

Everett glanced at Demetria to see her take on it. He was afraid that as soon as he said it was a jaguar-shifter day care, Devlyn would hang up on him.

Demetria shook her head, which Everett took to mean that he shouldn't mention they were jaguars.

"My mother had never seen the child or the woman before. I still think it was dumb luck that the woman brought the boy there, since he shifted twice after he was dropped off. He hasn't shifted back yet. Was she afraid someone was going to find her with the kid and she'd be arrested? In any event, it's all still a mystery."

"His mother must be a fairly newly turned mother, if she can't hold her form while her son is with a stranger. For her son's safety, she would have kept her human form otherwise."

"Yeah, the full moon must be making her shift and then her young son is shifting at the same time as his mother." Everett was trying to get confirmation that it worked that way with the wolf shifters, but he hoped he hadn't said anything that showed his ignorance.

"Sorry. Can't help you. We don't know any Arctic wolf shifters."

"We're at a dead end here. Can you give us the name and location of another wolf pack that might know where the pup belongs?" Demetria asked.

"A couple. Not that they've ever mentioned anything about an Arctic wolf pack, and they live even farther away from your location. A distant cousin of mine married a SEAL wolf located on the Oregon coast." Devlyn gave them her number. "No Arctic wolves that I know of in their pack either."

The pup was snarling and growling while Maya tugged him back and forth all over the living room floor with the rope toy, keeping him preoccupied.

"You said there was another?" Demetria asked.

"Leidolf's red wolf pack is in Portland, Oregon." Devlyn gave them his number too. "Oh, and a geneticist. He's been looking for wolf packs to test their blood concerning this longevity issue, if he hasn't located your pack already. Dr. Aidan Denali. I just have his card with his phone number on it. I don't know anything else about him. Still, he might have run across an Arctic pack while doing his research."

"Thank you." Everett felt somewhat relieved that they had a few more leads. But he sure wished someone knew of a wolf pack in Dallas.

"Thanks," Demetria added.

"Let me know when you find the boy's home," Devlyn said.

"Will do." Then Everett ended the call and let out his breath.

"Ohmigod, I can't believe you pretended we were werewolves," Maya said. "That was brilliant. And it worked!"

Everett smiled. "Who would have ever thought?"

"Agreed. We ought to call the geneticist first since he could be working with a ton of packs," Demetria said. "Then he can tell us if he found a white wolf pack."

"What if he wants to test our blood?" Wade asked.

"Wouldn't he be surprised?" Everett straightened his back and called the doctor. "Hi, Dr. Denali? I'm Everett Anderson. Devlyn Greystoke gave me your name and number in case you know of any Arctic wolf packs because of the research you are doing. We're attempting to find the parents of an approximately four-year-old male Arctic wolf shifter, blond hair, amber eyes. He was dropped off at my mother's day care in Dallas, Texas, by a woman who didn't leave an ID. She took off before anyone could talk to her. So we're trying to locate his family."

"The boy shifted? He didn't just smell like a wolf?" Dr. Denali sounded more than concerned. He sounded like he wanted to help too.

Everett was thrilled, yet his enthusiasm waned when he realized the doctor hadn't instantly said he knew of an Arctic wolf pack. "Yes. He's a wolf and he hasn't shifted back, so we can't ask who his parents are, what his name is, and if he knows where he lives."

"The full moon is out. His mother must be a fairly newly turned wolf."

"But he's about four years old."

"Right. Even though she would gain control during the rest of the month, she might still be having trouble during the full moon."

They could change *anytime* during the month? *Great.* Here Everett thought they'd have a reprieve after the moon waned enough.

"I haven't tested any Arctic wolves. I don't recall your name among the packs I've run blood tests on. Are you located in the same place as your mother's day care?"

"Uh, yeah. You haven't tested us." Everett was thinking that a doctor, someone who would be more scientific minded, might believe what they were when others wouldn't without seeing them in person.

"Dallas…"

"Yeah, and that's where the boy was dropped off. So we don't know if his pack is close by or the kidnapper brought him here from somewhere else. Devlyn gave us his distant cousin's pack's location on the Oregon coast, and I'm checking with them next. Another is in Portland, Oregon. But if those don't pan out, do you know of any others that might give us another starting point? Any wolf packs in Dallas?" Everett figured if he mentioned the packs, the doctor or others would believe he and Demetria were on the up-and-up. Hopefully, that would make more of them feel free to share what they knew.

"Only yours in Dallas. I would think you'd know if any others tried to encroach on your territory. There's a wolf pack in Silver Town, Colorado. More of the SEAL wolf team of the Oregon coast lives in Montana. A gray wolf pack claimed the Seattle territory, but they refuse to allow me to test their blood. Another is in Amarillo, but there were significant issues with them and…they've moved on. No Arctic wolves were among any of the packs I've met. What about you? Do you have a pack that you would allow me to test?" The doctor seemed eager to know about this newly discovered pack, as if he'd forgotten why they had called him initially.

"What is the longevity issue that you're testing?" Everett asked, ignoring the doctor's question and hoping his own question didn't trigger some concern on the doctor's part.

The doctor was silent, and so was everyone in the room listening in on the conversation, even the pup who had curled up in Maya's lap and was sleeping as she leaned her back against the couch and Wade's legs corralled her.

"You…don't know?" Now Dr. Denali sounded suspicious.

"Well, we haven't had any problem with it." Everett shrugged at the others, clueless about what was going on. They looked a little apprehensive.

"No changes in your longevity at all? I've got to test your blood. The larger the sample size, the better. I'm hoping I can determine why the change is occurring. But this is good news."

Everett took a deep breath. He hated to give the doctor hope that his kind could resolve whatever their issue was, but he was certain their blood couldn't.

"Dr. Denali, you're a scientific man, right? You believe in all kinds of possibilities if you can test them and prove they're correct, right? I mean, you're open to any new theories. You're not close-minded. Correct?"

"I like to think so. What's this all about?"

"What if I told you my kind have always had the same longevity as humans?"

"Then I'd be disappointed, but I would still want to check your blood to learn why you're so different from the rest of us."

"I can tell you why. But initially, I doubt you're going to believe me. We're shifters. Just not wolf shifters."

Silence.

"When we shift, we become jaguars."

Silence.

"That's why it's imperative that we find the boy's parents. Besides the fact that they must be frantically searching for him, if they are dead, raising a wolf shifter among jaguar shifters might be a bit of a challenge for us and for him."

"I'm sorry. I thought you had a legitimate situation you were calling about. I really don't have time for—"

"Wait, Dr. Denali. I thought you said you were open-minded. Do you have a secure cloud-based service?" Everett asked if the doctor used the same one he did.

"I do."

"Okay, I'll send you a video of the boy shifting into a wolf, and I'll send one of me shifting as a jaguar so you know we're for real and not on drugs or something." Everett sent the video of the boy to the doctor. Then he said, "I'll have someone take the video of me, and we'll send it to you so you'll know this is legitimate. It'll take just a few minutes."

The doctor didn't say anything.

Demetria said, "I'll video record Everett shifting to include Maya, Everett's half sister, with the wolf pup so you can see we're all here. She's been playing tug-of-war with him and wore him out."

Everett quickly stripped out of his clothes. They didn't video record someone shifting ever in case the tape got into the wrong hands, so he felt a little like a stripper while Demetria recorded it. Then he shifted, his muscles and bones heating and reshaping until he was standing before Demetria as a golden jaguar.

He couldn't help but notice the way she was smiling at him as if she was impressed and interested.

The pup had woken and was staring at Everett as if he'd suddenly turned into a giant-sized version of the jaguar cubs who had been clawing and hissing at him at the day care. Everett moved slowly toward him, trying to put the pup at ease and let the boy smell him, forgetting for the moment that his actions could have been videotaped for the wolf doctor. All that mattered was that Everett made sure that the pup knew it was just him and he was safe. And then the pup wagged his tail and began play-biting Everett. He hadn't expected that and lay down on his side so he could let the pup nip at him.

Everyone in the room laughed.

After that, Demetria said, "Okay, everybody ready?"

Everett thought Demetria had ended the video right after he shifted. He wondered just how much she had caught of his interaction with the pup.

"Yeah, go ahead," Wade said, rubbing Maya's back.

Everett nodded his jaguar head.

Demetria said, "Sending it now."

She waited until it went through. "Okay, as you can see, Everett shifted into a golden jaguar. The boy is perfectly safe with us and will be well-loved, played with, and fed, but we still need to find his family."

The doctor still didn't respond.

"Dr. Denali, are you still there?" Demetria asked.

Everett thought maybe the call had been dropped. He couldn't imagine the doctor had passed out or anything that drastic. He was just speechless, Everett guessed. He had to remind himself how he had felt when he first saw the boy shift and then shift again.

"How…how long have you known we exist?" The doctor sounded a little shaken up.

"As soon as the boy was dropped off at Everett's mother's day care and shifted this morning. Believe me, it was a shock for all of us. None of us believed it. If Everett hadn't caught the boy shifting on video, I'm sure none of us would believe it."

"I have to learn everything there is to know about you. This is just unbelievable. And incredibly wonderful." Dr. Denali sounded ecstatic.

Everett swore the man was smiling when he said it. Like he'd made the biological discovery of the century. Still, Everett suspected not all wolf shifters would be so pleased with the situation. The jaguars lived among humans. The wolves must too. Would a wolf pack feel threatened by jaguar shifters in their territory if they knew about them? Cat and dog fights? He could just see it.

"I'd still like to test your blood and learn more about you." Dr. Denali sounded eager.

"You can. But we still need to find the boy's family," Demetria said, emphasizing the importance of *their* mission. "Do you have a wolf police force that can look into it?"

"No. Packs police their own people or those crossing into their territory. I'll let everyone know about it. My brother hires private investigators for his business, completely discreet because of our secret wolf status. He'll have them search for the parents too."

"All right. When the boy shifts, we can learn his name and parents' names, and hopefully his address. We'll share the information with you in case that might help too," Demetria said.

"Would you like to have a wolf pack take care of him?" the doctor asked. "I'm sure any of the packs I work with would be happy to take him in. Well, except for the wolf pack in Seattle."

"No thanks, Doctor. We wouldn't feel right about doing that when he was left with us. And he's perfectly happy with us right now. What is the issue with your longevity, if you don't mind sharing?" Demetria asked.

"We used to have much longer lives. Now, on average, we age one year for every five human years."

Wade whistled. "Hell. What a deal."

The doctor laughed. "Our longevity did cause problems for us while we were trying to keep our slower aging process secret. I've got to work on some cultures, but I'll call my brother, Rafe, and tell him about your circumstances. He'll get his PIs on it right away. No one is going to believe this." He paused. "I want to make arrangements to see you as soon as I can. Welcome to our world of wolves."

"And to our world of jaguars," Demetria said, smiling.

Maya gave Wade a high five.

This wasn't the end, only the beginning, and who really knew how the wolves and jaguars would react?

It was like venturing into a galaxy far away and finding new alien life forms they would have to learn to get
along with.

Chapter 10

EVERETT SHIFTED AND QUICKLY DRESSED BEFORE HE called Hunter, the SEAL wolf on the Oregon Coast. Hunter didn't know about any Arctic wolf packs. Everett didn't tell him anything about the jaguar-shifter equation, just said they were trying to locate the family of the Arctic wolf pup. Hunter mentioned the rest of his SEAL team in Montana. Everett thanked him, though he already knew about them and was trying to look at this reasonably. Cases often required a lot of "footwork" before the agents could get to the meat of the situation.

After he ended the call with Hunter, who had asked him to be updated when they learned who the parents were and wished them well, Everett expressed his concern to Demetria and the others. "Three more to go. The pack in Montana, the Silver wolf pack in Colorado, and the red wolf pack in Portland, Oregon."

"We'll find the parents, Everett." Demetria reassured him. "Look at how we began. We had no idea about *any* wolf packs. Then Maya gave us a clue, and from there, we've had several to check into. It might take a little while, but we'll find them."

"She's right. This is the important groundwork. You'll locate his family," Wade said. "And you still have the possibility of locating the wolves in Dallas."

"Okay, Leidolf's pack, the Silver pack, or Paul's Montana pack first?" Everett asked.

"Toss-up between Leidolf's and the Silver wolf pack. If Hunter didn't know of any, the rest of his SEAL team might not either," Demetria said.

"Leidolf it is." Everett was certain that when he called the red wolf pack leader, he'd get more of the same. Instead, the wolf seemed really wary. Not that Everett blamed him. He imagined if someone he didn't know called out of the blue and started asking about his jaguar family and if they knew the parents of a black jaguar cub—because they were rarer, like the Arctic wolves were—he would be just as wary.

"I don't know who you are or anything about you," Leidolf simply said.

"Fair enough." Everett didn't blame the man one bit. "I have a video of the boy shifting. I'll send it to you. Maybe you'll recognize him." Everett sent the video and then waited for a response.

"I still don't know you. Are you a gray wolf pack? Red? Arctic? Mixed? The pack leader? What?"

Everett glanced at his companions. The wolf was already wary. He was certain if he told him they were jaguar shifters, he would hang up on Everett. But he didn't want to get off on the wrong foot and lie.

"Thanks for all your help. I've got to find the boy's parents. If you don't know anything about them, then I've got to make another call."

"Wait."

Everett's heartbeat ratcheted up a notch. Maybe it wasn't just wariness on Leidolf's part. Maybe he thought he might know where the boy belonged.

"I might know of the wolf pack. It's a long shot, but bring him here, and I'll look into it."

"It's my job, and my partner's, to locate the parents and reunite them."

"Good luck with that," Leidolf said dryly and hung up on him.

Everett looked at all the astonished faces watching him. Demetria said, "He's the first real clue we have."

"He may be wrong."

"He seems to know of an Arctic wolf pack," Wade said.

Everett shook his head. "He might know of an Arctic wolf pack, but I'm not turning the boy over to a red wolf pack all the way out in Oregon."

"They would be more likely to give him the care a wolf needs," Maya said.

"No, Everett's right," Demetria said. "We don't know Leidolf. He might decide to keep the boy in his pack if he's unsuccessful in his search. Then what? The boy would be living way out there, and we'd probably never know it. We have to resolve this ourselves."

"Agreed," Everett said. "I've got another couple of calls to make."

When he got hold of Lori, the female pack leader in Montana, she said, "As to your question, we don't know any Arctic wolves. One of our pack members was part of a gray wolf pack in Seattle. His name is Everett too. Everett Baxter. Maybe his former pack members know of an Arctic wolf pack."

That was the second time someone had mentioned a gray wolf pack in that area. Dr. Denali had said they weren't cooperative about the longevity testing, if it was the same pack. The way the packs were spread out, they didn't seem to like other wolf packs in their

territory. Everett wondered how they'd feel about jaguars being there.

"But otherwise, none that we know of," Lori reiter-
ated. "Good luck."

"Thanks, we'll keep you posted." Everett called
Lori's pack member after that. "Hi, Everett, I'm Everett
Anderson. I just spoke with Lori about trying to find
the parents of an Arctic wolf pup. She said you were
with a gray pack out of Seattle and maybe knew of an
Arctic wolf pack." He sent him the video of the boy and
explained what had happened.

"Okay, yeah, there *is* an Arctic wolf pack that I know
of. Well, they used to be humans and must have tangled
with an Arctic wolf shifter pack. I don't know anything
about it, except that as humans, they had a private-eye
operation in Seattle. When they returned from a trip
back east, they were Arctic wolves. My pack leaders
told them to find some other territory. You know how
difficult it is to keep what we are secret from the human
populace, but to have another wolf pack, all newly
turned, living in your territory? They didn't want to
be absorbed into the pack—not that my leaders were
offering—so they had to leave. I don't have any idea
where they settled. Since they're white wolves, I would
presume up near the border of Canada somewhere.
Maybe they even went to Canada."

Everyone's expressions had brightened.

"That doesn't explain how the boy ended up with us
in Dallas." But Everett was glad to hear that this might
be the real clue they needed.

"I don't think it'll help to call the gray pack leaders,
but here's their number just in case. You might not want

to mention I gave you their number. We didn't part on really good terms."

"Thanks, Everett. Dr. Denali mentioned them too, so we can say he referred me to them."

"I doubt that will go over big either. But good luck."

"Thanks." Everett ended the call. "That Arctic wolf pack might not be the one we're looking for, but the fact they're newly turned gives me some hope that they are."

"Why don't you let me call the Seattle gray wolf pack?" Demetria asked. "Since they had problems with both Mr. Baxter and Dr. Denali, maybe they won't feel as threatened by a woman."

"Sounds good to me," Everett said.

Demetria called and got hold of a June Greyhauffer, who told the same story as Everett.

"Are you kidding me? Well, I'm not surprised that they would be having a bunch of kids and losing them along the way."

How did one little boy turn into a bunch of kids? The woman was definitely hostile toward the Arctic wolf pack.

"So you don't have any idea where the pack has gone? What their names were?" Demetria asked.

"Cameron MacPherson is the pack leader, former private detective. He's probably doing the same kind of work, freelancing as much as he can, if they can't get their shifting under control. I'm just so glad we didn't allow them to stay here. What a mess."

"If you had, the boy probably wouldn't be with us now," Demetria said, her voice angry.

June snorted. "We have our own issues to handle. We don't need a newly turned pack to deal with too. As gray wolves, it's hard enough to hide what *we* are from the general human population without adding Arctic wolves to the mix. If you're out of Dallas, I imagine you know that better than the rest of us. It can't be easy to run pretending to be wild wolves where you live. At least here, if anyone spies us running as gray wolves in the forests, he or she will believe we're from the Idaho pack."

"There's an Idaho pack?" Everett asked, getting ready to jot down the location.

"I mean, *real* wolves. But Arctic wolves? They would stand out too much."

"I understand," Everett said.

"I feel sorry for the kid, but Cameron got himself into this mess."

Demetria didn't think the woman sounded sorry in the least. But if the boy hadn't fallen into the jaguar shifters' hands, he could have been in real trouble. "*If* the boy is his son."

"Well, of course."

Demetria suddenly had another thought. "What if the boy belongs to the Arctic wolf shifter who bit Cameron?"

"Possibly. I don't know anything more about Cameron's pack, and I know even less about the wolf pack they got mixed up with. Got to run. Good luck cleaning up the mess." Then June hung up on her.

"Wow," Maya said. "Sounds like they don't like anyone."

"At least she talked with us and we know about a real possibility. So, now we need to spread the word about this Cameron MacPherson and see if we can get any bites," Demetria said.

"We should share it on all the social networking sites," Maya said.

"You know what happened when you included a jaguar picture of yourself in the greenhouse," Wade reminded her.

"What happened?" Demetria never shared anything on social network sites, but she could just imagine the trouble that could cause.

"The biologist from the Oregon Zoo thought Maya had something to do with stealing the jaguar from his zoo when he saw her as a jaguar in the greenhouse," Wade said.

"Oh." Demetria snorted. "Like all jaguars look alike."

They laughed.

Then Everett got a call. Looking at the caller ID, he quickly said, "It's Leidolf. Putting the call on speaker."

Demetria smiled. So the red wolf leader wasn't as hard-nosed as he appeared to be.

"What's your address? I'm flying out tomorrow to see the boy," Leidolf said, not asking, but acting like a real alpha wolf.

Everyone smiled. But how would he react when he learned they were jaguars?

Wade motioned to Everett to give the nursery as the address.

Everett did, and Leidolf said, "I thought you told me you were from Dallas. Why are you near Houston now?"

"We're here trying to learn what we can from my half sister." Everett explained how the discussion with her about Henry had led them to Devlyn and then eventually to Leidolf. "We got a lead on a Cameron MacPherson and his Arctic wolf pack, but no idea where they are located. Do you know of them?"

Silence. Then Leidolf said, "Yes, but I'll discuss it with you in person. So you're not *with* a wolf pack?"

Everett hesitated to say, as if not wanting to scare Leidolf off. "No, we aren't. We're just…family."

"And you feel safety in numbers."

Everett looked like he was about ready to contradict Leidolf, but Demetria said, "We can meet you, just the two of us, if you'd feel more comfortable with that."

Everett smiled at her.

Like a typical alpha, Leidolf said, "No problem for me. I'll be there at noon. I'll rent my own car, so no need to pick me up at the airport." Then he hung up.

"Yes!" Demetria said. "I think he knows a lot more than he's saying."

"To fly out here, I'd say so," Everett said.

"So does he know about us, or does he just think you're a scaredy-cat wolf and not with a pack?" Maya asked, a teasing glint of the devil in her eyes.

"If so, he's going to be one confused red wolf," Everett said. "I'm going to call Dr. Denali back and let him know that we've got a lead on an Arctic wolf pack so his brother has another clue for his private investigators."

While Everett was making the call, Maya said to Demetria, "You know this could be a good time for the two of you to take a break. It might be a while before you find the boy's family. I can babysit him. I wore him out anyway."

"Sure, we'll take you up on that. Just a walk in the gardens so we'll be close by in case the boy shifts." Demetria smiled at Everett as he glanced in her direction, looking as if he was surprised to hear her agree with the suggestion. Then he ended the call with Dr. Denali.

"Okay, Rafe Denali is having his men search for a Cameron MacPherson who might have established another PI shop somewhere in the States."

"You would think that with a background in investigative work, Cameron would have been able to locate his son already," Wade said.

"You would think so. Who knows what lengths the woman, and I'm sure her accomplice, took to cover their tracks." Everett glanced at the wolf pup sleeping in Maya's arms. "Okay, let's go."

He and Demetria grabbed their jackets, pulled them on, and headed outside. The nursery was closing, and the last customers were leaving. Connor was carrying the toddlers on his way back to the house. "Best way to wear them out," he said, smiling.

Kat was locking up the garden shed and hurried to join him. "Did you have any luck with the calls you were making?"

"We might have a lead about an Arctic wolf pack that's newly turned." Demetria pulled a scarf around her neck and shivered.

"Oh, that's great news." Kat caught up to Connor, who had stopped to talk to them.

Demetria motioned to the house. "Maya's watching the wolf pup."

"Still a wolf then," Kat said.

"Yeah, but we've got a red wolf coming from Oregon tomorrow to talk to us about this Arctic wolf pack. That might give us a real clue to where the boy's family is." Everett zipped up his jacket.

"Did you tell him what we are? He's going to get quite the shock tomorrow if you didn't," Connor said.

"We didn't, but another wolf we talked to might have told him," Everett said.

"Oh wow, he's really coming here?" Kat took one of the toddlers from Connor.

"Yes, hope that's all right," Everett said.

"Sure. Great. Our first wolf man. Should be really interesting, but most of all, maybe you'll get somewhere with the case. Got to take the little ones inside now. Have a nice stroll." Kat walked off with Connor.

"So what are we going to do if Leidolf knows of the family and wants to take the boy with him?" Demetria was worried that he might insist because he was a wolf and knew the family, while Demetria and Everett were jaguar shifters. "He sounds like he has a personal stake in this. Why else would he fly all the way out here?"

"I agree that it could be a concern. It's our job to take care of this, or it will be a concern if not taken care of."

She looked up at him. "You mean with this new 'shift' in our world, we'll be just as ready to protect wolf shifters as our own kind? That should be interesting. Especially when it will take time for everyone in both camps to know the other exists."

"How would you like to be part of a new team that specializes in all shifters? We've got hands-on experience right up front."

She let out her breath, her eyes steady on his. "There might be a need for it." She wondered if there might be more to Everett's offer than a strictly business arrangement.

He pulled her in close. Yeah, like this.

"There might. Then again, there might not be. Still, we've already located several wolf packs and made first

contact. If any of them discover jaguar shifters causing trouble or in trouble, who do you think they would
call?" Everett asked.

"Us, because we've made first contact." She smiled.
"I don't know if my director would go along with it."

Everett's breath was frosty in the chilly night air.
"My director suggested I head the team. But I would
love to work with you, and we can do this together. We
could be the first to teach jaguars in the field how to deal
with wolf shifters, once we get the hang of it."

"We might even have a unified force, with some
wolves on the team eventually. Wow, the possibilities
are limitless."

Demetria shivered and Everett wrapped his arm over
her shoulders, pulled her even closer, and walked with
her down one of the lighted paths. "So what do we call it?
United Shifters Task Force? United Shifters Command?"

"I like *task force*, but it seems like it would be for
one job only. Like a police task force. *Command* sounds
powerful. What about United Shifters Force? The USF."
She snuggled closer to him. This is what she liked even
more. Being close to him, sharing the same heat, connecting. She wished things had ended differently for
them last night. She wished she'd been more with it
and had thanked him better for taking care of her mess.
Well, if she was wishing for things, she wished she had
seen him in the morning after she'd had a chance to look
more presentable.

"Sounds good to me, although the directors might not
go along with our idea," Everett said, looking down at her.

"Sure they will. They already have two experts in
the field."

"You want to shake on it?" Everett smiled, looking really happy and snuggling with her in a sweet way, but not pushing the dating issue. Maybe he was afraid she'd fall apart like she did at the movie.

"No. I want a kiss to seal the deal."

He pulled her to a stop next to a fountain shut off for the winter and ran his hands down her arms. "Demetria—"

"Unless you're afraid I might bite again." Or get upset again.

He laughed. "No way." Yet he seemed hesitant.

"Don't think. Just do it." Then she took his hand and kissed it.

He leaned down to kiss her mouth, the kiss nothing like a handshake kind of a kiss, brief and to the point. His mouth pressed hard against hers, his tongue seeking entrance, the chill instantly abating. He wrapped his arms snugly around her as if he were a bear shifter and not a jaguar, hugging her to his body, saying he wanted her, wanted the intimacy between them, just like she wanted all of it with him.

Demetria was ready to yank off her jacket because her body was already so hot. Instead, she ran her hands underneath Everett's jacket and warmed her fingers for a minute while he continued to kiss her. Yet despite how she'd wanted this, how she'd needed this, tears filled her eyes. She couldn't help it. She had to quit feeling like she was betraying Matt by kissing his best friend. If Everett had asked her out first, things would have been so different now. Yet she felt guilty that she'd even think that.

She pulled away and smiled, her eyes misty with tears, looking quickly away so Everett wouldn't see them. She loved Everett's kiss and knew he felt something for her, so why couldn't she let the past go?

When they separated, she took a deep breath, trying to steady herself. "Okay, good. I'll let my boss know I have a new job." She wasn't going to ask. She would tell him. If her boss didn't go along with it, she'd just put in a transfer to Everett's branch. She might be a super professional in any job she was committed to, but after she saw the way Everett had handled everyone—the teens, Howard, the wolf-shifter boy—she wanted this new job that would take her in a totally different direction.

Everett seemed to like the notion. *Even better*.

"So how do we handle Leidolf, since he doesn't know we are jaguar shifters? What if he wants to take the boy with him?" Demetria slipped one of her cold hands into Everett's jacket pocket as she held him close and they continued to walk.

"He can stay with us and help to find the boy's parents. Or he can return home to his pack. He's not taking the boy anywhere unless the boy's mom or dad is with him and the boy shows us that they're indeed his parents." Everett wrapped his arm around her shoulders and sauntered around the loop through the garden that would eventually take them back to the house.

"I believe we should meet with him alone, not with your family present. Don't you agree?"

"I do to an extent, though if we have any trouble with Leidolf, Wade can give us backup since he is a JAG agent. Maya can take the boy out of the picture so we can deal with Leidolf alone if he becomes unreasonable. I don't want the boy to be upset."

"Do you think Leidolf will become unreasonable?"

Demetria wondered how the wolf pup would even respond to another wolf if he didn't know him.

"He might. He seemed pretty hardheaded when we first talked to him. Though it's understandable if he's trying to protect a pack he knows personally. It's a real toss-up how he'll feel about us when he actually sees us and can smell what we are, if he doesn't already know."

"Okay. Maybe we should wait before we decide to form our own team and offer our assistance in any other mixed shifter cases. We need to successfully resolve a case first." But new team or no, she definitely wanted to see more of Everett. She tugged at him to walk faster and go back to the house, since she was getting chilled.

"Are you kidding? We'll do great."

She hoped so. "About…the room arrangement."

"Yeah." Everett let out his breath. "I'll keep Junior with me so you can get a good night's sleep."

She sighed.

"What?" he asked. "Wait… Hell, yeah, us together?"

Ohmigod, she couldn't believe he was really willing to do this. Or that she was. "What will we do with Junior?"

"Maya and Kat will take care of him, or one of them will. They're great with kids of all ages. They'd do it in heartbeat. Why do you think Maya wanted to give us a break by sending us out here to walk in the dark so we'd be cold and have to snuggle a bit?"

Demetria smiled, then she frowned. "Maybe we shouldn't…rush this. Maybe we should wait until we find the pup's family first."

"Rush it? We've known each other for years. *No way* are we going to wait to find the pup's family first."

She smiled as she watched the brick path they were walking along, no longer feeling the cold.

"I sure as hell am not waiting another couple of years." Everett squeezed her tight and relaxed his grip, but still kept her tucked securely under his arm.

She laughed. "If we stayed in the same bedroom, it might cause some speculation." She looked up at him, hoping he didn't care. This felt right between them. That was one of the reasons she'd always wanted to meet Tammy at her house first, not somewhere else. She had hoped Everett would be there. She wanted to be with him, hoping they'd both give up the ghost and start seeing each other.

"Don't worry about that. No matter what we do, they're already speculating," Everett said.

She raised her brows.

He pulled her to a stop again and smiled down at her. "What do you think the guys were talking about when we were cooking dinner? Us. A surefire mating, just because *they* got caught up with their mates on a mission."

Demetria groaned and began to pull away, but Everett pulled her tightly again. "I told them no *way* that would happen to us. Not on a mission." He kissed her forehead. "Not that I said anything about this to them, but it wouldn't happen that way. Because I've wanted to date you from the first time I saw you visiting Tammy, Demetria."

"But I was seeing Matt."

"Yeah. You and Tammy left to have lunch with some other Guardian agents, and when she came home, I subtly asked about you. She said you were dating Matt."

"Hadn't he told you?"

"Well, sure, but not by name. You can't imagine how

disappointed I was. After he was gone…you didn't date. I was afraid you weren't ready. And then after the movie the other night…"

She sighed and rested her face against Everett's chest. "I didn't go out without anyone else because I was hoping you'd… We'd… Well, I felt the same about you. I was afraid you felt we shouldn't date because of Matt. About the other night…I'm sorry."

"You don't have to be. The movie affected me too."

"About us tonight, I don't know. I mean, if we were alone…"

"We will be. Probably the only chance we'll get for quite a while if we don't find Junior's home soon."

Maybe she was pushing it too fast where he was concerned. "But your family. You know, I'm not used to that. It's just my mom and me, and I'm on my own, so I don't have to even worry about what she thinks."

"Do you want me to ask her for permission to date you first?" He fumbled to get his cell phone out.

She laughed. "No."

"We could get a hotel room."

She laughed again. "As if that wouldn't cause all kinds of conjecture!"

He smiled.

She loved when he smiled at her like that. "All right, if they're guessing already about us…"

"They are. They've already warned me it's a done deal. No backing out of it now. I mean, if you're really afraid of letting anyone know, I could wait until Junior is asleep and then slip into your guest room to see you."

"No. I'd rather someone look after him, to make sure he doesn't get scared or in case he shifts."

"All right then. We could wait until Maya goes with Wade to their home on the other side of the property and just ask Kat."

"No, Maya might be the one who'd like to take care of the pup. We'll let the ladies decide."

Everett breathed in a sigh of relief. "Is it time to go to bed?"

She laughed. "Come on. Let's visit with the others before we retire to bed at a *decent* hour."

"Don't be surprised if what I consider a decent hour seems rather early to you." He kissed her again with the same passion, his lips pressing hotly against hers, his hands stroking her arms, his tongue seeking entrance.

She opened up to him, their warm breaths mingling in the frigid air, and they kissed again, their tongues sliding and caressing each other. She groaned, not wanting to stop. She knew even if nothing came of this, they were making love to each other tonight. And it was way past overdue.

Being the practical person she was, she reminded herself that her fantasies about him would probably make the actual experience pale in comparison, but she was ready to give it a shot.

When they returned to the house, they were surprised to see Kat and Maya wearing their jaguar coats while they supervised the play between Kat's toddlers and the wolf pup. Even though he was older, the wolf pup was gentle with them, and they were learning how to play with him right back.

Along with Demetria, Everett smiled to see the shifters playing, his arm around her shoulders as if to show his family a change in the dynamic between the two of them. Yet, since Maya had orchestrated their walk alone through the garden, had she already known a change was coming?

Wait until they told them they needed a puppy nanny so they could do the naughty.

Not that they would come right out and say that, but the jaguars would all know.

Demetria should probably tell Everett first that her mother was downright furious with him, but she figured he'd know that soon enough.

Chapter 11

EVERETT COULDN'T HAVE BEEN MORE THRILLED THAT Demetria wanted to sleep with him. And more. Between playing so late on his video game, having to take care of Tammy and Demetria, and then his mom calling so early about the wolf pup this morning, he hadn't gotten much sleep. So really, bedtime needed to be early. Not just because he was dying to go to bed with Demetria. How would it look if he went to bed with her later, at what she thought was a decent hour, and in the middle of lovemaking, he fell asleep? Or he could barely stay awake?

Connor and Wade were sitting in the living room having beers and watching the shifter cubs and pup playing as the lights sparkled on the Christmas tree.

Everett led Demetria to the couch and they sat together, legs touching, his arm around her shoulders.

"Want a beer or a glass of wine?" Connor started to rise from his seat.

Everett shook his head. "I'm afraid it would knock me right out. I was up quite late last night playing a video game."

"I'm the same way when I'm on vacation. Once I start playing, Maya has a hard time getting me to take a break even to eat," Wade said.

"Yeah, same here. I wasn't expecting to have to do anything but sleep late this morning. But we were up really early when Mom called about the wolf-shifter pup, so we didn't get a whole lot of sleep."

"Want a cup of coffee?" Connor offered instead.

Everett shook his head. "Nah. That might keep me awake the rest of the night. We really need to retire to bed early with all the work we have cut out for us tomorrow."

Connor and Wade looked at Demetria. Her face flushed beautifully.

"If it wouldn't be too much of an imposition, and someone wouldn't mind taking care of—" Everett rubbed Demetria's arm in a soothing, possessive way.

"Everett's right. We did have a long night. Maybe Maya could tell us which two rooms we can use," Demetria cut in.

Everett gaped at Demetria. He didn't believe she had changed her mind altogether, but apparently she didn't want everyone to know what they were doing. If she wanted him to sneak into her room, he would. He just hoped she wouldn't turn all jaguar and bite him. Unless she really had changed her mind. He sighed.

Maya bolted out of the living room, her tail whipping about. He hoped that meant his half sister was coming to his rescue, not Demetria's. Kat continued to watch the cubs, the pup, Everett, and Demetria.

"Would you like anything to drink?" Connor asked Demetria.

"A glass of water would be good. Thank you."

Connor left to get her a glass, and Maya stalked back into the living room dressed in jeans and a sweater and barefoot. "So, Kat, do we toss for who gets to take care of the pup tonight?"

Everett smiled. He loved his half sister. From the

minute he and Huntley had learned Maya and Connor were their half siblings, they'd been just like his own brother and sister that he'd grown up with. Arguing, loving, and protective.

Wade folded his arms across his chest, smiled, and shook his head.

Kat growled a little at Connor, indicating she needed help with their toddlers. Connor returned with the glass of water for Demetria, then lifted one cub under each arm and headed for the toddlers' bedroom.

Kat smiled, showing her wickedly beautiful jaguar teeth, then followed Connor out of the living room.

Maya lifted Junior into her arms and cuddled him. He licked her chin and she laughed. "Your tongue is so soft and velvety. Our jaguar tongues are sandpapery. So what do you think, Wade? Do you want to help me look after the wolf pup tonight?"

Wade sighed in an exaggerated way. "Man, does this bring back memories."

Everett knew he didn't mean about babysitting. He meant about falling for a woman during a mission.

"Of course, honey. Anything for progress. Besides, this will probably be the only time we'll ever have the chance to babysit a wolf-shifter pup. We can tell our own kids about it when we have them one of these days."

Maya snuggled next to Wade on the couch, cuddling the pup in her lap. He had gone to sleep, worn out after all the playing with the jaguar cubs. "I've gotten a couple of rooms on the west wing of the house ready for you. Why don't you head over there? You'll be all growly when you have to meet Leidolf tomorrow if you don't get a good night's sleep. We'll be over there in a couple of hours."

Everett really loved Maya.

Wade smiled and nodded. "At *least* a couple of hours. The way the house is laid out, you won't even hear us come in. We'll see you in the morning. Sleep late. Leidolf won't arrive until the afternoon, and we'll keep the boy well entertained. Oh, and in case you feel the need to get a little exercise before you sleep…"

Demetria's face flushed again.

"The pool is good and hot, the air nice and cold. You might want to swim as jaguars. Maya and I do most nights before we retire, any season of the year."

"Thanks, man. Sounds like a good idea," Everett said, never having given it a thought. When he had a home of his own with a big treed yard, that's just what he was going to have put in.

"Good night. Pleasant dreams," Maya said, smiling.

And that was their cue. Though Everett wanted to say good night to Kat and Connor too.

He rose from the couch and helped Demetria up. Kat rushed out to give them both a hug. "So glad you're both here, and thanks so much for bringing the pup. My kids adore him, and he seems to love them just as much. Don't worry about the business with Leidolf tomorrow. Maya and I will take care of the pup while you're getting to know Leidolf. Connor will be working with customers, but Wade will be here as extra muscle if Leidolf doesn't like what we are."

Connor joined them and shook Everett's hand. "Night, old man. Remember what I said." He gave Demetria a hug. "See you in the morning."

After saying their good-nights and hugging a sound-asleep Junior, Everett and Demetria grabbed their jackets, pulled them on, and headed out to her car. She was still red-faced, but Everett was thrilled his half sister and brother-in-law had stepped in to take care of the pup. Plus, they would be in the same house as Everett and Demetria, so if Junior got homesick for them, Maya or Wade could come get them or bring the pup to them.

"Ohmigod, Everett," Demetria said as she backed out of the parking lot.

"Great, isn't it? Turn back down that road. It winds around for about an eighth of a mile. Maya and Wade's place is about a hundred and fifty acres away from Kat and Connor's home, so they all have privacy but are close enough to help each other out." He smiled at Demetria. "We could have done the sneaking bit, but once it was out in the open, I figured it was better to just be honest about it. And you saw how they were."

"Yeah. Like they thought we were mating."

"They know we aren't. Just baby steps. You really didn't want to cancel on us tonight, did you? They have three bedrooms in the west wing, and if you really wanted to sleep separately, I can tell Maya we changed our minds after the fact."

"No, it's already a done deal."

"No, it isn't. It's totally up to you. Not that I won't cry on my pillow tonight if you decide to sleep elsewhere, but I'll take it like a—"

She laughed. "A hot alpha jaguar shifter doesn't cry into his pillow at night—not over something like this." She reached over the console and offered her hand to him. He gripped it and squeezed. "We'll only use one room." Then she frowned. "Since we had very little sleep last night, we probably need to just swim, hit the sack, and…sleep."

"Yeah, we will."

"You don't mean that."

"Yeah, I do. After we get some cuddling and kissing in." And more, if she really was ready for it.

She smiled.

They saw the Christmas lights wrapped around the eaves of the one-story, ranch-style house, trees lighted out front, and white lights framing the four front windows, warm and welcoming.

"Despite the fact the pine trees and grass are green, it still looks like a Christmas card." She pointed to the right of the house. "Oh, oh, look over there. Deer!"

Sure enough, four deer were watching them, but they took off as Demetria drove into the parking area and parked.

"They don't usually hang around when they smell the jaguars' scents." Everett grabbed their bags and carried them into the house. "You can pick whichever guest room you want."

When she didn't say anything, he snagged her hand and pulled her with him. She was looking at the evergreen Christmas tree in the living room covered in everything gold—balls, beads, and a gold crown on top.

Everett smiled at her. "It's a joke between Connor, Maya, and Kat. The natives revered Connor as a jaguar god in the Amazon, but in native legends, there was also a jaguar goddess. And the ladies reminded him of it every time he got a big head about being a jaguar god."

She laughed. "I love your family. The tree is just beautiful. Just as beautiful as yours, I might add."

"I'm glad you like it. It always makes me feel cheerful when I get home from work, no matter how stressful the day. Yours was really nice too."

"Thanks." She peeked in the first room with a queen-size bed done up in jungle fabrics. "Oh, I love this." A little Christmas tree was decorated in jaguars and parrots and toucans. The scent of Christmas spices came from a red glass bowl on a chest of drawers, and red and green towels were folded next to it. He thought this was the room she wanted to stay in.

"Wait, stay here. I just want to check out the other rooms." She headed out of the guest room. Everett set their bags on a chair and followed her into the hall, curious as to what she was looking for.

The next room was decorated in candy canes, furnished with two single beds, and had a tree decorated in candy canes and other candy ornaments. The last guest room had another double bed, in subdued forest green and burgundy, more of a manly room, featuring a countrified Christmas tree covered with miniature snowshoes, pinecones, feather-covered balls, Texas brass stars, and a garland of wooden beads.

"Jungle room or this room?" she asked, taking hold of his hand and squeezing.

"As long as it's not the candy cane room, I'm good with either."

"I bet you anything you'd even go for that if I had my heart set on it."

"Hell, yeah, you know it. I'd just have to do a little furniture rearranging, or we'd have to share a single bed."

She laughed and led him to the patio door, turned on the pool lights, and looked longingly at the shimmering blue water. Jaguars loved the water.

It was damned inviting, the water calling to his jaguar nature. "Do you want to undress and shift in the bedroom so we can go swimming?"

"Yeah, let's swim a few laps and…sleep," she said.

"Right." But he really didn't think she meant to only sleep.

They returned to the jungle bedroom. He shut the door and began to untie her scarf. He was sure she didn't have him undressing her in mind, but he wasn't giving up the opportunity for anything.

She pulled at his jacket to slip it off and then tossed it to the floor. He didn't remove her scarf just yet, but slid the sleeves of her jacket down her arms, pulling it off the rest of the way and throwing it on top of his jacket.

He remembered that first day he'd seen her with his sister, smiling and having fun, and damn if she hadn't tossed a smile his way in a flirtatious manner—even if it hadn't been intended for him. Their gazes had latched on each other, and right then and there, he knew he wanted to see more of her. But once he'd learned his friend was dating her, that was the end of that. Now, he was going to make this right between them.

Everett pulled Demetria close for a kiss. She hooked her arms around his neck and tilted her face up in anticipation. Even if her desire to have him was just a fantasy she'd built up in her mind, she had to know for certain. Would Everett be the one and only one for her?

Right this very minute? Yes!

He kissed her gently, as if preparing her for more.

Then taking a breath, he parted his lips, his warm, sensuous mouth inviting her in. She took advantage, stroking the side of his tongue, teasing it with the tip of her own, and then pulling out and kissing him full on the mouth, nothing soft about it.

His hands shifted from her hair to her ass, pulling her tight against him, encouraging her to feel his growing need for her. He was hot and hard, his erection pressing against her belly, letting her know just how aroused he was. She reveled in it, sweeping her tongue against his lips again. This time, he slid his tongue between her parted lips, stroking and teasing. His hands kneaded her buttocks, his arousal jerking against her belly.

It had been over a year since she'd been with anyone like this, but no one could compare to Everett's touch, the way he made her hot and wet and needy all at once.

He slid a hand up her sweater and cupped a breast, his thumb rubbing over the silky, thin bra as if it wasn't there at all, her sensitive nipple stretched out for more.

He pulled off her scarf and then her sweater, eyeing her bra for a second as if he'd never seen one before, or at least not her red bra with the tiny, candy-cane appliqué sewn in the center, the fabric silky and barely there. Her nipples were poking at the fabric, the darkened dusty rose nipples visible through the lightweight material.

Unfastening her bra, he slipped it off and tossed it on a chair. He studied her breasts before he placed his hands over them and massaged them, making her groan. She slid her hands up his black sweatshirt and tweaked his nipples. She craved the feel of his soft skin against her palms, the feel of his pebbled nipples against the pads of her thumbs.

She wanted his sweatshirt off. As much as she didn't want to disturb where his hands were glued to her breasts, lifting and massaging, she needed him to be naked now.

She peeled off his sweatshirt and skimmed her hands over his naked skin, feeling the muscles beneath her fingertips, his smooth skin, and the light hair trailing down to his jeans. Which she was ready to tackle next.

Everett lifted her up before she could begin to work on his belt and set her on the edge of the mattress. He pulled off her black boots and her socks, then began unzipping her jeans. Her hands were on his belt buckle at the same time, yanking it free. Then she pulled his zipper down, his erection clearly defined against the soft denim cloth.

She stroked him for good measure, making him groan this time, inspiring her to stroke him again. She slowly pulled his jeans down, kissing his belly, then tugging the jeans farther down his legs. He kicked off his shoes and finished yanking off his jeans and socks.

Black boxer briefs fit over his package, the hard ridge of his erection swelling with eagerness.

He pulled her up from the mattress to remove her jeans and red silk panties.

Her heart was pounding, her body yearning for him, needy, wanting. Her pheromones were on maximum overdrive, pushed and pulled by his own as they tangled sensuously, revealing their compelling desire for each other.

He kissed her neck and throat, her shoulders, making her skin tingle with heady anticipation. His warm breath brushed against her bare skin like a hot summer's soft breeze. She barely breathed, running her hands over his muscular arms and feeling scarcely aware of anything but his hot mouth against her skin. She arched her back as he moved his mouth lower until he captured a breast in his mouth, licked and suckled, and moved to the other as he ran his hand over her free breast.

She purred in a rough jaguar way, never having made that sound of pure delight before. Everett did that to her—carried her away from this time and place and made her feel loved, wanted, needed.

"Ready?" he asked.

Before she could get her lust-filled mind to work out a response, he dipped a hand between her thighs, poked a finger between her feminine folds, and whispered in his rough-hewn voice, "Yeah, so hot, wet, and ready."

Then he was tossing the comforter aside, lifting her onto the bed, and joining her.

"I've wanted you forever." He brushed her cheek with a kiss and began to stroke her feminine nub, his mouth caressing hers with hungry, long-lasting, deep-delving kisses.

She was on fire, but the house quiet, the only sound their frantic heartbeats and raspy breathing as he stroked until he catapulted her into another realm.

She cried out his name, her hands cradling his head, and kissed him deeply.

Demetria's skin was warm and soft and welcoming, and her dark eyes willed Everett in. Her pink lips parted, and she pressed his body against hers. He wasn't lying that he'd wanted her like this forever, dreamed about it even.

He crushed her tightly against his already aroused

body, loving how she had awakened to his touch. He felt and heard her heart beating wildly, matching the breakneck speed of his own. He tasted her sweet mouth as his fingers speared her long hair and luxuriated in the feel of the silky strands.

Her mouth was pressed against his, her tongue sliding against his, telling him she wanted this intimacy as much as he did.

This was what he'd wanted with Demetria. Not just working cases with her or admiring the way she was ready to deal with anything in a good-natured and responsible way.

"Ready?" he huskily asked.

"Yes," she breathed out.

He started to leave her to grab a condom, but she seized his arm. "Have it covered."

He resettled and nudged her opening with his thick erection, pushing deeper until he was all the way in. He held himself still, and then he began to thrust deep inside her. She wrapped her arms around him, holding him close, and lifted her hips to match his thrusts.

Heat consumed him as he drove into her slick, warm sheath. He felt he was claiming her in a raw, primal jaguar way. Wild jaguars claimed a jaguar mate in their territory, or even two females when territories overlapped. Jaguar shifters often preferred to find a mate to stay with forever. Like Everett did. Like his parents had. But did Demetria feel the same way? He wanted this connection, the intimacy between them, to never end.

He felt the end coming, held himself still, and felt her nearing orgasm. The way she was barely breathing. The way she was tense, on edge. He drove into her again and again, turning and twisting to wring the climax out of her.

And she murmured a soft moan of pleasure, giving him the go-ahead to release.

He continued to thrust, feeling her fingers stroking his back until he'd given her all of him, the state of climax washing over him in a warm wealth of bliss.

He lay on top of her, and she held him tightly to her body.

"My only regret is we didn't do this sooner," she said on a tired sigh.

"My thoughts exactly."

She smiled at him. "Would you be too tired for a swim with me?"

"Jaguars are always ready for a swim. *Always*."

He rolled off her and stood, then pulled her from the bed. By the time he stalked to the door and opened it, she'd already shifted. She nipped him on his bare butt and bolted out the door. He smiled and called on the shift, his muscles warming and stretching until he dropped onto all four paws, realizing he'd have to shift back when he got to the patio's french doors. But then he heard them open and knew Demetria had shifted to human form to do so. He lunged through the bedroom door to reach her and saw her glorious naked backside before she blurred into her jaguar form and raced out. He didn't want to leave the patio doors open and let all the cold air in, so he shifted, shut them, shifted again, and hurried to join her as she dove into the pool.

She was a beautiful black jaguar, with brown rosettes that barely showed at night, even in the deck lights, as she leaped into the pool, sending the water splashing everywhere. He joined her, his splash even more widespread before he swam after her. Even though they paddled, which for humans could be slow, jaguars' legs were powerful and allowed them to move silently through the water after their prey—caiman, ancient catfish, turtles. In this case, Everett was after one hot she-cat.

Sensing he was after her, she whipped around and smiled at him with her wickedly deadly teeth fully exposed. No sneaking up on another jaguar. But this was half the fun. He swam toward her and licked her face, and she licked him back.

They rubbed their bodies together. Then she swam away and pulled herself out of the deep end of the pool with her powerful forelegs. She turned and sat near the tiled edge. He watched her, eyeing her body language, deciphering what she was up to. She crouched slowly. She was going to lunge at him, her gaze fastened onto him. He paddled in place, just waiting, the anticipation of the hunt giving him a rush.

If she lunged straight for him, should he move to the right? To the left? Meet her head-on and pull her under like he would his prey? He opened his mouth and smiled.

Her whiskers twitched a little, her nose sniffing the air, and then she leaped with the power of a jaguar, her strong muscles bunched, then stretched as she lunged straight for him.

He met her head-on as she encircled his neck with her forearms. He mouthed her face, nuzzling, before she twisted and pulled him under as if she were going to drown her prey. The playing was instinctual, and neither of them used their claws while they hugged each other as big cats underneath the water. In their element. Their sensitive whiskers brushed each other's like antennae, feeling, sensing, and connecting. Their tongues stroked, not like jaguars would, but like shifters that wanted more of the human interaction.

That was what was so wonderful about what they were. Not only did they love their jaguar side for all that the courtship meant to them, but they also cherished the human side even when in their jaguar coats.

She released him, heading to the surface for air, and he joined her. He licked her mouth, and she licked his back. But she wasn't done playing and put her paws around his neck, nipping at his cheek in a gentle, playful way.

He paddled to keep them afloat, and then she pulled him under again, such a natural instinct. He went eagerly, hugging her back. She licked his nose, let go of him, and swam to the surface. He grabbed her tail with a gentle tug, then joined her. What he wasn't expecting was for Demetria to shift.

She paddled in place, smiling at him. He shifted too, then pulled her into his arms and kissed her like a man needing a woman, this woman, in his life.

The warm water collided with the air touching it and produced a mist, like being in a misty pool of water in the rain forest.

Demetria kissed the big cat back, her naked body pressed against his, feeling his arousal all over again, only this time in the silky, warm water brushing against her skin. She broke off the hot kiss. "Are you tired?"

"I think I'm waking up." He rubbed his erection

against her belly as he kept them afloat, and she wrapped her legs around him.

"I think you're right." She rubbed her mons against his stiffening cock.

"Here or…" he ventured.

"Here."

They moved to the shallow end so he could stand on the bottom of the pool. They made love in the swimming pool, the heat and passion building all over again as the stars filled the night sky, and their breath was as misty as the air above the pool. After she reached climax and he had finished deep inside her, they pulled apart and she shifted, nipping his hair, and swam for the stairs. He shifted and nipped at her tail, and she growled at him in fun.

This was the best time she'd ever had. And she realized then just how much more willing she was to try new things she'd never experienced with Matt. This was a wondrous night to cap off an unbelievable day that she'd never forget.

They shook off the water on the patio before Everett shifted and opened the french doors, and they returned to their guest bedroom.

They took a quick shower to wash off the chlorine, and after drying, Everett said, "Meet you in bed. I'm going to dry the wet floor before Maya and Wade come home."

She was going to help him, but he kissed her cheek. "I'll be right back. Warm the bed for me, will you?"

She smiled. "Just don't be too long, or I'll likely be sound asleep and totally growly if you wake me."

He laughed. "I think I hear a challenge. And I'm *always* up for that kind of challenge if it's coming from you."

She smiled and climbed into bed. When he returned, he slipped under the comforter, pulled her into his arms, and yanked the comforter over them.

The jungle print made her feel as though she was with her big cat in paradise. If they hadn't had such an important mission to take care of, she would gladly have spent her whole holiday vacation with Everett, relaxing and making love.

She hoped he wouldn't have any regrets in the morning and wanted to pursue this attraction they had for each other like she wanted to. She was used to being independent and unattached, so she didn't know where she really stood with him as far as making any kind of commitment. Was he even ready?

He kissed her breast and she smiled. Maybe.

Everett made love to Demetria two more times during the night, though she initiated one of the lovefests when he was sleeping soundly—she'd awakened and it had been too early to get up. It didn't mean she was in love with Everett. Just like she hadn't been in love with Matt. Though this sure felt like something more than she'd felt for him. A need to see more of Everett. A desire to fulfill this sexual craving only he seemed to be able to quench. It was more than that though. He'd asked her to help run this special operation for dealing with both kinds of shifters. Not anyone else, but her, as if he felt comfortable working with her and confident she could help him successfully manage the cases.

It was an honor to be asked, especially by someone she respected so much. He just got along with everyone, even Howard, who was known to be a real hard case to deal with.

What's more, she couldn't quit thinking of Everett, wanting more with him. But a mating? Could she truly be in love? After seeing her father and mother split up, she just wasn't sure.

She didn't know if Maya and Wade had returned to their home with Junior or not, because the house had remained quiet the whole night.

She hoped their love bouts hadn't been heard in the rest of the house. With as little sleep as they'd both had the night before, she couldn't believe how they'd had enough energy to make love to each other two more times during the night. Even if she was in doubt about Everett being the one and only for her, she sure could get used to this.

She glanced at the clock in the room. Nine. She groaned. Way past time to get up.

Everett pulled her tight against his body, telling her he wanted her to stay, cuddle, be with him. Yeah. She *really* could get used to this. So she kissed his whiskery cheek, snuggled against his hot and sexy body, and drifted off to sleep.

An hour later, they heard Junior growling menacingly in the living room. Demetria hurried to get out of bed to take care of the pup.

Everett threw on a pair of boxer briefs. "I'll check on him."

Appreciating that Everett seemed as concerned about the boy as she was, Demetria rushed to take a shower and get dressed instead. She was just pulling on her sweater when Everett returned.

"Maya's fixed cereal and fruit for everyone. We'll have lunch when Leidolf arrives. We're going to meet him at Kat and Connor's house though."

"Okay, sounds good. What was the pup growling about?"

"Maya was playing tug-of-war with him. He gets really growly when he's trying to win."

"Is he still going after her hands?"

"Nope. She was wearing her jaguar teeth, just lying on the floor and holding the rope toy between her teeth while he tugged on it."

Demetria laughed. Not only would they have the experience of a lifetime to share with their own kids someday, but so would the wolf pup.

"I'm showering, and I'll join you for breakfast in a few minutes." He pulled her in for a hug and a kiss first. "Sure wish we were completely free for the next two weeks."

"No way. You'd get bored in no time." She broke free and headed for the door.

"No way in hell."

She laughed and left him to shower.

After they all ate breakfast, Demetria, Everett, and Junior drove over to Kat and Connor's house, with Maya and Wade following in their own vehicle.

Demetria couldn't help how apprehensive she felt about Leidolf's arrival. How would he react toward them if he knew what they were? She wanted to act normally around him. But it wasn't every day she met a full-grown wolf man. Though they tried to talk about other things that morning, all conversation returned to the issue of Leidolf's arrival and how hopeful everyone was that he knew where the boy's parents were.

When the time approached and Everett got a call from Leidolf saying he was fifteen minutes from the nursery, Demetria said, "I'm going outside." She had to brace herself for the meeting while Connor waited on customers in the garden shop and the others were in the house taking care of the kids. Everett joined Demetria outside and rubbed her arm in a way that said he was trying to relax her, but she noted he was just as tense.

A few minutes later, they heard a vehicle driving along the private road to the nursery. A black mini-SUV appeared and continued on its way to the house.

"Are you ready?" Everett asked, and she glanced at him. He gave her a small smile. She swore he looked a little nervous too. "So what do you think? Does he know, or doesn't he?"

She watched the car park. "I'm going to guess he already knows."

Then Leidolf got out of the car, frowning at them. He had chestnut hair that glinted in the afternoon sun, and his olive-green eyes assessed Everett first, just like jaguar shifters would check out the bigger threat. Then he glanced at Demetria and nodded a greeting.

"I can't tell from his expression. Could go either way." Everett stepped off the porch to greet Leidolf.

Demetria followed him.

Leidolf stretched out his hand to shake Everett's, but then the wolf man lifted his head and smelled the air. Or rather, Everett's scent.

Demetria smelled Leidolf's at once too. A wolf for sure. Different than the pup's smell. But still a wolf.

Leidolf immediately dropped his hand before he shook Everett's outstretched hand. "You're not a wolf shifter." His gaze took in Demetria, and he smelled her scent too. "You're not either." His eyes narrowed. "What the hell is going on?"

They knew they had to smell like cats, and they'd thoroughly confused him. Humans who worked with big cats at a big cat reserve? That's probably what he assumed. And somehow they'd learned about the wolf shifters.

"Why don't you come inside and see the wolf pup and share what you know," Everett said, "and we'll talk about this more. Customers are at the nursery now, and we should keep this private."

Wade and Maya raced out of the house as jaguars through the cat door.

Demetria's mouth dropped open. None of them had planned this. But she guessed they'd been listening and decided to "help" out a bit. Luckily, the bend in the road kept customers at the shop from seeing the house. But voices could carry.

"We're jaguar shifters," Demetria quickly said.

Leidolf was standing his ground, probably realizing that running for his car would be a big mistake. His jaw had dropped and his eyes were nearly black with concern as he concentrated on the male and female jaguars.

"All of us are jaguar shifters. We thought Dr. Denali might have told you. He said he was going to spread the word to the packs he knew of," Everett said.

"He must have forgotten to let me know." Frowning deeply, Leidolf didn't appear to be happy with the situation at all. But what could he do? They were what they were, and he and the other wolves would have to get used to the idea, just like the jaguars would about the existence of wolves.

"We weren't sure you would believe us if we told you over the phone," Demetria said. "We wouldn't have believed your kind existed if it hadn't been for the boy shifting in front of Everett."

"All right," Leidolf said, sounding a little bit anxious. "Let me see the boy."

"He's still a wolf," Everett warned. "It's like he's stuck in that form. If it's anything like our shifter kind, children only shift when their mothers do until the child reaches puberty."

"It's the same with us."

They all entered the house, and Everett led them into the living room. Kat, her toddlers, and the wolf pup were out of sight.

Wade and Maya ran down the hall in their jaguar forms and returned a few minutes later as humans fully dressed.

"I don't believe it." Leidolf shook his head as he took a seat on one of the chairs.

"Do you want one of us to shift in front of you?" Demetria asked, willing to do anything to help convince him they were for real.

"No. I know you wouldn't have trained a couple of jaguars to come out, greet me, run back into a room, and then have the two of you come out in their place," Leidolf said to Maya and Wade.

Introductions were made all around, and Everett explained about their policing force that now included the United Shifters Force he and Demetria headed. At least they would once they solved their first real mixed-shifter case and told Everett's boss they wanted to be in charge of it.

Kat brought in her toddlers and the wolf pup.

The pup greeted everyone and wagged his tail when Leidolf leaned over to pet him. "He's not afraid of anyone."

Which Demetria took to mean he wasn't afraid of the big cats. "No. He's learned we're all good guys. So what information do you have to share about an Arctic wolf pack?"

"I helped take down some werewolf hunters, but in the process, I came across a couple who had been recently turned. The woman's father was part of my pack for a while, having been bitten by one of my widowed females. So he was a red wolf, his daughter, an Arctic wolf. Cameron MacPherson had a PI business in Seattle. But when they tried to return, the gray wolf pack there wouldn't allow it," Leidolf said.

"We learned about Cameron from the Seattle pack. We wondered if the wolf who turned him could be the boy's parent," Everett said.

"I doubt it. They were an old pack. Since the boy is shifting during the full moon when he's not with his pack, I assume the mother is a more newly turned wolf. Cameron might not be his father, and the boy could be from someone else's pack, but Cameron's is the only one I know of that could fit the scenario. Since the boy was dropped off in Dallas, I would check Dallas and the surrounding areas to see if there's a PI by his name closer by. Maybe check all of Texas and the surrounding states."

"So you don't know where the Arctic wolf pack is?"

Demetria had hoped he knew but hadn't wanted to give away their location over the phone.

"No. Faith's father and his mate left my pack. I thought they intended to join Faith and Cameron, but we never heard back from them. We tried to locate them but never could. We have enough problems taking care of our pack, so unless I learn they are in trouble, I wouldn't search for them."

"Does the boy look like he might have been Faith and Cameron's son?" Everett asked.

"He could be. They were both blonds. And from the video Everett shot of the boy before he shifted, he does look like he could belong to them. If we could, we'd run DNA testing, but without either of the parents' DNA, we have no way of telling," Leidolf said.

"Lunch?" Kat asked. "Connor's waiting on customers."

"I'll help make lunch," Maya said.

"I've got babysitting duty," Wade said. "I've been told that I have to practice at this before our own kids show up." He smiled at Maya, then took the toddlers to the den.

The wolf pup ran back to Everett, wanting to get in his lap. Even if he wouldn't have allowed an animal on the furniture, the pup wasn't just an animal. He was human too, and a shifter would have a difficult time understanding that one part of him wasn't allowed on the couch, while another part of him was. Besides, Everett knew Kat and Connor didn't have any problem with it. Their own jaguar cubs sat on the couch when they were in their jaguar forms, though they'd been strictly taught not to scratch the furniture. Everett lifted the pup into his arms.

"I would never have thought a wolf pup could get along with a big cat." Leidolf smiled a little.

"I think there's hope for all of us," Everett said. "If we can just set aside our differences and appreciate our similarities, I think most of us will welcome knowing there are more of us out there."

"I'm certain some will. Since I knew Cameron and Faith and I am a wolf, I'm willing to act as a liaison. I think we'll have better success at this if we do."

"We'd appreciate it," Demetria said.

Leidolf told them about his kind, how the phases of the moon affected them, and about their increased longevity. Otherwise, they were similar to the jaguar shifters, both either being born as a shifter or turned by a bite. Their offspring didn't shift on their own until puberty, and they homeschooled their kids. But the wolves didn't have an organized police force that dealt with their shifter kind. Instead, the packs dealt with problems in their territories like little wolf kingdoms on their own.

The red wolf pack leader seemed surprised that with the jaguar shifters, family was just as important as the wolves' families, but they didn't have packs like the wolf shifters.

"Now that we've made contact with you and other wolf packs through Maya's help, I suggest we return to Dallas where the boy was dropped off at the day care and see if we can track down the woman who left him there," Everett said.

Demetria showed Leidolf the recording of the woman dropping off the boy.

"All right," Leidolf said. "I'd like to leave right after lunch and get started on this."

As soon as they'd had lunch and thanked Everett's family for the meal, they left for Dallas, with Leidolf following in his rental car. Demetria drove while Everett held the pup in his lap.

"He sleeps a lot on drives," Everett said.

"Good for us. I was afraid we'd have to keep stopping to let him out to potty." She let out her breath. "I'm glad Leidolf came, though I was worried about how he'd react to us. After the initial shock, he seems to be okay with it." The pup began to squirm on Everett's lap. "Do you need me to pull over?"

"Hell, yeah! Something's wrong. Wait. Hell, the boy's shifting!"

Demetria hastily looked for the next exit. "Hold on for a quarter of a mile."

"Not happening," Everett said, and sure enough, the cute little wolf pup was now a little boy sitting naked on Everett's lap, while Everett was fumbling to get the zipper open on the boy's bag, one hand around the boy's waist to keep him secure while Demetria drove.

Chapter 12

NORMALLY, EVERETT WAS LEVEL-HEADED IN A CRISIS, but he wasn't used to dealing with young children, and he'd never had to deal with a child shape-shifting on his lap while he was a passenger in a car.

Instead of pulling onto the shoulder of the interstate, Demetria signaled to take the next exit and merged onto the access road. She got an incoming call on her car link from Leidolf and hurried to say, "The boy's shifted. Pulling off to locate a good place where we can dress him and ask some questions quickly."

"Okay, following you."

Everett was glad she was thinking clearly because he was fumbling with the bag while holding a four-year-old tightly against his lap when the child should have been in a car seat. He just hoped a patrol car didn't spot them.

Demetria quickly asked, "What's your name?"

Hell, Everett should have asked that right away, but he couldn't get the zipper open on the boy's bag with one hand while holding on to the boy with the other.

"Demetria wants to know your name." Everett assumed the boy thought she was asking Everett when he didn't respond. "I'm Everett, by the way." He figured the boy had heard someone use his name any number of times, but just in case he hadn't…

"My name is Corey," the boy finally said.

"What a beautiful name." Demetria drove into the

closest gas station, which had a parking area much farther away from the pumps. The nearby grassy area was
perfect, so she pulled into a parking spot. Everyone was
either getting gas or inside buying snacks, having parked
right next to the building. So at least they wouldn't
have anyone else on top of them while they took care
of Corey. "What's your *last* name?" She took the bag
from Everett and unzipped it, then handed him the boy's
blanket to cover him until she could fish out his clothes
and dress him.

"MacPherson," Corey said.

Everett swore they both let out their breaths at the same
time. Demetria smiled broadly, and Everett couldn't
have been gladder to finally make a breakthrough.

"Leidolf, the wolf in the car following us, knows
your parents," Everett told Corey. "Is your mommy's
name Faith?"

"Uh-huh. But I call her Mommy."

"What about your daddy?" Demetria asked.

"I call him Daddy."

Demetria smiled. "What's his name?"

"Cameron."

Leidolf pulled alongside them, leaving room
between the cars to help shield the view of them from
the access road.

Demetria opened her car door. "I'm taking him into
the backseat so he can get dressed easier." Then she got
out of the car, came around to the passenger's side, and
opened the door to pull Corey into her arms.

Everett hurried to get out of the car and opened the
back door for her. She set the boy on the seat, then
moved inside with him. Everett handed her the bag and

shut the door for her so she could help Corey dress. As Leidolf joined them, Everett quickly informed him, "He said his name is Corey MacPherson. His mom is Faith, and his dad is Cameron. Before he shifts again, we need to learn all we can." As fast as Corey had shifted before, Everett definitely was worried about it.

He climbed into the backseat with Demetria and helped her dress Corey while Leidolf got into the front passenger seat and shut the door.

"Where do you live, Corey?" Demetria helped him into a pair of underpants and then jeans.

Corey lifted a shoulder.

"You don't know your address?" Demetria tugged a shirt out of the bag.

"We keep moving. We live in a big cabin now." Corey spread his arms wide to show it was really big.

"Do you know what town it's in?" Everett was disappointed. He'd really believed that once the boy could talk to them, he could tell them his address and they'd be able to locate the family pronto.

Corey shook his head.

"What's the name of the lady who brought you to the day care?" Demetria pulled the shirt over his head.

"Belinda."

"She wasn't a shifter. Did you know her?" Everett figured they didn't have much to go on without her last name.

"No."

Everett found a pair of socks for Corey. The car was still warm, thankfully, so he wouldn't get chilled while they were dressing him. "Was there anyone with her?"

"Paddy O'Leary."

Now they were getting somewhere. "Did you know him before?"

Corey shook his head.

"Was he a shifter?" Everett asked.

"Nah. She was *so* mad at him. And he was *really* mad at her."

Demetria frowned. "Why were they mad at each other?"

"I was in the trailer, and I wasn't s'posed to be."

"Trailer? What trailer?" Everett searched in the bag for Corey's shoes and found the sneakers stuck in a fold of the bag, along with a receipt for shoes, a blanket, the bag, and toys.

"The one I sneaked into."

He looked up at Corey. "Did she take you shopping?"

Corey nodded. "She got me coloring books and shoes and crayons. And that blanket. I told her I wanted one with wolves on it, but she said there weren't any wolf blankets. She said little kids are s'posed to have cute things on their blankets, like sheep or bunny rabbits or something. She asked what kind of a kid likes wolves, and I told her a wolf." Corey raised his hands palms up as if to say it was a no-brainer that he would love wolves. "But then she woke me up before I was awake, and I forgot to take my coloring books and crayons."

"Why did she get you sneakers? Didn't you have shoes?" Everett asked.

"I took them off in the trailer, and I didn't remember where I put them and she couldn't find them."

Everett thought it sounded like him and his brother and sister when they were little. Their mom was always looking for one of their missing shoes. But she shifted so they would have to shift and use their noses to search for them too. "Okay, about the trailer... What kind of a trailer was it? A really big one?" Everett asked.

"A camping trailer. We had one once. I wasn't s'posed to be in it, and Paddy O'Leary got mad at her and said she shoulda locked it, and she got mad at him and said he shoulda locked it. Then they quit fighting, and they both looked at me and were frowning."

Everett slipped on Corey's socks. "And then what did they do?"

Corey let out his breath. "I got hungry."

Demetria and Everett exchanged looks.

Corey shrugged. "I ate some graham crackers and marshmallows and chocolate bars and a hot dog. But I didn't like their hot dogs. My mommy gets better hot dogs. Belinda was mad 'cuz I made a mess. Said I had chocolate, marshmallow, and graham cracker crumbs all over my face. Then she got mad 'cuz I made a mess on the floor and their bed. I got cold and hungry and ate on the bed. Then I fell asleep. Oh, and I got thirsty and drank some of the water, and the trailer was bouncing, and I fell and spilled water all over. It wasn't my fault."

"It's a wonder you didn't make yourself sick eating all that stuff." Demetria pulled a sweater over his head.

"Mommy says I can eat anything and never get sick. She says I have an iron stomach."

They laughed.

"Okay, so what did they do after they saw you and all the mess you made?" Everett could just imagine having to clean it up. All of this was bringing back some memories.

"Paddy O'Leary said it was *her* mess to clean up 'cuz *she* left the trailer unlocked. And she said *he* left the trailer unlocked, so *he* could at least clean up the trailer and *she'd* clean me up. But he just turned around and went to the front of the trailer and kept making it move. Then he got in a big truck"—Corey spread his arms wide—"and drove off really fast. Daddy woulda said he had road rage."

Everett finally managed to get one of Corey's sneakers on. "What did Belinda do after Paddy left?"

"She looked at me and was frowning. And then she started to laugh. And then she started to cry. And then she took my hand and led me into the house so she could get me all cleaned up. She said she never had any kids before, and she never knew what a mess one little kid could make. She said after seeing me, she never wanted a kid. She gave me a bath, and then she said she'd take me to a place the next day to play with kids. It was too late that night 'cuz they were closed. I wanted to see my mommy and daddy, and she said they would pick me up."

"She didn't say she was going to pick you up later?" Demetria asked.

"No. She said I was a *big* mistake." Corey spread out his arms to indicate just how big. "But she didn't tell me..." He turned to look at Everett.

Everett raised a brow at Corey as he finished tying the boy's sneakers. "What?"

"Those little cats were trying to scratch me. You smelled like them. Different. But like them."

"We're jaguar shifters. Like you're a wolf shifter."

"*Lupus garou*," Leidolf said.

They had a fancy name for their kind? Why hadn't the jaguars thought of creating a fancy name like that?

Everett was certain this had all been a big mistake. For whatever reason, the woman was afraid to turn the boy over to the police and explain how he came to be in her trailer. But he didn't believe for a minute that Corey's parents knew where he was, or they would have picked him up or sent word or something already. "I doubt Corey's parents knew anything about where he ended up."

"Why did you get in the camping trailer?" Demetria set Corey in the car seat.

"I was playing hide-and-seek with my brother and sister while Daddy was chopping wood. I tried to find the bestest hiding place 'cuz my sister, Angie, always finds me. So I found the bestest hiding place. Only I guess I fell asleep on the bed waiting for them to find me. I woke up when I felt the trailer shaking. I tried to open the door, but it was locked. I yelled, but no one heard me. Then I got hungry and ate, and I fell asleep again."

Demetria pulled a hairbrush from her bag and brushed Corey's blond curls.

"Do you have uncles?" Leidolf asked, changing the direction of the questions, but it reminded Everett that Leidolf knew the family.

Corey nodded.

"How many?"

"Three." Corey held up three fingers. "Uncle Owen. Uncle David. And Uncle Gavin."

"Do you know all of them, Leidolf?" Everett suspected Leidolf did or he wouldn't have just asked about uncles, but aunts too.

"Yeah, I do. They're Cameron's PI partners out of

Seattle," Leidolf said. "What about a granddad and grandmom, Corey?"

"Yeah."

"They're red wolves, not white like your mama and daddy and uncles when they turn into wolves?" Leidolf asked.

"Yeah."

"Do you have any other brothers and sisters?" Demetria asked.

"Just two." Corey held up two fingers.

Demetria smiled. "How wonderful. I don't have any sisters or brothers, so that must be nice. How old are you?"

He held up three fingers.

Everett thought Corey looked too old to be just three. "When's your birthday?"

"December 20."

"Tomorrow," Demetria said. "How exciting. So you'll be four."

"Four." Corey held up three fingers. She showed him how to hold up four fingers.

"We'll have to have a birthday party for him," Everett said.

Demetria smiled at Everett.

"I'll ask my mom if she could have the kids in her day care attend it. Maybe she can even have it there because the kids can go out back and play. No worry if he shifts again."

Demetria agreed.

"So this sounds like the family you know of that was newly turned?" Everett asked Leidolf. He was busy texting.

"Yeah, just letting my wife know what's going on."

"You said your parents were staying in a cabin. And you slipped into a camping trailer that was nearby. Were you camping?" Demetria asked Corey.

He shook his head.

"Were you on vacation?" Demetria asked as she buckled Corey into the car seat.

He shrugged.

"Did the trailer move for a long time?" Everett asked.

"Yeah. I dunno. I was sleeping. Riding in a car makes me sleepy."

"Any other questions?" Everett asked Leidolf.

"Yeah. Corey, did you ever turn into a wolf in front of Belinda or Paddy O'Leary?"

Good question. As jaguar shifters, they would want to have that clarified if one of their own had shifted in front of humans.

"No. Mommy said I wouldn't shift ever when I wasn't with her. I never did before. Then I couldn't help myself when I was at the day care. I never seen anyone turn into cats before. Their mommies probably couldn't help it either. My mommy and daddy and uncles can't either during the full moon. They said that's our time to be wolves and stay far away from humans."

"If we knew a location for the MacPhersons, we could put an ad in the paper. The personals. 'Searching for Cameron and Faith MacPherson. We've found your puppy. Taking good care of him, but trying to locate you to return him,'" Demetria said.

"Not sure the MacPhersons would even be reading a local paper. And it would take some time before the ad ran, if we even had a clue about where to run it," Leidolf said. "What if it wasn't the correct newspaper?"

"I've searched networking sites. No sign of them, or I would have just started contacting anyone with that name. Cameron MacPherson, yes. But not one married to a Faith. Unless they're divorcing over losing their son," Demetria said.

"We mate for life like real wolves do," Leidolf said dryly.

"Oh." Demetria sighed. "I don't know. I just want to do something more."

"If we could pinpoint the location better, we could do more. Let's get on the road then." Everett climbed out of the backseat.

"Sounds good to me." Leidolf returned to his car.

Demetria got back in the driver's seat while Everett sat in the front passenger seat, and she headed the car back to the interstate.

"Corey, tell us all about your sister and brother," Demetria said.

"And what you want for your birthday," Everett said, which earned him another smile from Demetria. If he were Corey, that's what he would be interested in.

While Corey was giving his birthday list and talking about his brother and sister, Everett called Howard and asked him to check on Paddy O'Leary and Belinda. He didn't know if the two had the same last name, but it was a start. He thought it was odd that every time Corey mentioned the man, he gave a first and last name, as if they went together like that always. Which made him think Belinda had called him that in anger.

Then Everett called his mother about the birthday

party, letting her know what Corey wanted and asking her if it was okay to have it at her day care.

"Is that all he wants for his birthday?" His mother chuckled. "Sounds like you and your brother and sister's birthday lists. I'm glad you're getting somewhere on this and that he's back to being a little boy again. And yes, I'd love to throw him a birthday party here. We often have them for the children who stay with us. Have you had any news about his parents?"

"We've got a wolf here helping us now, and he personally knows the family."

"Ohmigod, that's wonderful. Since you're returning to Dallas, bring him over for dinner. Is he an Arctic wolf too?"

"Red wolf."

"Oh, wonderful. He's got to shift for us."

Everett smiled. "I don't think so, Mom."

She let out her breath. "All right. But don't be shocked if I ask."

He laughed and they ended the call. At least for now, they were making sure Corey was having fun so he wouldn't have time to be homesick for his family.

Chapter 13

WHEN THEY ARRIVED AT HIS MOTHER'S HOUSE, Everett wanted to make arrangements for the boy's care so he could help look into the situation with Belinda and Paddy O'Leary. His mother had baked homemade chicken pot pies for them, so they sat down to eat dinner first.

Maybe his mom and Demetria could take care of Corey while he and Leidolf did some searching. Everett had already done Internet searches for private investigators named Cameron MacPherson. Tons of Cameron MacPhersons were listed on Facebook, and one was an athlete in the news. Many more private investigators were listed either by personal names or by location names. Many did government, insurance investigations, and missing persons investigations.

Mary turned to Leidolf. "My son says you wouldn't want to do it."

"Mom," Everett warned, knowing just what she was up to. He wondered if Dad would have shaken his head at her, if he'd been here. Probably not. He pretty much let his wife have her way because he was gone so often on "fishing trips," as he called them. They all wondered if he'd ever get tired of all the covert operations and retire for good.

Demetria smiled at the two of them, unsure what was going on.

Leidolf chuckled. "What's that? Shift?"

"Oh, would you?" Mary was so hopeful that Leidolf laughed.

"For you, yes."

Everett just shook his head. He should have warned Leidolf that his mother might suggest it.

After they finished dinner, Mary showed Leidolf to a spare bedroom, and though Everett hated putting the leader of a pack of wolves out, Leidolf didn't seem to mind. Maybe he was even proud of showing off his wolf self. He came back out to see them. Beautiful red coat. Beautiful wolf.

"What a handsome wolf," Mary said, her eyes alight with excitement.

Demetria was smiling just as much. "Beautiful."

Everett frowned.

"You look like my granddad," Corey said.

Leidolf licked his cheek.

Then Corey hugged him around the neck and released him. Leidolf returned to the bedroom to shift and dress. When he was back and ready for business, they all settled in the living room. Mary had set up a dinosaur puzzle for Corey to put together on the coffee table.

Then Everett called Rafe Denali, putting the call on speaker so Demetria and Leidolf could listen in. "Hi, I'm Everett Anderson, the man who's trying to find the Arctic wolf pup's family."

"My brother, Aidan, sent me the video of you. Unbelievable," Rafe said.

"Right. Just as unbelievable as your wolf kind are to me. So I was wondering... Since you have PIs working on this, do any of them know this PI, Cameron MacPherson, from doing business?" Everett asked.

"No. The men who work for me are strictly undercover. They're Special Forces and the like, so they do more than just collect information. Although I've shared the name of the couple with them, they have never heard of them. The MacPhersons were human before this, and my PIs didn't come in contact with them then either. Now that they're wolves and can't control their shifting, the MacPhersons may no longer be in the business. Or they might have to operate more discreetly. They probably wouldn't have a shingle hanging out in front of an office," Rafe said.

"They still could do a lot of searching via the Internet," Everett said.

"True. But can you imagine them trying to meet with clients, but not being able to during the phase of the full moon?" Leidolf raised a red brow. "One of the PIs hadn't been turned." Leidolf identified who he was to Rafe and how he knew the MacPhersons. "Unless he's been turned since then, he's still strictly human." Leidolf gave Rafe the first names of Corey's "uncles," the other men who had been with the private investigative agency. "I don't recall their last names. Gavin was the man who hadn't been turned."

Demetria asked Corey, "Is Gavin a wolf now?"

Corey nodded.

"Gavin's a wolf." Demetria explained that Corey had a brother and sister and about how he had met Belinda and Paddy O'Leary. "Corey said he doesn't know his address because he moved around a lot."

"So you're sure the boy wasn't stolen?" Rafe asked.

"No, from what Corey says, he was a stowaway," Everett said.

Corey was happily putting the stegosaurus puzzle

together. Everett's mother was well prepared to have him there. She had all kinds of toys for him to play with, plus animated videos to watch and coloring books—enough to keep him happy and occupied for hours.

"Can you tell us what Belinda's house looked like?" Demetria asked Corey.

"It had a red door."

"Was it a brick house? Wood siding? White, red? Two-story? One-story? Stairs?"

"Two-story." Corey continued to put the pieces of the puzzle together as he talked. "I had to walk up the stairs to go to bed. Don't remember about the rest. Snowman on the door. Red door."

"Was the door red, or was it covered with red paper with a snowman printed on it?" Demetria asked.

Corey twisted his mouth in thought and looked up at the ceiling, then back at his puzzle as he tried the wrong piece in a slot. "Red with a snowman on it."

Demetria continued to press Corey for details. "Paper, or was the door painted red?"

"Paper, I think."

"Did the yard have trees? Lots of space around it? Or were the houses really close to one another?"

"Close. I saw a kid peeking out a window next door. He was really close. He didn't come out to play with me. Belinda rushed me inside. She said the boy was mean and I wouldn't want to play with him. But they had a huge backyard." Corey spread his arms wide. "And lots and lots of trees. Like a forest."

"Did Belinda take you out to eat anywhere? A pizza place or a burger place?" Mary asked.

Demetria glanced at Everett's mother and she smiled.

"Nope. We couldn't eat out." Corey wrinkled his nose. "She didn't cook good. I didn't like her food."

"What did she fix?" Mary asked.

Corey shrugged. "Stuff with red stuff all over it. But it tasted yucky." He looked up at Mary. "It burned my tongue. My mommy doesn't put all that spicy stuff on food. And no meat. She said meat wasn't good for us when I wanted some. I told her my mommy said it was good for us."

"She was a vegetarian?" Demetria asked. "Did Paddy eat her food?"

"He didn't come home till real late. And he smelled like hamburgers. I wanted one too. Then he grabbed a brown bottle out of the fridge, frowned at me, and stomped up the stairs. I know it was called stomping 'cuz Nick does it when he doesn't get his way. He stomps and Mommy tells him to stop his stomping. Belinda yelled at Paddy O'Leary, 'Won't she take you in tonight?' And then he slammed the door upstairs. We get in big trouble if we slam the doors."

Demetria frowned. "Was he mean to you?"

Corey shook his head. "As soon as she made me go to bed, they started fighting in another room. He said they were going to get in trouble over me. He said he was leaving her if she didn't get rid of me. I was scared. But the next morning, he was snoring in another room, and she left me at the day care. Then you and Everett came and got me. I was glad. When do I get to see my mommy and daddy?"

"As soon as we can find them." Demetria gave him a hug. "What does Belinda look like? Color of eyes? Hair?"

"All brown."

"What about Paddy?"

Corey looked at Leidolf and pointed a puzzle piece at him. "Like him."

"Red hair? Green eyes?" Demetria asked.

"Yeah. Only…Paddy O'Leary's hair was…redder."

"Do you remember what the truck looked like?" Everett asked. "What color was it? Did it have two doors or four doors?"

"It was black with wolves painted on it, and it had a big cover on the back. I smelled fish in it. It wasn't pretty like my dad's car. It's shiny blue."

Then Everett began questioning about his dad's car.

"Big. Lotsa doors. Lotsa seats."

"Did it have black seats? Was it light colored? Gray?" Everett asked.

Corey shrugged.

"What difference does the color of the seats make?" Leidolf asked.

"Asking for more details sometimes helps someone remember something else that might really help with an investigation," Demetria said. "What about Belinda's car?"

"White."

"Did it have a door to the backseat, or did it only have doors to the front seats?" Everett asked.

"It had a door to the backseat. She didn't have a kid seat to sit in. I told her my mommy wouldn't let me ride in the car unless I sat in one. She said it was okay just for a short ride."

"Too bad he didn't see the license plate and memorize it," Rafe said, and everyone turned to look at the phone Everett was holding.

Demetria had forgotten the wolf was listening in on the details.

"I saw it." Corey smiled. "We played games in my dad's car. Who could see the most different license plates for different states. I won lotsa times. I looked at hers, and she had a star on it. I asked her what it was, and she said that means Texas."

"What was on your mommy and daddy's license plate?" Everett asked.

"It has a mountain on it. And Mommy said the little words said Evergreen State."

Demetria looked up license plates on her cell phone. "Washington State. The Evergreen State. They must still have the license plate from when they were living in Seattle."

"What about the trailer? Color?" Everett asked.

"White."

"I found Pat O'Leary in Dallas. No Paddy. But I don't think it's the guy." Leidolf showed a picture of the senior vice president of a firm to Corey, but he shook his head.

Rafe said, "There's no listing for a Belinda O'Leary either."

"Nothing on searches on Facebook. The guy probably doesn't mess with stuff like that," Leidolf said.

Mary was typing on her laptop keyboard. "There are a couple of P. O'Learys. Both in the Dallas area."

"What do they do?" Leidolf asked.

"Don't know. It just shows address listings for them," Mary said.

"As much as I hate to bring him along, what if we take Corey with us and see if he recognizes one of the two homes?" Everett asked.

"It's the one with the red door," Corey said, as if that was a surefire way to locate it.

Everett smiled and ruffled the boy's hair. "What do you think, Demetria?"

"I agree with you. It would probably be the best way to ensure we have the right place, if he can recognize it."

"Wish I could be there with you," Rafe said. "Let me know what happens. I'm feeding my PI team all the particulars of the case."

"Thanks, Rafe. Out here." Everett pocketed his phone.

"Why don't we take two cars?" Leidolf said. "That way, if Corey can verify one of the places is correct, Demetria can take him home while we speak with the couple who found him."

"Sounds good. I'll call Howard to let him know where we are with this, in case we need backup." Everett explained who Howard was to both his mother and Leidolf.

"All right." Leidolf tucked his phone away.

They looked at Demetria. "Okay with me. Thanks so much, Mary, for the delightful supper, as usual." She'd had so many meals there that she felt like she was almost family.

Corey looked longingly at the puzzle he was working on.

"It's going to be time for bed when we get back, but you can work on the puzzle again later," Demetria said.

"Remember, the birthday party is tomorrow," Mary said. "You're going to need a good night's sleep so you can play with all the other kids."

Demetria hoped Corey wouldn't shift again around the jaguar kids.

"And, Leidolf, I don't know what arrangements you've made, but I want you to stay here. I promise I won't ask you to shift again," Mary said.

"Thanks, but—"

"No buts. You're in Texas now, and we aim to be downright neighborly. We all need to stick together, you know."

"Yes, ma'am."

Mary beamed. "Good."

Demetria was glad Leidolf was fine with it. She wanted to be with Everett tonight, but he might have been thinking of putting Leidolf up for the night instead. She was glad he didn't. She knew they would have talked about the case, and she would have been left out.

Then Demetria buckled Corey back in the car seat, and she and Everett took the lead while Leidolf followed them in his car.

Chapter 14

"SO ARE YOU TAKING COREY TO YOUR HOME TONIGHT?" Everett asked Demetria.

She wanted them to stay together, but maybe Everett wanted to cool things down a bit until they got the boy home.

"Yeah. Unless you want to take him." Everett seemed really attached to Corey, and the boy seemed to feel the same way toward him. Either way, she was going to miss them if they stayed together and she went home alone.

When had she begun to feel like that? That she would be lonely in her own home when she loved her freedom? She did as she pleased, with no one else to worry about.

"I can take him." Everett looked happy to take care of him. Demetria didn't think she'd ever seen him that way with little kids. Well, perhaps with Lacy. "Maybe it will be dark enough on the way home that we can see houses decorated with Christmas lights."

"Yeah!" Corey said.

"That would be nice." But she suspected that if they found the O'Learys, Everett would stay with Leidolf to deal with them, and she would be heading back to her house with Corey.

When they reached the first house on their list, Demetria saw that it was a two-story with brick and white siding. A white car was sitting out front, and a white camper parked off to the side. Her heartbeat drummed as she heard Everett's start to beat faster. Her gaze was riveted to the front door—a shiny, red, aluminum poster, door size, with a big snowman in the center. She couldn't help feeling both excited and hopeful and was barely breathing in anticipation. "I think this is it."

"I think so too."

It was getting dark out, but a porch light and their cat night vision made the house fully visible.

Demetria let out her breath and studied the place for signs of life. A couple of rooms were lit up. "Corey, is that the house?"

Everett was taking pictures of the car, the license plate, the camper, and the house.

Corey didn't answer so she glanced back over the seat. He was sound asleep.

Everett looked back over the seat. "Hey, Corey. Wake up, bud. Is that the house where Belinda lives?"

Corey's eyes opened, but not very wide, and he looked really tired. She hated that they had to wake him.

"Is that the house you were staying at, Corey?" Demetria asked.

Corey turned his head and looked out the window. He nodded, then laid his head back against the car seat and closed his eyes.

Demetria drove slowly past the house with Leidolf following her and then called him on the car link. "It's the right house. I'll park up the street a bit and Everett can join you. I'll just wait. Take pictures of the couple and send them to me. I want to show them to Corey just to be sure."

"All right," Leidolf said.

She parked a couple of houses down from the house, not wanting to get so far away that they couldn't watch to make sure neither Belinda nor Paddy got spooked and left. Paddy's truck wasn't visible. Maybe it was parked inside the garage. Or maybe the woman Belinda was mad about had finally let him stay the night with her.

Everett got out of the car. "If anything goes wrong, take Corey to your place. I'll catch up to you there."

"Okay. Be safe." She was really surprised he'd offer to join her. She had thought he planned to either take Corey home alone or let her take him, but she was glad he wanted to be with them both.

Everett called Howard to tell him they had found the house and would need to take the couple into custody, if they were home. They'd take them back to an exam room at JAG headquarters. Even though they were human, these people had taken in a shifter. So Everett couldn't very well turn this case over to the police. Everett also sent Howard the license plate number to check out.

Everett got into Leidolf's car, and Leidolf turned it around, parking the rental behind Belinda's.

"Ready?" Everett asked.

"Yeah, let's do this." Though Leidolf wouldn't have any idea how JAG agents dealt with a situation like this.

"We'll take them into custody, which means I'll need to drive us straight to JAG headquarters with the couple, and you can text Demetria and my boss to let him know what our next plan is."

"Okay, works for me."

He and Leidolf headed for the front door. The yard

was well maintained, and there were colorful Christmas lights on the house and a sparkly Christmas tree in the front window.

Leidolf rang the doorbell, and a woman answered the door after a few minutes. "Yes?"

She looked like the woman Corey had described. Brown hair, brown eyes. And she smelled like chocolate chip cookies.

"Ma'am, we work with the FBI and are trying to verify some information from you concerning this boy." Everett showed her his badge and then pulled out the picture of the boy and showed it to her.

"Oh?" Her eyes lit up.

Everett took a deep breath of the air, like he always did to catalog someone's scent. She was definitely human and terrified. "Can you tell me anything about this boy?"

The woman looked at the picture and swallowed hard, tears filling her eyes, but she didn't say anything.

"Okay, here's the deal. We know you dropped the boy off at the day-care facility. We have security tapes that show everything. That's how we tracked you here so easily. We're going to take you in for further questioning. Does a Mr. Paddy O'Leary live here?"

"Yes. He's my husband."

"We need to speak with him too."

"He's not here." She snorted. "Who knows when he'll be home. He's out drinking with his buddies. Or sleeping with his girlfriend. Could be middle of the night, tomorrow morning, or after work, if ever."

"Okay. Come with us. No need to cuff you. Unless you give us trouble."

"I–I didn't steal the boy." She sounded panicked.

"You also didn't let any law-enforcement agency know you had a child in your custody. Instead of informing someone, you just dropped him off at the day care and let them deal with it. What if they hadn't called us? What if he had left the building and was nabbed by someone else?"

She locked her door and walked with Everett to the vehicle. "I didn't steal him. He got in the trailer. He was trespassing. That's against the law."

"A four-year-old?"

She twisted her mouth and got in the backseat.

While Everett drove the rental car to JAG headquarters, Leidolf used Everett's phone to text Demetria and Martin. Demetria followed behind them.

When they arrived at headquarters, Everett parked and got out of the car, along with Leidolf and Belinda. Demetria parked in a distant section of the parking area, staying out of sight with Corey. Two more men in suits met up with Everett and escorted Belinda into the headquarters.

Everett noticed that Leidolf was checking out the people in the area, smelling that they were all jaguars, and they were doing the same with him.

Everett said to Leidolf, "Let me get Demetria and the boy. I'm sure they'll take Belinda to a room with a two-way mirror so he can positively identify her."

Howard hurried to join them. "I ran her license plate. She's got a few moving traffic violations. Her husband has been in a few fights at O'Flaherty's Pub and has been arrested for it, but no other scrapes with the law. Neither has spent time in jail. He's a construction worker, but also a middleweight boxer in his spare time. She is a homemaker."

"She said he might be out drinking with friends or with a mistress," Everett said.

"Okay, as soon as we know more, I'll check it out." Howard studied Leidolf for a moment and shook his head. "Since I was little, I always said there could be all kinds of different shifters out there—bear, cougar, fox." He smiled. "Wolves."

Leidolf returned his smile. "Total shock to me."

Everett went to get Demetria and Corey while Belinda was escorted inside the building.

"He's sound asleep." Demetria got out of the car and pulled open the back door.

"I'll get him." Everett was certain Corey would wake, but he just snuggled up against Everett's shoulder and continued to sleep. He was a cute kid.

The agents were all smiling at the boy.

"I can't believe I was ever like that. Now if anything wakes me, I have a hard time getting back to sleep," Demetria said.

"Me too. I'm sure meeting all the new people, all the activities he's been involved in, and the long trip here from the Houston area wore him out." Everett led the way into the building. The whole place was lit up and several people were there. Normally at that hour, everyone was home with their families unless they were on a mission. He suspected the large turnout was because of having a red wolf and the little boy who was an Arctic wolf in their midst.

"Exam room five." Howard led them all into the viewing room.

Belinda was sitting at a wooden table, the lights in the exam room bright and harsh. Everett's boss was talking with her.

"Corey," Demetria said softly. "Wake up for just a minute, honey. We need you to tell us if that's the woman who was taking care of you."

After much coaxing, Corey finally and reluctantly opened his eyes, stared at the woman, and nodded.

"That's Belinda? The woman who dropped you off at the day care?" Demetria asked.

"Yeah."

"Okay, you can go back to sleep."

Corey snuggled again against Everett's shoulder, and Everett smiled.

Howard called Martin. "Corey identified the woman."

"Okay. Have Demetria and Everett talk to Mrs. O'Leary." Then he said to Belinda, "Just tell the agents exactly what happened, and you'll be free to go as soon as we can get your husband to corroborate your story." Then Martin left the room.

Howard said to Everett, "Do you want me to take the little tyke?"

Demetria couldn't believe he'd offer.

"Yeah, sure." Everett handed over Corey and then said, "Okay. Demetria, are you ready?"

"Am I ever."

They walked into the exam room and shut the door. They believed Corey's story, but since the O'Learys hadn't contacted the police, they must have had something to hide.

Tammy returned to the room carrying a poster that pictured Corey. She tacked it on a wall, and then she left.

Belinda stared at the picture as if it were of some alien being, her eyes wide, her face ashen.

"We're investigating how this boy came to be in your possession," Demetria said. "We want to know the whole story. But mostly, we want to know where you were when the boy climbed into your camper and you locked him in."

Demetria flashed her badge. "We're with an agency of the federal government that specializes in child endangerment cases," she said, her voice soft, trying to lull the woman into believing they didn't really think she was a kidnapper. "Tell us what happened in your own words." Demetria took a seat across from Belinda as if she were just a concerned friend.

"I didn't endanger any child."

"All right. We believe you. Just tell us how you ended up with Corey and then left him off at the day care."

Belinda clenched her hands together, so pale that she looked like she was ready to pass out. "All right. I didn't do nothing wrong. Paddy, the bastard, had been sleeping with a mutual friend of ours."

Demetria wondered what that had to do with anything, but she knew to wait unless the woman was straying too far from the story. Everett leaned against the wall and folded his arms, staying out of the picture for the moment. Demetria wasn't used to interrogating a suspect quite like this.

"Well, I knew he was sleeping with her, and I was trying to get him to fess up. And he kept denying it and denying it. But I'm no dummy, and I knew he was sleeping with her. So I kept pushing. And he finally confessed. He got tired of me asking about his late-night phone calls from her. He'd said the call was from one of his poker buddies, who was upset about getting a divorce. I asked him where he'd been because I'd gone to O'Flaherty's looking for him and he wasn't there."

"What has any of this to do with—"

"I'm getting to it. You told me to tell my story in my own words, didn't you?"

"Go ahead."

"Okay, so he said he was seeing Millicent O'Brian. She's a friend of mine from school. His too. And they've been sneaking off together and doing it. Well, I hit him with my fishing pole, and he got mad and said, 'Fine. We'll just go home. Can't go anywhere without you making a fuss.' Fuss? I wasn't fooling around with a friend of his! So he started tearing things down and throwing everything mad-like onto the sled."

"Sled?" Demetria didn't fish, but a sled sounded like snow to her. And there wasn't any snow this time of year in this part of Texas, if ever.

"Yeah, yeah, it's the easiest way to haul all that stuff to the river."

"Snow? It was snowing there?"

"No, it wasn't snowing."

"But if you had a sled…"

"Yeah, it was snowy, but it wasn't snowing. Not until we left."

Demetria wanted to throw her hands up in exasperation. "Where were you?"

"Minnesota, but don't ask me where in Minnesota exactly. I don't like to drive in snow, and if I'm not driving, I got to take motion sickness pills, so I was sleeping. He knows where he's going, and he doesn't need me to navigate for him. Well, most of the time."

"Minnesota. You said Paddy might be out drinking. Where?"

"O'Flaherty's Pub. He drinks and plays poker in a back room."

"What's Millicent O'Brian's address?"

"Are you kidding? How would I know where that traitor lives? If I did, I'd have a knock-down, drag-out fight with her."

Everett was already on his phone. "Do whatever we have to so that we can locate Paddy O'Leary. Apparently, he's the only one who knows where they picked up the boy."

The woman told them about how they'd driven home in a hurry, angry with each other over the whole mess with him and her friend. "We never heard the boy make a peep. Believe me, if I'd heard some kid in there crying or hollering to get out, I would've unlocked the door and checked it out."

"Why didn't you stop at a campsite on the way home?"

"Once we drove out of the snow, I took the wheel. We alternated between driving and sleeping. I just wanted to get home and kill him. When we got home, I went to grab the food out of the fridge in the camper. But when I unlocked the door and opened it, there was this little boy sitting on the bed, a half-melted chocolate bar in hand, taking a bite of it, and a mess everywhere. Took me days to clean it up too. I never seen such a mess." She went on to explain in detail the mess, taking the boy to clean him up, buying him a couple of things, and then taking him to the day care. "Oh, I finally found his snow boots."

"Snow boots." If they'd had those all along, they

probably would have had a clue he'd been up north before he'd even shifted.

"And I've got his coloring books and crayons. Which he can have."

"If you hadn't done anything wrong, why didn't you report this to the police so they could reunite him with his parents?"

"I've been in trouble with the law before. Nothing much. Just petty stuff. But when you get in trouble, people look at you differently. I've never stole a kid before, but what if someone thought we had done that this time and then just chickened out and called the police?"

"Corey told us how he was playing hide-and-seek with his brother and sister. You would have been exonerated. We want you to look at some maps and see if you can give us any direction, any idea of where you drove. Was the same route you took to Minnesota the same as the one on the way back?"

"I don't know. When I take that medicine, it makes me sleepy. But I get so nauseated, I have to take it. I can show you where I drove through on the way home. And on the way there. But once we hit snow, I didn't drive. Paddy's from Minnesota. He's used to it. Not me. I was freezing. I'm from Texas. Never lived anywhere up north. I don't travel well, so I don't usually go anywhere but on really short drives. Paddy wanted to get away. I think he was mad at Millicent, because when he got mad at me and we returned home, he left and I thought he was staying with her, but he came home again."

"Where in Minnesota is he from?"

"St. Paul, I think."

"St. Paul," Everett said. "Big city, no help there. Family there still?"

"No. Parents passed away. No brothers or sisters."

As if on cue, Tammy came in with a large map of the States and spread it out on the table in front of Belinda. "Leidolf wants to talk to the two of you, and Martin suggested I try to learn what I can from her about where they might have traveled while you take Corey home. Howard is going to look for this girlfriend of Paddy's and check out the pub."

"All right. Thanks, Tammy," Everett said.

Demetria knew he wanted to stay and work the case, but they needed to get some sleep and take care of Corey.

Chapter 15

EVERETT TOOK CHARGE OF COREY, THANKING HOWARD for taking care of him. "Good luck on your search."

"A bunch of us are searching. I'm in charge of this part of the investigation until we can bring Paddy O'Leary in," Howard said.

Leidolf pocketed his phone. "I've got pack trouble at home. I need to take the next flight out of the Dallas area. Keep me in the loop on this, will you? And I'll keep trying to track down the MacPhersons with my own resources."

"Absolutely," Demetria said.

"Sure thing. Appreciate you flying all the way out here to help us." Everett balanced Corey and shook Leidolf's hand.

"I'm sure we'll have more dealings with one another in the future." Leidolf nodded to Demetria and Howard, then left the viewing room.

"That's the problem with being a pack leader," Demetria said. "It might be neat to have a pack-run mini kingdom, but when the king is away…"

"Yeah. Hope it isn't anything too serious," Everett said.

Howard said, "I'll let you know if I track Paddy down and get a location. Or find the girlfriend."

"Thanks, Howard." Demetria took hold of Everett's arm. "Come on. Let's get Corey home to bed."

Everett smiled at her.

"Yeah, yeah. If we come up with any ideas in the middle of the night, we can discuss them." But Everett was still smiling, as if he knew that any ideas they came up with would have nothing to do with the case and wouldn't lead to any discussion at all.

Martin met with them before they left. "We're keeping Belinda in a separate wing of a correctional facility for jaguars so our agents can continue to question her, promising she'll be released without criminal prosecution as soon as the family is found. We can't release her until then, in case she's afraid she'll be prosecuted for not turning the boy over to police and tries to disappear."

"Sound good," Demetria said.

"Are the two of you good with taking care of Corey while you're still on the case? Do we need to call someone else to take care of him in the meantime?"

"No, we're good," Everett said. "I don't think it would be a good idea to keep handing him over to different families. We're giving him a birthday party tomorrow, taking him to see Santa, and checking out the mall again. Though I suspect that since Corey's family is in Minnesota, they have nothing to do with the woman and her children that smelled like wolves at the mall."

Martin glanced at Demetria. "Yeah, we're good, sir. He loves us, so no problem with that. He's been great," she said.

"Okay. We had a lot of offers to take the boy in, and even more tonight when they saw him sound asleep in Everett's arms, so just checking. It's late. Why don't you get some sleep and get to work on all of this in the morning."

"Yes, sir," they both said.

As she drove them to Everett's home, Demetria made a detour and traveled through one of the more highly decorated home developments so she and Everett could enjoy the Christmas lights. Corey was in the car seat fast asleep.

"Beautiful," Everett said. "Haven't done this in years."

"Me either. We'll have to do it again when Corey's still awake."

She parked at Everett's town house shortly after that, but still no word from Howard.

"Why don't we put Corey to bed while we wait for Howard's call?" Everett had every intention of having Demetria stay with him. "We can decide where everyone's staying the night." He carried Corey into a guest room while Demetria grabbed Corey's bag. "We'll just put him to bed in my spare bedroom, and we'll have some decaf coffee or hot chocolate or eggnog."

"I have to warn you, I don't do well with too little sleep."

He smiled. "I thought we did well last night. You can just doze, and I'll wait for the call and wake you."

She sighed. "I wouldn't be able to sleep. Hot chocolate sounds good to me." Demetria began to undress Corey and put him in pajamas.

Everett pulled her into a hug. "We'll solve this one." He kissed her tenderly, and she kissed him back. "And you and I need to talk. About us."

And about Matt. Everett wanted to clear the air with her, to tell her how he'd felt about her from the first moment he'd seen her. He wanted her to know the feelings he had for her were real, and he hoped she felt the same way about him.

Everett left the room and made hot chocolate for them, turning on all the Christmas lights as he went.

When she joined him, he still hadn't heard from Howard. "This could take a while."

They sat close together on the couch, their legs touching, mugs of cocoa in hand.

He wanted to ask her how she was feeling about Matt, and yet he didn't. He wanted to know more about her father and what had prompted him to leave, why they were concerned about him returning home, and how she felt about her parents' divorce, because things like that would affect any relationship she might have in the future. Like with him. But he was afraid to pry.

The situation concerning Matt was tough. He wasn't just some guy she had dated and fallen in love with. He'd been Everett's good friend. Losing him on the mission had affected Everett even more. No matter how much he told himself that he couldn't have stopped what happened to Matt, that he could easily have been the one shot and killed instead, he still felt bad about it.

He finished his cocoa and set his mug down, ready to get down to business, when she said, "Everett..."

He braced to hear what she had to say.

She finished her hot chocolate and set the mug on the Christmas-tree coaster on the coffee table. "I know how close you were to Matt. Like blood brothers. He talked about you all the time."

Okay, so Everett really didn't want to hear this. He'd thought with the passage of time he could deal with it. But hearing her talking about him, sharing how much Matt had cared about him, and knowing he hadn't been able to save Matt's life...

She sighed again and took Everett's hand. "Matt mentioned you'd always wanted to date me. He talked about it constantly."

Everett stared at her, shocked. He hadn't remembered ever telling Matt that. Maybe in jest, or perhaps an off-hand comment. But he didn't think he'd been that obvious about showing his interest in her.

"I think he knew I wanted to date you. I think that's why he tried so hard to make it work with us. But we just didn't fit together, not like I feel with you," Demetria said.

Everett had wondered why they hadn't married before the last mission.

"He knew I felt it wasn't working out between us. But I think he was afraid to let go of me because then you and I might have dated. He was afraid of how that would have affected your friendship. I didn't want to ruin the friendship the two of you shared either. When you weren't off doing things with Huntley, you were with Matt. We had fun, Everett. I won't deny it. We had a lot of great times. He was a good friend. Like he was a good friend to you."

A good friend. Not a lover. Not the man she wanted to marry?

Everett stared at her now, not believing what he was hearing.

She took a deep breath and let it out. "I really hadn't thought he planned to ask me to marry him over the holidays. Not until he hinted at it right before the two of you took off. I would have said no." A teardrop rolled down her cheek, and then another.

Everett had felt much the same way, torn between

wanting to date Demetria and maintaining his close friendship with Matt. Everett pulled her into his arms, and she sobbed against his chest.

"I felt bad that I had planned to end things between us. I'd waited because I didn't want to do it right before a mission. I hated to hurt him, worried I'd even upset you, and if I dated you? I was just torn up about all of it. But I never expected him to die."

"I'm sorry, Demetria. I didn't know you felt that way about him. I felt guilty that I was lusting after his girl-friend. And then, I thought you needed the time to heal."

"I did. I had to sort out my feelings about all of it. And I felt you did too."

He agreed.

She smiled up at him through her tears. "And I think you were afraid I'd bite."

"You did."

She growled a little. "You shouldn't have dated my cousin."

"I thought maybe she was like you. That I'd capture what I'd lost when I learned that you were dating Matt."

She slugged Everett on the shoulder. "I'm not *any-thing* like her."

"No, you're not." He pulled her close again. "It was my grave mistake."

Demetria snuggled against his chest. "I couldn't have married him. I didn't love him. We had fun, but I needed something more. He was a jokester, never serious. I find humor in situations all the time, but I need some-one who's more serious like me, not so laid-back. I felt terrible when he died. I had planned to end it between us, and then there you were, depressed, disconsolate, bringing me the horrible news that we'd both just lost a dear friend. I thought you'd hate me for what I had intended to do to him, and I just couldn't…deal with it.

"I felt guilty I hadn't ended our relationship sooner. Like I'd led him on. I had tried to break it off a couple of times, and he just begged me to give him another chance to make this right between us. He was always competing with you. I don't think he could have handled the idea of us dating as well as you did him dating me."

"Like hell I could."

She smiled. And that smile cheered him to the marrow of his bones.

He'd wondered if something was wrong between Demetria and Matt. Matt had been so evasive about how things were going with Demetria. Everett had never suspected *he* had been the reason for her reluctance to fully commit to Matt. Everett thought the world of her for having held back in the hopes that he and she could make something of the muddled mess.

"And now?" he asked, wanting to make this work between them and feeling they had to make up for lost time.

"I won't forget the good times I had with him, but I really am ready to move on. Are you?"

Hell yeah, but he knew it would still be tough because of the close ties they had to Matt. "I am." Everett rubbed her shoulders, looking down into her liquid brown eyes, dark, mysterious, sexy. "Where do you want to go on our first official date?"

"We have this case to take care of."

"We don't know how long it's going to take us to find Corey's family. We'll work around the case. Here's the deal. Tomorrow is the big birthday party. While Corey's at the party, we'll see if we can learn anything more about Paddy's whereabouts, but we can have lunch out, your choice of place. The next day, we could go Christmas shopping with Corey. Help him pick out presents for his mom, dad, brother, and sister. Maybe his uncles. He can sit on Santa's lap and give him his Christmas list and have a picture taken. I want to be ready when we finally find his family and can bring him home bearing gifts.

"We could look for the mother and her triplets. And if you don't have any really warm gear, we should pick some up because I'm sure we're going up north with Corey as soon as we have a better idea where he's from. I'll need to pick up a few things too. Then he could stay with my mom and work on that puzzle with her while we take a break and go out to dinner."

Demetria smiled. "I think somewhere in the schedule, we need to go see my mother. That is, if you're up to it."

"Have I mentioned I love it when you challenge me?"

Chapter 16

DEMETRIA HEARD EVERETT'S CELL PHONE'S FAMILIAR jingle as she was dozing on the couch with him. To his credit, Everett was trying to answer it without disturbing her. She was so tired that she felt like she had a hangover. When she pulled away from him, he realized she was awake and put the call on speakerphone. Then he pulled her back into his arms. She'd never imagined that working a case with a teammate would be quite like this. She snuggled against his hot, hard body and listened to what Howard had found.

"We checked out O'Flaherty's Pub. Paddy wasn't there, and no one knows where he went. One of his fellow poker players is Lucian Covington. He wasn't in the least bit cooperative, but no news there. We have Paddy's place under surveillance. Millicent O'Brian isn't home either. She's a retired clerk from the city water department, so no one's missed her at a job. Her car is gone. We've checked with her grown son and daughter. They knew about her affair with Paddy, but they haven't heard from either of them. They figured Paddy and their mother went off somewhere together, but they have no idea where. In the meantime, we have her place under surveillance too."

"Okay, good. If anyone finds him, no matter the hour, we want to question him right away."

"Gotcha."

After they ended the call, Everett asked Demetria, "What do you want to do about tonight?"

She looked at the clock. "Midnight." She snagged his hand and got up from the couch. "I think we're beyond first dates." She smiled up at him. "Don't you?"

"Hell, yeah." When they entered his bedroom, he turned the light on, and she looked at the room for a moment. It was masculine—black and white with touches of red—with a large, fake zebra rug at the foot of the bed, zebra throw pillows, and a matching zebra-striped chair.

"Nice. Love the zebra touches. And I'm glad you don't have a caiman skin framed on the wall."

"Rite of passage. Matt was proud of taking down his first caiman as a jaguar. I got rid of mine a few years ago."

She smiled up at Everett, and he wrapped her arms around his waist and leaned down to kiss her, his arms sliding around her back to pull her close. Even snuggling with her on the couch had aroused him. Touching her, breathing in her scent, seeing her cast him an interested glance his way—they all turned him on.

He devoured her mouth, her jaw, her neck. Groaning with need, he tackled her clothes and then his own, tossing them aside. Then he jerked the covers to the side and they fell onto the mattress. Kissing her full lips, he pressed her body into the soft mattress with his, claiming her, possessing, pinning her in a way that said *mine*.

Their hearts were pounding, their breathing labored, as he held her arms to each side and began to kiss her throat and breasts with a fever, dragging in the scent of her soft skin, hot and she-cat sweet.

He nuzzled her breasts with his whiskery cheek and

she moaned, wrapping her legs around his before he began to rub his stiff cock against her mound. He swore he had been doomed to love her from the first moment he saw her.

He moved over, releasing her arms so he could stroke her into oblivion, rubbing her harder and smelling her pheromones wild with excitement. Her arousal called to him, and his responded with the same jaguar jungle craving.

She clawed at his back like a jaguar in love. Her breath hitched, and she gripped him tighter before she called out in bliss. He quickly covered her mouth with a searing kiss, but too late to muffle her cry of rapture. He paused for a moment, waiting, making sure that Corey didn't come in to check on them.

When Corey didn't, Everett nudged Demetria's legs wider, pushed into her tight sheath, and felt the ripples of climax tightening around his cock. He captured her mouth with his again, tonguing her, and sliding in and out. He pushed his cock deeper, rocking her against the soft mattress. Her hands caressed his back, her foot sliding up the back of his leg, her body moving with his. He pumped harder, pushed in and pulled out, and thrust again. He felt the end coming, uttered a deep growl before he released, and growled again with hot satisfaction at the last.

Moving off her, he pulled her tightly against his body, enjoying the feeling of her softness planted against him, the silkiness of her skin, her heat, her heart beating steadily, and then he yanked the covers over them.

"I will never be the same," she said, cuddling against him.

"Is that good or bad?" he asked, kissing the top of her head and rubbing her back gently.

She kissed his chest, her warm lips stirring him up all over again. "I'll let you know in a little while when I wake you up again."

He chuckled. "I'll never be the same again either."

Demetria felt eyes on her when she finally woke that morning after making love again to Everett in the middle of the night. They were two tired old cats after that and had slept just a little late. But her jaguar senses told her they were not alone.

She opened her eyes to see Corey in his pajamas, watching her.

She smiled. "Need some breakfast, honey?"

"Yeah," Everett said and tried to pull her back into his arms.

"We have a little boy to feed," she warned Everett, chuckling.

He peered over her and smiled at Corey. "Good morning, bud. Why don't you go in the living room, and I'll be right there to fix you breakfast."

"Okay." Corey padded out of the bedroom and headed down the hall.

Everett hugged and kissed Demetria. "Are you thinking what I'm thinking?" He pulled away and hurried to get dressed.

She folded her arms behind her head and watched the sexy jaguar as he pulled his boxer briefs on. "Depends on what you're thinking." She smiled a little and raised her brows in question.

Everett was buttoning his shirt as he leaned over to kiss her. "The future. Our future."

"A wolf puppy in our future?"

Everett laughed. "I'm thinking more of a jaguar cub."

She groaned. "You haven't even met my mother yet or taken care of my dad."

"You haven't told me what's going on with your dad. And your mom? I'll do everything in my power to make her love me." Everett finished buttoning his shirt and tucked it in.

She smiled at him, then sighed. "My dad left us, but every once in a while, he shows up out of the blue. My mom starts thinking he's here to stay, but then he's gone again. It's a real roller coaster, and I don't want him upsetting her."

"How does your mom feel about it?"

"She just tells me she's a grown woman and can deal with it, but she gets so upset."

"Has he visited you?"

"A couple of times. I told him off."

Everett smiled at her.

"Well, he deserves it!"

"Okay, I'll talk to your dad and see what his problem is. And then we can see your mom at some point. But first, I need to feed a hungry wolf pup."

"What did I tell you about trying to save the whole world at once?"

Everett smiled at her. "For you, I can handle it." Then he headed down the hallway. Demetria sighed, climbed out of bed, and walked into the bathroom to take a shower.

If she could have a mate like Everett who would take

care of the little ones while she had a leisurely shower before work, and he dropped them off at his mother's day care, well, that could work, couldn't it? She smiled and poured shampoo onto her hair, wondering if this was still a pipe dream and she'd wake up and it would all be over. But if Everett could reason with her dad and make him stop coming around and upsetting her mom, she was keeping him.

Everett fixed "the family" breakfast—eggs, sausages, toast, and hash browns, thinking how he could handle being a papa jaguar. How he could make love to his sleepy wife, take a quick shower, make breakfast, and rouse the kids. Then he'd drop off the kids at his mom's day care and still make it to work on time with his lovely teammate. And they had plenty of family around to take care of the kids when they were on missions out of town. In any event, all of this could work out.

After fixing breakfast, he was still smiling about it and talking away with Corey, who was busy coloring in one of the coloring books that Demetria had picked up for him.

"So what does your mom fix you for breakfast?" Everett asked. They talked about favorite foods and swimming and Corey playing with his brother and sister, and Everett shared what it was like playing with his too. Even though Corey was a wolf and he was a jaguar, they shared a lot of common likes and dislikes, played the same kind of games, and loved to fish and swim.

"I caught a fish once but it got away," Corey said.

"Sounds like me and a caiman I caught when I was

little." Everett showed him the picture on his cell phone of what a caiman looked like. "I grabbed for him but didn't quite succeed in gripping him in the right place with my teeth, and he got away. Next time, the caiman I went after wasn't so lucky."

Corey looked at the caiman, wide-eyed.

"Jaguars' teeth can kill a caiman. But I wouldn't recommend going after one as a wolf."

"Never seen one before," Corey said.

That gave Everett an idea. "Have you been to a zoo?"

Corey shook his head.

"Maybe we can take you to the one here. They have lots of animals and probably even a caiman."

"Now what are we planning?" Demetria asked, smiling as she joined them. "Oh, wow, this looks good." She sat down to eat with them. "A trip to the zoo?"

"Yeah," Corey said. "To see the animals."

She smiled up at Everett as he served the rest of the food. "I'm game." Demetria took a deep breath and then turned her attention to Corey, who was busy eating his sausage. "Do you have any idea what Belinda and Paddy were fishing for?" She finished her eggs and set her fork on the plate.

"I smelled walleye in the truck. I saw mooses out the window of the camper. I wanted to stop and get out and see them."

"Moose?" Everett asked.

"Yeah. Three of them." Corey held up three fingers.

"Okay, so your parents live in the wilderness where they have lots of forests? Not too many people? So they can run as wolves? Arctic wolves? White wolves?" Demetria asked.

"Yeah. So we don't get shot."

"You live near a river," Demetria said. "Do you know the name?"

He shook his head.

"What about lakes?" Everett asked.

He nodded.

"There are ten thousand of them," she reminded Everett. "Are there other wolf packs there?"

"Yeah."

Demetria frowned. "Like yours?"

"Nah. They're real wolves. We got to be careful of them, Daddy said."

"Okay, so his parents settled in Minnesota because there are no other wolf-shifter packs there. Not near a town—" Everett said.

"An old town."

"An...old town?" Demetria asked. "Small though? Not many people live there?"

"Just ghosts. Only got one house left." Corey raised one finger.

"A...ghost town?" Demetria asked, her jaw hanging.

"Yeah, but I didn't see no ghosts."

"But it's called a ghost town?" Everett asked.

"All the people left, and the town just blew away. That's what Mommy and Daddy said. 'Cuz Angie got scared we'd see ghosts. But there aren't any. Nick said he saw one, but Mommy said he was fibbing 'cuz there aren't any ghosts."

"Do you live where the ghost town used to be?" Demetria asked.

"Nah. Daddy and my uncles builded cabins. We live in them."

"Do you know the name of the ghost town?" Everett asked.

Corey shook his head.

Demetria did a Google search. "Okay, an incomplete listing of ghost towns in Minnesota gives us fifty-one."

"The list is *incomplete*," Everett said.

"Right." Demetria started listing them to see if Corey recognized any of them.

Corey just shook his head at the names each time.

"That's a lot of ghost towns, and it's not even all of them," Everett said.

"Let's go over the maps of Minnesota and see if we can locate ghost towns near lakes and rivers." Everett cleared the table of dishes and looked up a map of Minnesota.

"And since towns need water to survive," Demetria said, raising her brows at Everett, "and because the state has ten thousand lakes…"

"They probably all are by some source of water."

"We need more to go on," Demetria said, sounding exasperated.

After breakfast, Everett and Demetria took Corey to his birthday party at the day-care center. Mary had decorated everything with a dinosaur theme, since Corey had been having so much fun putting the dinosaur puzzle together.

But the best part? Demetria noticed that three new figures had been painted on the jungle mural. One was a little white wolf pup poking his nose at a leaf covered in raindrops, while below that, a jaguar cub was catching the falling drops on his tongue. And peeking out from behind a tree was a jaguar wearing angel wings.

"Look, Corey, that's you," Everett said, taking the boy by the hand and showing him the picture.

Corey pointed to the jaguar cub. "That's Lacy 'cuz she always wears wings."

Demetria and Everett smiled at the painting. She loved seeing the new additions. It was like a new beginning between the wolf and jaguar shifters.

"Okay, Corey, we're going to look for your parents some more. Are you going to be all right playing with the other kids and with my mom?" Everett asked.

Five other moms were there to help out, all smiling at Corey.

"You're not going to stay?" Corey asked.

"We'll come back and get a piece of cake and a scoop of ice cream in a little while and see all the cool presents you got," Demetria said.

"Okay." Corey gave them a thumbs-up.

Everett laughed and ruffled his hair. "Okay, we'll be back in a couple of hours."

Demetria gave Corey a hug, but he wanted one from Everett too.

"He'll be fine," Mary said. "We'll have fun."

"Thanks, Mom."

They returned to JAG headquarters, where Everett worked with a sketch artist to draw a picture of the woman and her triplets he'd seen at the mall. Demetria verified that the picture looked like the woman and kids. Then they'd make a copy and send it to all the agents in the branches. They figured there was always the possibility that the MacPhersons had run across a pack in Dallas at some point, as much as they moved. Martin also wanted to touch base with any wolf shifters in Dallas to offer them the branches' services if they needed them.

Howard hadn't been able to find any sign of Paddy but was still on the case.

Tammy had a little more information that Belinda had recalled about the trip up north. They had stopped to eat at a couple of places, and she had receipts for gas. This was good news and got them closer to the location where Corey's family lived. But one thing was troublesome: Paddy had apparently taken a wrong turn, having no signal for the GPS out there, and they'd ended up somewhere they'd never been before. They'd had to take lots of winding country roads and he'd sworn constantly, worried they weren't going to find their way back to civilization before they ran out of gas. Would Paddy remember the location if they could find him?

They sure hoped so.

Chapter 17

WITH THE NEW INFORMATION FROM BELINDA, EVERETT and Demetria studied the map of the States again. The more Tammy had talked with Belinda, the more the woman had recalled about the route she and Paddy had taken. They'd started out on Interstate 35 from Dallas all the way to Highway 61, which took them to Gooseberry Falls State Park in Minnesota, where they camped for a few days.

But after that, the route they took became a blur. They had been headed to Bear Head Lake State Park but missed their turnoff and took another road. Belinda had taken medication for nausea because of all the winding rural roads Paddy was driving on, and she had slept for the duration, so she wasn't sure where they had ended up.

Paddy had told her he'd given up on trying to find the right road, parked, and fished on the river where he and Belinda had the fight. But he hadn't known the name of the river.

"It could be anywhere up in that area," Everett said. "We still need to narrow it down." He glanced at the clock. "Want to have lunch at the mall?"

"Yeah, sure. I suspect we might become regulars there while we're trying to track down wolf shifters, when I rarely went there before. I was thinking maybe now would be a good time for you to talk to my dad."

"About him getting out of Dodge?" Everett wasn't sure if she meant that, or if she wanted him to tell her dad what his intentions were. He was ready for either.

"Yeah. Tell him to quit coming home and upsetting Mom."

"I can do that. What do you want to do in the meantime? Do you want to come with me, or do you want me to drop you off at the day care and you can watch Corey?"

"Let's have lunch, and then you can drop me off at the day care and see my dad."

They ate at a fish-and-chips restaurant, which reminded Everett of Belinda and Paddy and fishing. Everett hoped that when they found Paddy, he'd recall where he and Belinda had camped so the JAGs could get closer to the actual area where Corey's parents lived.

Both Everett and Demetria had been taking deep breaths practically the whole time they were walking through the mall, but neither had seen any sign of the mother and her young boys who had smelled of wolves or even caught a whiff of others who smelled like that. But they did see lots of jaguar agents and jaguar families wandering through the mall.

"If they live in this area and shop here, the wolves are going to wonder why they're smelling so many cat lovers all of a sudden." Demetria waved at yet another family with small children that they knew.

"They'll never suspect a thing unless Dr. Denali gets in touch with a local wolf pack in Dallas and shares the news about our existence."

"True."

After enjoying lunch, Demetria said, "Okay, I texted my dad and he's going to meet you at O'Flaherty's Pub."

"Wait… The same place Brayden Covington's dad, Lucian, goes to? And Paddy O'Leary?"

"Yeah. I suggested it to my dad so you could still be working the case if Paddy's there."

Everett paid for the meal and smiled at her. "You are such a taskmaster."

"You love me for it. Besides, I'm the Guardian so I'll be doing my job by staying with Corey for a while. I don't want you to be goofing off."

He laughed. "Works for me." He was glad she had thought of it. They made a great team.

When Everett left her off at his mother's day care, Demetria gave him a hug and kiss. "Don't kill my dad. Just tell him he's not welcome."

"Will do." Everett gave her a hug and kiss back, thinking they should have gone to his place or hers for a little extra loving before they went back to work. He figured she wouldn't go for it if he suggested it now.

She smiled at him as if she knew very well what he was thinking. "Yeah, too late now. Later."

<center>~~~</center>

Everett arrived at the appointed hour to meet with Demetria's father, Joel MacFarlane, at O'Flaherty's Pub, which was dark and smelled of testosterone, cologne, sweat, and alcohol. An Irish drinking song played overhead as conversations filled the air. Christmas lights reflected in the dark mirror behind the bar. Some of the men drinking at tables glanced in his direction, checking out the stranger in their midst.

A group of four homicide detectives that Everett recognized were sitting at one table.

The shifters didn't really work with the police on cases, but they shared information with them if they came across a case that strictly had to do with humans. The police appreciated their help because they never stuck their noses in the police department's business beyond that.

One of the detectives raised his beer to Everett, and he smiled and nodded in greeting. He really hadn't expected to see anyone he knew, let alone that might be on the police force.

Riley Keefer, a homicide detective, motioned for him to have a seat with them, which indicated to the rest of the patrons that Everett was welcome. He joined them to say hi but told Keefer he needed to meet someone.

Then he saw Demetria's dad, same dark hair and eyes as she had, but his face was chiseled granite, his eyes narrowed at Everett. He didn't look happy to see him. Everett felt likewise.

Everett took leave of the detectives and headed to Joel MacFarlane's table. He reminded himself that he had to handle this right. He wanted to get her father's approval to marry Demetria, even if her father hadn't been there for her and her mom. It was just something Everett had been brought up to believe in. And he really didn't know her father or his issues, so in all fairness, Everett wanted to keep an open mind.

"So, what do you want of me?" the man growled.

"Are you Joel MacFarlane?"

"Yeah, and you're the guy chasing after my daughter."

Everett took a seat at the table. "We're working together on a mission."

"You're doing a hell of a lot more than that."

"I'm Everett—"

"I know who you are. You were best friends with Matt, the guy my daughter was seeing before he was killed in Costa Rica a year ago, trying to save a little girl. And yeah, I know you brought them both home. I know about your current mission, who your family is, and a hell of a lot more."

"Demetria told you—"

"My daughter and I don't speak much."

"Hell, you sound like my dad." Then Everett frowned, thinking suddenly how much he thought the circumstances could be the same. Some covert operatives maintained families, like his father. Others, afraid their families would be at risk, abandoned them. Like Demetria's father?

"Yeah, I know Roy Anderson too."

Everett raised his brows. Her father didn't say he knew *of* him, as in researched his background, but knew *him*.

"Here's the deal. It's none of your damn business why I'm back in town unless you think you're trying to protect my daughter. But she doesn't need protecting. Not from me."

"And her mother?"

Joel smiled in a sinister way. "You don't know anything about me. But what I want to know is, where is this going between you and my daughter?"

"We're getting married." Everett didn't know why he said that so definitively, especially when he hadn't even discussed it with Demetria. But Everett intended to, first chance he got. He wished he'd done so before he had said anything to her dad. Then again, she and her father didn't talk to each other much, so Everett figured he was safe.

"When?"

A server came to take Everett's order. "Beer." When the woman left the table, Everett said, "We haven't set a date yet."

"Well, set it already. My daughter's not getting any younger. I'll give you an early wedding present so you can get down to business. White wolves have been spotted up near Blue Hill."

"How do you know—"

"Let's just say I have my sources. You need to get that kid home to his family, and you need to set a date."

The server brought Everett's beer and he paid her. After she left, he asked Joel, "Why are you here?"

"My daughter asked me to meet you."

"Why are you in town?" Everett asked, exasperated.

Joel leaned back in his seat, finished his beer, and set the empty mug on the table. "You tell me."

Everett drank some of his beer. "You still love your wife, and you love your daughter. You come around to check on them, sometimes letting them know and other times not. It's not something you're happy with, but if you ever decide to retire from the job, you'll return to your family. In the meantime, you're trying to keep them safe by making it appear that you don't care anything about them."

"How do you figure?" Joel asked.

"One of my father's friends in the business is the same way."

Joel gave him a little smile. "Keep treating my daughter right, and you'll live a long and healthy life."

"We'll send you a wedding invitation. Do you think you'll show up?" Everett finished his beer.

Joel rose and tossed a tip on the table, grabbed his leather jacket and pulled it on. "You ought to ask my daughter if she's going to marry you first, don't you think?" He chuckled darkly and stalked out of the pub.

Everett stared after him. Hell. Then he glanced around the pub to see if Paddy was in the place, just in case. He called Demetria to say things went well with her father, but that he needed to ask her an important question.

"Hey, Demetria, still at the pub. Met with your father and everything seems to be fine with him."

"Concerning?"

"Everything with you and your mother. He loves you both. I'll explain when I get there."

"And about the wedding?"

Everett glanced back at the door to the pub. Hell. How had her father told her already?

He left a tip on the table. "Uh, yeah, about that…"

"My father gave you permission to marry me."

"Yeah." Everett cleared his throat. "About that. I meant to ask you first—"

"But you're your father's son, Everett. And you wanted to get my dad's permission even if you didn't need it."

"Yeah. Hey, can you hold on for just a second? I'm checking the poker room for Paddy." Everett pulled open the door to the room where the guys played poker. Lucian was there, but Paddy wasn't among the players. He must have suspected he might be in trouble and was lying low. Lucian frowned at Everett and began to rise from his chair as if he thought to have a word with him about his son. But then Everett noticed one of the players at the table was missing. Was it Paddy? Was he in the men's room?

"Has anyone seen Paddy O'Leary?" Everett asked.

"What's it to you?" one of the men asked, but Lucian's brows rose a bit.

He was probably wondering why the JAG agent would be interested in a non-shifter.

"He's missing. We're worried about foul play," Everett said.

"Why would that concern you?" Lucian asked.

"He's a cop. Can't you tell?" one of the men said. "He has it written all over his face."

Detective Riley Keefer came in behind Everett. "You need any help?"

Everett shook his head. "I've got this one. But thanks, Riley."

"No problem."

Then Everett gave Lucian a hard stare, wondering if the man really did know where Paddy was but was holding out until they gave him his son back.

Everett turned and left, heading for the men's room.

At the sink, a red-haired man was mopping up a bloody nose.

"Are you Paddy O'Leary?"

The man narrowed his green eyes at Everett. "What's it to you, buster?"

"Cheating at poker?"

"I don't have anything to say to you." Paddy pressed wadded-up toilet paper to his nose and looked back at his reflection in the mirror.

"Let's have this conversation somewhere more pleasant." Everett flashed his badge.

"Okay, so are you supposed to be the good cop and the other guy was the bad cop? Only he didn't flash any kind of a badge, just a fist."

"What other guy?" Everett asked. No one on the force would have beaten this man for the truth, unless maybe he was a frustrated Enforcer agent.

"The big guy wearing the leather jacket. Hell, he must've been a middleweight boxer the way he laid into me before I even had a chance to come out punching."

Demetria's dad? "What did he ask you?"

"About..." Paddy grew silent, as if he realized Everett might not be there for the same reason.

"He was asking about where you'd picked up the little boy?" Everett asked.

Paddy's eyes rounded a little.

"So what did you say?"

"Blue Hill, okay?"

So that was where Demetria's father had gotten his information. His source. The man himself. With one punch to the nose. Everett smiled, then he frowned at Paddy. "You're coming with me. Don't give me any trouble, and we'll get along just fine. Or I can cuff you. Your choice."

"The kid just got in the damn trailer. It wasn't my fault."

Everett grabbed Paddy's arm and hauled him out of the men's room. "Yeah, but one of you didn't lock the camper door. And a little boy was taken from his home because of it. Now we're trying to find that home. And you're going to help us."

"You can't charge me with nothing," Paddy said as Everett walked him through the pub.

"Child endangerment? I'll see if I can get the charges dropped if you help us." Everett nodded to Riley and the other police detectives, who were staring after them. "Getting him some medical attention," he said to the detectives. "Someone popped him good. But he probably deserved it."

They just smiled at him.

When he got out of the pub, Everett zip-tied Paddy's wrists, just in case.

"I thought you said you wouldn't handcuff me if I went with you," Paddy complained.

"Changed my mind. Get in." Everett helped him into the car and then shut the door. "Hey, you still there, Demetria?"

"Yeah, you got Paddy?"

"Yeah, taking him to JAG headquarters before I join you. I'll question him on the way over there."

"Hallelujah. But I'm still waiting to hear what's up with us."

He smiled. "I love you and I want to marry you—and please say yes."

She laughed. "I wonder how many women are asked to marry a guy who proposes over the phone while he's drinking at a pub! Oh, great, your mother and half the women here supervising the birthday party just heard. That's the trouble with our hearing." She moved to a somewhat quieter location, though he could still hear the noisy kids playing in the background.

"Is that a yes? I'm taking you out and doing something really special, or we can do this at home, wherever you prefer, but I wanted to tell you before—"

"Dad told me?"

"Well, yeah, but—"

"You forgot?"

He laughed. "I haven't thought of anything else. I'll be there in a little while."

"Your mom is frowning at me. Not sure if it's because she's not keen on me marrying you or that you proposed to me over the phone."

"She loves you like a daughter. It's definitely me proposing to you over the phone."

She laughed. "I'm not squaring it with your mother. That's your job."

He chuckled. "She loves me for all my faults."

"Me too. See you in a little bit. Oh, and great news about the location of the ghost town. Dad told me. I've been looking over the map again and figure it's time to take a trip to the cold north."

"So do you feel better about your dad?"

"That depends on what you have to tell me when we can really talk privately."

Chapter 18

EVERETT TALKED TO PADDY ALL THE WAY FROM THE pub to the headquarters, asking him all kinds of questions to help clarify where he had gotten lost and how he had ended up at the river he didn't know the name of.

Everett had called Demetria back on his car link so she could listen in and ask questions too. With the promise that they would drop all pending charges against Paddy if he would help them, he was giving them even more details.

"All I saw out there was snow on the ground, the roads, trees covered in snow, a river half-frozen, no homes, no people, no towns. It was a real wilderness area."

Just perfect for Arctic wolves. "But the road you took was passable enough that you could get there, right?"

"Yeah, sure. Not saying that it would be now. Saw on the news a new snowstorm hit there last night." Paddy leaned back against the seat. "There was a snowmobile rental place and a blue-and-white hotel near the road I took. The rental place caught my eye because I wanted to do some snowmobiling, but I knew my cantankerous wife wouldn't go along with it. She hates the cold, but she doesn't want me to leave her home alone. So I take her and put up with all the bellyaching about how cold she is the whole time. *She* was the last one in the trailer and should have locked the door."

"You know, all that matters is we get the boy home to his parents," Demetria said.

"All right! If I think of anything more, I'll let you know."

At headquarters, Tammy and Howard took over questioning Paddy, while Everett headed to the day care, feeling sure that they would locate Corey's family now. It would take some time to get up there, and it would take time searching for where the wolf pack was staying, but he was certain they'd locate the boy's parents.

When Everett arrived at his mom's day care, everyone was leaving the party. Demetria smiled at him, while a few of the mothers cast him amused looks. Thankfully, no one had commented on the situation between her and Everett, but she was certain they were dying to know what was going to happen.

His mother especially.

Demetria asked Corey to show Everett all the presents he'd gotten. He was eager to do so while Everett cut them both a slice of cake and Mary got a scoop of ice cream to put on top.

"I thought Santa was a wolf at the North Pole," Corey told Demetria. "But he smelled like a jaguar."

"Huh. Santa's a wolf, eh?" Everett smiled and looked at his mother.

Mary shrugged. "He was the only one available to fill in for Santa on such short notice."

"So Santa's a wolf though," Everett said to Corey.

"Yeah, 'cuz they have Arctic wolves at the North Pole, Mommy said."

"I see. Makes sense. What did you ask him for Christmas?" Demetria thought they could get him some of the Christmas presents he wanted.

Corey gave him a long list.

Mary laughed. "You just got a ton of presents for your birthday."

Corey smiled.

Demetria took her paper plate and sat down on the couch, and Everett joined her.

Corey showed Everett one of the puzzles he had gotten for a birthday present—an Arctic wolf family of six adults and four pups standing in the snow, the sun shining on the snow-covered pines.

Everett looked up at his mom. She smiled and nodded. She was so good with kids, thinking about how Corey probably missed his family and would love a wolf puzzle that reminded him of them. "He told me that the wolves pictured on the puzzle weren't his family," Mary said, smiling, though her eyes were tearful.

Everett set his plate down and gave his mother a hug. "We'll find them," he promised her.

"Hey, Corey, do you want to go to the zoo now?" Demetria was afraid it was the last fun thing they would do with Corey before they returned him to his family, and she wanted to make his last day here memorable. After that, she and Everett would be driving to Minnesota, a very long drive, and it wouldn't be any kind of a vacation.

"Yeah! And see the caimans!"

"Caimans?" Demetria asked, casting a raised-brow look at Everett.

He smiled at her. It was a guy thing. "Mom, do you want to go with us?"

Mary shook her head. "I'm going to clean up here and get the day care ready for tomorrow."

"We'll help you with everything," Demetria said.

"Yeah, Mom, what do you need us to do?"

"Take Corey to the zoo. You need to enjoy this time with him. Straightening up won't take me any time at all. And when you get home from your trip to Minnesota, I want to talk to you, young man, about the art of proposal."

Everett's ears tinged a bit red, and he laughed. "Uh, yeah. Well, I promised to do it right."

Demetria loved him and wrapped her arms around him. "You did it just right." And she kissed him before they bundled up Corey's presents, which helped to clean up the day care substantially before they left.

"After the trip to the zoo, we can go to the mall and shop for Christmas presents for Corey and his family," Everett said.

"And have dinner there. I need to pick up a few warmer clothes. Do you have cold-weather gear?"

"I'll need a couple of things. As a jaguar, Texas is about as far north as I get. Everything else is south of the border. And we'll get a few things for Corey. I don't think he needs to see the mall Santa," Everett said, "since he's already seen the one here. Even if he was just a pretend jaguar Santa."

When they arrived at the Dallas Zoo, Everett eyed the jungle-print zoo strollers. "Can you walk, buddy, or do you want us to get a stroller for you?"

"I'm too big for a stroller. Mommy said when we were four years old, we wouldn't need one anymore."

"Can we get one for me?" Demetria asked.

Corey frowned and pointed his finger at her. "You're way too big for one."

She laughed and said to Everett, "Let's get one, because we'll pick up some things at the gift shop for Corey and his brother and sister, and we can use it to carry the packages if someone doesn't get tired and need the stroller."

"Good idea," Everett said, smiling at her.

They saw black-and-white ruffled lemurs, chimpanzees, and spider monkeys swinging from trees. Corey thought they were pretty cool and wished he could do that.

"That's what we see in the jungle when we visit it," Everett said.

Corey was wide-eyed as he watched the bobcat in the exhibit watch him back. He loved the cheetah and compared its spots to what he recalled of Everett's. He thought the ocelot was just a little kitty cat. "You look more like the tiger, only he has stripes instead of spots," Corey said. Then he pointed out the lion. "That's the daddy 'cuz he has a mane. And that's the mommy..." He frowned because there were three females lying on rocks nearby. "One of them is the mommy. And the others are..." He shrugged.

"Maybe her sisters," Demetria said and smiled at Everett.

Corey loved the donkeys, hogs, and meerkats. Corey's mouth hung open as he watched the giraffes stretch their necks to reach baskets of food.

"You haven't ever been to a zoo before?" Demetria asked.

Corey shook his head. "I seen lots of these in a book Mommy showed us. But not the caiman."

They took him to see the reptiles next, and Corey studied the caiman in the water. "They look like alligators. How big was the one that got away?"

Everett pointed to one that was similar in size. "But I was young, so it might have just looked really big to me."

"That's big." Corey spread his arms wide to show how big.

They stopped at the gift shop and bought stuffed animals for Corey and his brother and sister, and Demetria tucked the packages in the stroller. She caught Corey eyeing it. "There's lots of room in there for you too, Corey."

He looked at Everett as if he thought he needed permission.

"If I were smaller, I'd sure go for a ride," Everett said.

Corey grinned at him. "You're too big." Then he looked at Demetria again as if making sure it was all right.

"Hop aboard. Everett will push you. We still need to go to the mall to pick up clothes and gifts, but instead of eating dinner there, did you want to eat at the Serengeti Grill here? They have big glass windows so we can see the lions," Demetria said.

"Do they have hamburgers?" Corey settled into the stroller, looking so cute.

Demetria laughed. "Yes, and hot dogs and other stuff."

Everett pushed the stroller. This seemed so natural for him. It would be nice to bring their own kids here someday.

"Sounds good to me," Everett said.

After eating hamburgers and watching the lions, they started for the gate but had to stop to see more of the elephants. After leaving the zoo, they headed to the mall while Corey slept in the backseat.

"I hope he sleeps like that on the way to Minnesota," Demetria said as she drove.

"We'll take bathroom, gas, and meal breaks." Everett had his phone out and was punching in stuff. "Okay, it's about eighteen hours to that area of Minnesota. Figure at least twenty hours to accommodate breaks."

"If we split up the driving, we could make it without stopping for the night. I drove fifteen hours to Omaha, Nebraska, in the summer to see the wildlife park near there. Well, it wasn't quite that long a drive—wasn't supposed to be, but closed roads, detours, closed lanes, and GPS direction malfunctions added five hours to the trip."

"Okay, so that's a good point. It could take us even longer to get there. You went by yourself?"

"No, with Mom. But she doesn't like to drive. She wanted to see the buffalo in the drive-through safari park, but I was fascinated with the wolves. We stayed in Omaha, then drove out to the wildlife park after that. We left about four in the morning or earlier."

"So if we left at four in the morning, we wouldn't get into the Blue Hill area until very early the next morning. And that's not accounting for GPS error or road delays."

Demetria parked at the mall. "Then we'll plan to stay the night at a hotel around six and finish the drive early the next morning so we can spend the rest of the day searching for their cabins in the wilderness. We only have a few more days left before Christmas."

"We could just pick up what we want at the mall, pack up our gear, and head out tonight. We could drive until eight."

"Okay. Let's see how long it takes us to shop and get ready to go."

"Be sure and pack a bathing suit," he said.

She frowned at him. "Why?"

"We'll have to stay at a hotel. We'll be tired of driving all day. If we can find one with an indoor pool, we can get a little exercise."

"We don't have a bathing suit for Corey."

Everett glanced back at him. He was sound asleep in the car seat. "If we can't find a swimsuit for him at the mall, he can wear his underpants."

"Maybe we can find some pajama shorts for him. They would be kind of like swimming trunks."

"Sounds good."

By the time they'd bought all the things Corey wanted for his family, picked up more warm clothes for the trip, and gone their separate ways to pack, it was nine that night. Too late to drive.

"I'm going to do a load of wash and really sleep," Demetria said over the phone to Everett as she started her washing machine.

"Don't tell me you're not joining us tonight." Everett helped Corey into his new fleece shark pajamas.

"Yeah, I know just how *that* would go. Shoot, and we haven't seen my mom yet either."

"Want to run over there tonight?"

Demetria loved how eager Everett was to please her. "No. You just put Corey to bed, right?"

"Yep."

"And we need to go to bed early."

Everett sighed heavily into the phone. "All right. When you wake up in the middle of the night and go to cuddle with me and I'm not there to pull you into my arms and snuggle with you, just remember we had this conversation, and it was *your* choice."

She laughed. "I love you, Everett. See you really early in the morning." She finished everything she had to do, packed her car, showered, and went to bed. And watched the clock. That was the problem with knowing she had to get up so early to go. She was afraid she'd sleep late, despite setting the alarm clock.

She tossed. Turned. Tossed. Look at the clock again. She must have fallen asleep for a little while because when she looked at the clock again, it was midnight. If she stayed with Everett tonight, he wouldn't have to take a detour to her place to pick her up in the morning. That would save a little on gas. And time.

She closed her eyes.

But they needed to sleep. And being with him was not conducive to sleep. Yet, damn it, she wasn't sleeping anyway.

She rolled over onto her back and stared up at the ceiling, then closed her eyes. If she was at his place, she wouldn't sleep in. Surely one of them would wake up, and then they'd be all set. What if Everett didn't wake up, and she was waiting for him but he didn't show?

She groaned and got out of bed and stared at the darn clock. *Okay, all right*. She called Everett. "I'm coming over. Don't read any more into it than it'll save us time and gas."

He laughed. "Sounds like a good plan to me."

"And so I don't sleep in. One of us will surely wake up when it's time."

"Agreed."

"Okay, I'm already on my way. See you in a few minutes." She was glad Everett was so flexible. But he was right. She really missed snuggling with him. This was becoming a really nice habit, which was a good thing because when they got home, they had some talking to do about living arrangements.

———

At four the next morning, they were sleeping soundly when Corey tugged on the comforter.

"What's wrong, Corey?" Demetria half opened her eyes.

"A big caiman tried to eat me."

She turned to look at Everett, who smiled at her. "Sorry. You should have just called me, Corey, and I would have taken care of it."

Demetria narrowed her eyes at the clock. "Ugh, we need to get up. Corey, you can sleep on the couch while we finish getting ready. It's too early for you to be up. You can sleep in your pj's in the car."

So much for sleeping last night. When two wild jaguars got together to snuggle, there's no way it would stay at just that.

That morning, it was smooth driving while Everett took the wheel for the first several hours so Demetria could sleep, and then they stopped for gas, a bathroom break, coffee, milk, and doughnuts. Then Demetria drove while Everett got some shut-eye. So all in all, staying the night at his place had worked well, even if they hadn't slept the whole time.

When he woke, they began talking about the house situation.

"A home with a big yard and trees, out somewhere

in the country so we have our privacy, and with a swimming pool, don't you think?" Everett asked.

"Oh, I think that sounds pretty good. Especially the pool part. Did you check with your boss to tell him we were on our way to Minnesota?"

"Yeah, and we'll let him know when we get in."

"Okay, told my boss too. I haven't mentioned the shifter team we're forming, not until we have a good resolution with this case."

"We will." Everett rubbed her back. "We've made good time. Sunset will be about five. We have a couple more hours to drive before we stop, if that sounds good to you."

"Yeah. I'd rather drive more today and then have more time to search for Corey's family when we get there tomorrow. Maybe six or seven, if you can find a good stopping point."

By the time they reached a town, it was six thirty and dark out. Everett pointed out one of the fancier hotels. Corey hadn't shifted or given any indication he was going to, so Demetria hoped he would be fine, but she was thinking it would be better to have someplace easier to sneak in a wolf pup if he shifted.

"Why this one, Everett?"

"Internet and an indoor, heated swimming pool."

She laughed. "All right. The swimming pool won me over."

After checking into the hotel, they let family and work know where they were and got dressed to go swimming. Corey was raring to go. They'd found a pair of swim trunks for him at a sporting goods store at the mall in Dallas, and he was so excited that he was pulling

Everett along by the hand in the direction of the pool room while she tried to keep up.

A couple of people were swimming, the plants around the pool giving it a semitropical appearance as the cold wind whipped around outside. Demetria had never expected to be swimming in a pool with a wolf boy and a hot jaguar in a cold, cold wintry place like Minnesota with Christmas Day looming. She was certain Corey would remember this forever. She and Everett would. She only wished she and Everett could swim as jaguars while Corey swam with them as a wolf. Wouldn't that shock the hotel guests?

They played with Corey in the water until they wore him out. And then they washed up, dressed, and had dinner in the restaurant. After they finished dinner, they took him back to the room and got ready for bed.

"Are you sleepy, Corey?" Everett helped him with his pajamas while Demetria made up the pull-out sofa bed for the boy.

"No."

"How about we watch a little TV? But not for too long. We have to get up really early again to find your family," Everett asked.

Corey rubbed an eye and nodded.

Demetria smiled and climbed into bed. Corey scrambled into bed between them as Everett joined them and turned on the TV, switching channels until Corey pointed at an animated feature.

They all settled back and watched until Corey was sound asleep.

Demetria whispered, "Time for him to be in bed." She turned off the TV.

Everett agreed and carried Corey to the sofa bed and tucked him in, kissing him on the cheek.

Demetria smiled at him. "You are going to make the perfect daddy. Only not right away."

He laughed. "But I'm going to have fun working at it until you're ready, just to have lots of practice."

She smiled and they cuddled. "I sure hope we don't have any trouble locating Corey's family."

"We'll find them. No trouble at all."

They snuggled and fell asleep. Demetria woke to the sound of the wind howling and ice pellets striking the window. She half drifted off, hoping they wouldn't have a terrible ice storm during the night that would keep them from driving. In Dallas, when they had ice storms, travel was downright dangerous.

A small body moved over hers, waking her, as Corey climbed in between her and Everett like a wolf pup looking to snuggle with his parents.

"Were you scared?" Demetria pulled the covers over him.

He nodded and cuddled against her.

"The wind?" Everett asked, running his hand over Corey's back.

Corey nodded.

"Ice pellets are hitting the window, that's all." Demetria hoped they would all melt before morning. But she was sure it would only get colder tonight. She just hoped there wouldn't be a lot of accumulation. She sighed and tried to sleep but then began to hear thunder.

She glanced at Everett. Thunder during a snowstorm?

Everett and Corey were sound asleep.

Chapter 19

THE NEXT MORNING, EVERETT AND DEMETRIA LOOKED out the hotel window to see flurries and a few inches of snow on the ground.

"Let's get some breakfast and head out." Everett helped Corey put on his clothes. "Glad Howard picked up Corey's snow boots from Belinda's place and dropped them off before we left."

"And my coloring books and crayons," Corey said.

Everett patted his shoulder. "You can bring one down to color while we're waiting for breakfast."

Demetria tucked her phone away and pulled her hair back. "I just checked the weather conditions. Massive storm front headed toward the area where we'll be searching."

Everett finished packing his bag and Corey's. "We'll get as close as we can to the location and go from there."

After eating a hearty breakfast of eggs, bacon, fruit, and hash browns, Everett threw their bags in the car and Demetria buckled Corey in.

Then they were off again. The day was gray, and a heavy, threatening low cloud clung to the earth, taunting them. *Come any farther and you'll regret it.*

While Everett drove, Demetria played the license plate game with Corey. "Aww, everyone has the same old one," he grumped.

"Let's look at all the different colors of cars then," she said. And for a while they did that.

Then they sang Christmas songs. Demetria had to pull up lyrics on her phone because she couldn't remember most of the songs. Even Everett sang along on a couple of them.

When they stopped for lunch, the waitress said, "Hope you're not headed up north. They say it's going to clear out tonight, but for the next few hours, it's a real blizzard." She motioned to the service station restaurant. "That's why nobody's here. They're all at the grocery store."

"Where is the grocery store?" Everett asked, thinking they should pick up some groceries for Corey's family as a way to show friendship.

"Just down the road. Take a left on Main Street, go through two signals, and it's straight ahead on the right after that."

"Thanks."

"Are you thinking we're going to be stuck somewhere and need to have provisions?" Demetria asked Everett.

"No. I just thought we'd take some food as a gift. And they may need some anyway. I don't want to impose on them if they want to share a meal with us."

"Okay, good idea."

While grocery shopping, Corey told them all the things he wanted to eat before they got on the road.

"What do you think? Two more hours?" Demetria asked, looking at the swirling snow that was starting to envelop them.

"If we don't get stuck anywhere. Why don't I drive the rest of the way? You're keeping Corey entertained."

"All right. If you don't mind."

Then they headed into the brunt of the storm. A whiteout. Everett had been in one in Amarillo once, and it had been totally disorienting. He hadn't been able to see the shoulder, the centerline, or the traffic approaching until he was practically on top of the other vehicles, just like now.

Demetria had grown quiet, watching the road. Corey had fallen asleep.

"Maybe we should stop," she said, sounding worried.

"We only have about a half hour to go now, and it looks like it's clearing ahead." Everett drove farther, then after about twenty minutes, he thought he saw some of the landmarks that Paddy had described. "We're almost... Wait, I think this is it. There are the blue-and-white hotel on the corner, the snowmobile rental, and the two-lane country road leading north that Paddy described." Then he saw the barrier closing the road.

Demetria let out her breath on a frustrated sigh. "But the road's closed."

Everett glanced in the direction of the snowmobile rentals where a couple of men were taking some out. At least they still had an option.

"You want to go by snowmobile?" she asked. "I've never ridden one, have you?"

"No, but we can take a lesson. Looks like they're open for business." Everett pulled into the parking lot where four other vehicles were parked, covered in snow.

Corey woke while Everett was taking him out of his car seat, and Everett held his hand as they all walked inside the snowmobile rental shop.

The bearded employee greeted them, his long hair tied back in a tail. "Where are you headed?"

"Up north." Everett told him the approximate area they were going to search. "We've got friends living in cabins out there, but we should be returning tonight."

"I'll make the rental through tomorrow, in case you decide to stay. Then you'll be covered. If you have any trouble, call this number, but with the snowstorm in the area, reception can be iffy. It's isolated up there. Most of the roads are closed because of the snowstorm, and we're still getting a bit of snow." He paused, then smiled. "Do you folks need a lesson?"

"Yeah. I'll buy lessons for us."

"You might want to rent a sled for the boy."

"We do. We're taking Christmas presents and food for a feast."

"Hey, Kent! Got some more lessons to give."

A young man jerked a jacket on and smiled. "Let's go."

After Demetria and Everett took the snowmobile lessons, they headed north for the final trek, eager to locate Corey's family. Everett pulled the sled and Demetria followed behind. They'd bundled Corey up on the sled until he was barely visible. Christmas presents, his birthday presents, and bundles of food were all tied down behind him. Blankets surrounded him to keep him nice and warm, and he had a pillow to snuggle on.

They rode for miles through snowdrifts and forests, past rivers, creeks, and lakes. Behind them, Everett could see the snow was settling in again, but ahead of them he saw clear blue sky. Everything was white. Serene. Beautiful. They spied a herd of moose. Everett had never seen them for real before. He was amazed at how big they were, even off in the distance.

They'd driven all over the area, smelling for smoke from chimneys and listening for sounds of people talking or laughing or crying. According to his odometer, they had traveled nearly a hundred miles, but a lot of it was canvassing the area, back and forth, searching for any clues that the white wolves lived here. Everett felt uneasy as the sun began setting, coloring the sky in reds and oranges and then disappearing beyond the forest. The air was colder now, the wind whistling through the trees. He'd really believed they'd find the wolves' cabins before this. He didn't know what they were going to do if they had to stay out here in the dark all night. Probably shift. Demetria could stay with Corey on the sled to keep him warm.

Everett saw a clearing in the forest and headed for it. A lake came into view, shimmering with ice in some places and covered with snow in others. And then across the lake, he saw cabins tucked into the woods. Smoke was curling from one chimney, but the breeze was carrying it away from them, north.

Demetria pulled up alongside him. "Is that where they live, do you think?"

Everett was about to ask Corey, but then the most remarkable thing happened. A broad band of colorful light turned the blackness into something magical, surreal, spectacular.

"The aurora borealis," Demetria whispered, as if saying it too loud would make it disappear. She quickly pulled off her helmet.

Everett took off his helmet and pulled out his cell

phone. "I don't think I can take a good shot in the dark," he said, but she'd had the same idea and was fishing her phone out to take pictures too.

She sighed. "Our families won't believe it. It's beautiful. Just beautiful."

They just stared in awe. The northern lights. The wide bands of purple and red and faint yellowish-green, the broad spectrum of colors, shimmered across the blackness, reflecting off the ice-covered lake for double the pleasure.

"It's stunning." Demetria took more pictures of the lights.

Even as concerned as he was about locating Corey's family tonight, Everett wouldn't have missed this moment for anything in the world. They were witnessing a natural, magical light display that man could never replicate in a million years.

Wanting a better shot of the northern lights reflecting off the lake, Everett lowered his cell phone and made the focus more distant. And stared at a large, male white wolf standing on a snowy part of the frozen lake in his viewer, watching him as if the colorful lights had beamed him down. One minute he wasn't there, and the next he was.

Everett blinked, expecting the wolf to disappear, thinking that the snow had affected his vision and he truly wasn't seeing what he thought he was. But the wolf was still there. Slowly, Everett lowered his cell phone even farther so that he was peering above it, looking directly at the vision. Sure enough, the wolf was staring at him like Everett was staring back. "We have company."

Heart pounding, he cut off the engine.

Demetria was staring at the wolf too, and she slowly reached out to cut her engine.

Then the wolf bolted into the woods and disappeared.

Everett glanced back at Corey to see if he'd seen the wolf and recognized him, but he was sound asleep, mostly buried beneath woolen blankets.

Hell. Everett was afraid the wolf was warning the pack that snowmobilers were in the vicinity, and they needed to remain in human form or out of sight.

"Wait! We have Corey! The Arctic wolf!" Everett shouted. He was certain that if the wolf was a shifter, he would hear him. Wolves had exceptional hearing just like jaguars did. Everett assumed the wolf had to be part of Cameron's pack or Cameron himself, because real Arctic wolves didn't live in this part of the world.

"We're trying to locate Cameron and Faith MacPherson! We have Corey MacPherson with us, and we're trying to return him to his family!" Everett called out.

Corey sat up and was peering at the woods now. Then a howl sounded in the distance, eerie and hauntingly beautiful at the same time. Corey tried to unwrap himself from the blankets and leave the sled.

"No. Just wait, Corey. They'll come and greet us as soon as they've gathered the pack." Everett hoped they wouldn't do so in a hostile manner. "Which wolf is howling?"

"Uncle David." Corey sounded excited, but a little worried too.

He was probably afraid he would be in trouble. Maybe a little, but Everett knew Corey's family would be so relieved to see him that he wouldn't get into *too* much trouble.

"Is that one of your cabins across the lake?" Demetria asked.

"Yeah, Mommy and Daddy's." Then Corey tried to take off his helmet.

Everett joined him and removed it for him. Corey cupped his hands around his mouth, tilted his head up, and howled. He sounded so small, and it made Everett realize just how little he was. Even so, his wolf's howl would carry farther than if he called out to them as a boy.

Everett just hoped Corey's wolf family wouldn't gather the pack to take down whoever had their little boy. Would the wolves think he and Demetria were the kidnappers?

Several howls sounded from farther away, and then the pack drew closer, barking and howling.

Corey howled again in greeting, but his small wolf pup's howl didn't last as long and wouldn't carry as far as the adults'.

The adults grew quiet as if waiting to hear the boy's howls again.

"Go ahead, Corey. They're waiting for you to howl." Demetria sounded thrilled but a little concerned too.

Corey howled again and the wolves all sang a response, much closer now, as if they'd been on the move and not just listening for his howl.

"Hope you're making a nice, happy howl and not one that says you need rescuing," Everett said.

Demetria chuckled a little bit.

Corey smiled at him. Then another howl and Corey said, "Daddy." He stood up on all the blankets, watching for them, eager, happy, though he was frowning as he peered into the dark woods. "And my uncles."

"But not your mama?" Demetria asked.

"She'd have to shift and then I'd shift in the cold. She tries to warn us first. And she won't do it outside when it's snowing. We have to take off our clothes in the house."

"She's probably staying home with your sister and brother," Demetria said, "waiting for your daddy to bring you home."

Then four big, male white wolves suddenly appeared in the woods, peering at them and eyeing Corey.

"Daddy!" Corey jumped off the sled and sank into the deep snow.

Everett and Demetria both went to rescue him, but the wolves raced to protect Corey, growling.

Hell. Everett wished he was wearing his jaguar coat so he could show that he could protect himself and Demetria with his punishing claws and teeth. It wasn't the way to handle new beginnings between their kinds, but the natural jaguar instinct to protect came to bear, even though he knew the wolves' natural instinct was to protect one of their own.

"We've been looking for you so we could bring your son home to you," Everett said, just as growly, annoyed that the wolves would take such a hostile stance when it had to be rather evident that they were taking good care of Corey. "And we've got Christmas gifts for him and for your family. We even celebrated his birthday with him."

The wolves looked at Corey. He grinned and pointed to all the bundles on the sled. "I helped pick out Christmas presents for everyone."

"Leidolf was trying to help us track you down, but

then he had a family emergency and had to go home. We need to talk. Just lead the way. We'll take your boy on the sled to your place. You can't very well take him in these snowdrifts when he's running as a boy, and he's going to have a hard time making it through them as a pup. Let us help with this." Everett understood their need to take charge of the boy, to protect him when they'd lost him for so long. But under the circumstances, it just wasn't viable.

This sure was a far cry from their usual missions in the South American rain forests.

The wolves greeted Corey, who gave them each a big hug. They licked his face and nuzzled him, then looked at Everett. He didn't know if they were agreeing or not. He guessed if he tried to lift Corey out of the snow and the wolves attacked, he'd know they weren't.

"Come on, Corey. Let's ride a little longer in the warm sled so you can see your mom and brother and sister too. Okay?"

Corey nodded and Everett lifted him out of the snow, brushed him off, and situated him back on the sled, making sure he was warm and secure. He secured Corey's helmet again.

"Okay, lead the way," Everett said to the wolves as he secured his own helmet.

The wolves were smelling the area where Everett and Demetria had stood. Everett added, "We're jaguar shifters, police officials for our kind out of Dallas. Everett Anderson and Demetria MacFarlane, at your service. We can explain it all to you when we reach your place. Leidolf, Dr. Denali, and several other packs have learned about us while we've been trying to locate you."

Then one of the wolves raced off into the woods, another led the way for the snowmobiles, and the other two ran parallel to the sled. Everett suspected the wolf that ran off was informing Corey's mother that he was safe and coming home.

They had to go a long way around the large lake before they reached the other side. They traveled another couple of miles and finally arrived at a log cabin, the same one they had spied across the lake with smoke curling from the chimney. White Christmas lights framed the windows, real frost covered part of the panes, real icicles dripped from the eaves, and a Christmas tree all lit up stood in front of one of the windows, making the cabin look cheerful and welcoming.

The lead wolf stopped, but no one came outside. Everett cut the engine of his snowmobile and Demetria parked next to his. He got off his seat, removed his helmet, went to the sled, and removed Corey's helmet. Then he lifted Corey into his arms and carried him through the snow to the cleared wooden front porch.

The door opened, and a woman rushed out to hug Corey. She was a pretty blond, green eyed and petite, wearing jeans, boots, and a sweater, tears spilling down her cheeks.

"Mommy!"

"Ohmigod, Corey. We thought you'd drowned in the river." Tears filled Faith's eyes and she held her son tightly, kissing his head as he wrapped his whole small body around her. "Everyone searched for you for days. Oh God, I can't believe you're home."

Demetria joined Everett on the porch, and he wrapped

his arms around her shoulders, the heartwarming reunion making this the best Christmas ever.

"Faith? I'm Demetria MacFarlane, and this is my partner, Everett Anderson. We've been searching all over for you."

"You're..." Faith sniffed the air, the chilled breeze carrying their scents to her.

"We're from Texas, bringing Christmas presents for everyone, but we're not used to this cold," Demetria said, shivering and rubbing her arms.

"Come in, come in." Faith ushered them inside and put Corey down to greet his brother and sister. "Where in the world did you find him?"

"He was dropped off at my mother's day care in Dallas," Everett said.

The cabin was toasty warm, a fire burning at the hearth. A blond-haired boy and girl ran to hug their brother. The boy was a little shorter than Corey, his eyes green just like his mom's, and freckles dotted his nose and cheeks. The girl was taller than both boys by a half inch or so. Her hair was in two long braids, and her eyes were a purer blue.

"They're jaguar shifters," Corey said proudly.

"Don't be silly, Corey. There's no such things as jaguar shifters," Faith said, but she looked concerned, realizing their visitors weren't wolf shifters. That meant that Everett and Demetria knew what they were.

The lead wolf came inside and headed down the hall. Faith shut the front door.

Everett assumed the other wolves would join them after they shifted and dressed.

"Just like for our kind, you don't exist," Demetria

said. "Corey's right. We *are* jaguar shifters. So your secret about being wolf shifters is safe with us. Your son's presence in our life has been a real eye-opener for all of us. We're thrilled he was part of our lives for even a short while, and we want to offer our assistance to your kind in the future in any way possible."

"They're real, Mommy. I played with kids who were jaguar cubs when I turned into a wolf," Corey said. "Show Mommy."

"Later," Faith said, sounding like there was no way that she was going to believe it. "Have you eaten?"

"No," Demetria said. "We didn't want to impose so we brought some food with us to give to you too."

"Oh. Why, thank you. We go into town for supplies when we need to, but this is wonderful. We can't ever thank you enough." Faith scooped Corey up again and hugged him tight. "How in the world did he end up there?"

"Wait." Cameron joined them. Everett could see why all the kids were blonds; Cameron was also a blond, with blue eyes. "Let's get their supplies unloaded before the food attracts bears or wolves. The others are joining us too, so you can tell us all what happened when they're here."

"I'll start cooking the meal," Faith said.

"Can I help?" Demetria asked.

"I'd love that and we can talk," Faith said.

"I'll help with the supplies." Everett joined Cameron outside.

"I don't know how we can ever repay you." Cameron started untying the bundles on the sled. "I can't believe he's alive. That he ended up all the way in Texas. Or that he shifted and ended up with…" He glanced at

Everett as if he couldn't believe anyone could be a jaguar shifter.

"Jaguar shifters. Seeing Corey home with his family is thanks enough." Everett was untying another bundle. "We had every intention of making his Christmas special, but we knew him being home with all of you was what everyone needed most. Though I will say he's had fun while he's been with us, so no worries about that."

"We all had trouble keeping our human forms, if you didn't know. Not just Faith."

"I totally understand. We were born as shifters, so we don't have that difficulty. Not only that, but our kind is not affected by the phases of the moon."

They carried some of the bundles into the house, then put them in the living room to sort out.

"We searched for him forever. We thought he'd fallen through the ice and drowned, and we wouldn't find his body until spring thaw. You can't know how devastated we've been. Thank you for bringing him home to us." Faith wiped away a couple of tears and sniffled.

Three more men entered the house, and Cameron introduced them. David Davis, a man with shaggy brown hair and dark-brown eyes, nodded at them but gave them a dark look. Owen Nottingham had nearly black hair and blue eyes and kept sniffing the air wherever the two jaguars had been. And Gavin Summerfield, a redhead with green eyes, freckles, and fair skin, studied them warily. They all gave a helping hand and carried the rest of the bundles inside the house.

Demetria and Everett took turns explaining what they were, how they'd come to have Corey with them, and how glad they were to find Corey's home and return him there before Christmas.

"We haven't heard about this Dr. Denali," Faith said. "I guess if he wants to test our blood, even though we're newly turned, it's all right with us."

"He wants to test ours too. Not that it will have anything to do with your longevity issues," Demetria said. "We have the same life spans as humans. He's just curious about us."

"Oh, wow, yeah, I'm sure he'd be fascinated to see the differences between our kinds," Faith said. "We can't ever thank you enough."

"You can't know how happy we are to have finally found you," Demetria said. "But Corey was an angel. We had more fun with him."

Faith smiled at her son.

"I have to say one little boy found the best hiding place of all while playing hide-and-seek," Demetria said.

"About that," Faith said, "your daddy was in just as much trouble for not watching you better."

Cameron looked a little sheepish even though he was smiling.

After the family opened their Christmas presents and thanked the jaguars for everything, they sat down to a feast. It was like celebrating Thanksgiving between jaguars and wolves.

Once they finished eating and cleaning up, Corey asked, "Can we play in the snow? As wolves?"

"Tomorrow," Faith said. "It's getting really late, and it's too dark out for you to play in the snow. Tomorrow after breakfast."

Corey looked glum.

Everyone glanced at Demetria and Everett to see what they wanted to do. Demetria swore the wolf shifters appeared both curious and wary.

"Your mom's right," Demetria said.

"You're staying the night with us," Faith said.

"Well, we thought we'd head out after this, so we can let our families and our workplaces know we got Corey home okay," Demetria said.

"No. It's too late. You're not familiar with the area so you're liable to get lost. You have to stay, and in the morning, you can have breakfast with our family and then—" Faith said.

"Play in the snow with us." Corey took his mom's hands in his and danced up and down. "They never been in snow before. They never builded a snowman."

"Then that's what we need to do, if Demetria and Everett would like to. Come on, kids. Let's get your baths. And, Demetria, Everett, the last room on the right is yours. If you need anything, just let us know." Faith hurried her kids off to another room.

Everett smiled at Demetria and wrapped his arm around her.

Cameron said, "We want to reciprocate your kindness somehow."

"You don't have to do anything. We're just glad we could get Corey home to you," Demetria said.

"We'll do something. Have a good night's sleep. We'll see you in the morning."

Then Cameron and the other men threw on their jackets, and they all walked outside, shutting the door behind them. To discuss the jaguars in their midst? Demetria wondered if they still didn't trust them being jaguars. Or maybe they wouldn't truly believe it until they saw them in their jaguar coats. She figured there was no sense in showing the video of Everett shifting when the wolf shifters could see it for real themselves. Tomorrow.

Chapter 20

EVERETT WRAPPED HIMSELF AROUND DEMETRIA IN THE queen-size bed in the guest room and kissed her hair. "I know why you wanted to go to a hotel tonight."

She smiled up at him. "Yeah, no way can we fool around here without all the wolves in the household hearing us."

He chuckled, then sighed. "I guess I can get through one night without."

"I couldn't."

"You mean when you came over to my house to 'save time'?"

She smiled. "You couldn't either."

"I was overjoyed you had changed your mind. I was trying to figure out a good reason why I had to pack up Corey and join you instead."

She laughed. "I'm glad I went to your place then. I'm so relieved to see the family together. Aren't you?"

"You bet."

After that, they fell asleep, and the next morning, they woke early to have breakfast with the whole pack so they could make a snowman and get on their way. But to show goodwill, they agreed to play in the snow for a bit—as jaguars.

"We'll be right out," Demetria said, and she and Everett retired to their guest room, stripped and shifted, and loped down the hall. Everyone but Corey stared at them in shock. He ran up and gave each of them a heartfelt hug.

Everett licked Corey's hair with affection, and he swore everyone was holding their breaths.

"Can we go out and play in the snow now?" Corey asked his mom.

"Sure. Let's go shift." Faith and the kids went down the hall.

Cameron folded his arms and stared at the two jaguars. "Well, I'll be damned. Unreal. Even though I knew you had to be telling the truth last night, it's just not the same as seeing it for real. I'll let you outside, and we'll join you in a minute."

Everett bowed his head a little, and then Cameron opened the door for Everett and Demetria.

As soon as he leaped through the snow, Demetria lunged right after him. She tackled him, pulling him down into the snowbank, just like she'd done in the water. He was her prey, and she was going to have fun. She hoped the wolves wouldn't join them too quickly. Not when she and Everett had never had a chance to play in the snow like this. And certainly not as jaguars. As isolated as it was out here, it was perfect. The breeze shook the snow-laden fir branches, sprinkling snow down on them, creating a mini snowstorm. They sank in the cold, wet stuff, but their coats kept them plenty warm. They might not have coats as thick as the wolves, but they felt fine.

Better than fine as Demetria pounced on Everett, and he was caught between walls of snow where his body had sunk. He somehow managed to flip her over and was on top, nuzzling her face in a familiar, loving, jaguar way. She wrapped her forelegs around his neck and nuzzled him right back, then licked his mouth and stroked his long, sandpapery tongue. She loved him, and she was smiling at him as they were both covered in snow and looked like a couple of snow jaguars instead of snow leopards.

Then she wriggled out from underneath him to sprint across the snow, and he chased after her. She hadn't thought about it, but the wolves were probably even more surprised to see a black jaguar since they were so rare. She whipped around and tackled her pursuer, and he roared a little in utter delight. Everett was so much fun.

She pinned him down and licked him again, thinking how much fun this was, but also how much she'd love to make wild and reckless love with him again. But it was important to spend this time with the wolves, to prove to them that the jaguar kind could truly live in peace with them. Then she wondered what had happened to everyone. Were they afraid to come out and play with them? Afraid their wolf pups would be hurt?

Jaguars were formidable predators. Between a wolf and a jaguar, the cat would win. She turned to see if anyone was coming, and there they all were, the whole white wolf pack, standing on the porch watching them play. The whole lot of them were beautiful. Which made her wonder where Corey's red wolf grandparents were.

Everett brushed up against her, and they waited for the wolves to join them.

Corey looked eager to do so, but he hadn't had his mom's permission to move, and Demetria suspected that after losing him, Faith and Cameron had laid down the law about him going anywhere without their permission.

Everett grunted at Corey, and he looked at his mother.

Faith barked at him, and apparently, that was a signal telling him he could play. He dashed off to join the cats, sinking deep into the snow. Normally, Demetria would have handled this like any day when she played with cubs, but he was a wolf pup, not a jaguar cub, so he played a little differently. Not only that, but they had a bunch of anxious wolves looking on.

Even so, she did what came naturally and rushed to pull him from the snow as Cameron did the same.

She got there first and lifted Corey out of the snow-bank and onto the packed snow.

Corey growled and went after Demetria's leg in good fun. She tumbled him with her paw in a gentle manner. The wolves looked tense, Corey's brother and sister staying close to their mother.

Then Demetria ran off, and Corey chased after her.

Everett was sitting in the snow, watching her play with Corey. But he wasn't going to get out of all the fun, so she tackled him. A few minutes later, Corey caught up and tackled him too.

Corey's brother whimpered and barked. Angie did too. Then Faith barked, and Demetria thought Corey's mother was calling him in. But then Demetria saw the other two pups running to catch up to the jaguars and Corey. They were shyer and not as alpha as Corey was. Corey played with Everett, and Demetria greeted the other pups, rubbing her whiskers against theirs and gently letting them get to know her so they could see she and Everett were safe.

Then she ran a little distance, and they chased after her. She turned and chased them, and they yipped and barked at her, half running, half trying to stand their ground. She turned and let them chase her again.

The adult wolves never joined them, just sat or stood on the porch watching, as if ready to protect the pups if the jaguars got too rough.

Demetria collapsed next to Everett, trying to catch her breath. It was hard work playing with wolf pups. The wolf pups sat and watched them, their tongues likewise hanging out as they panted, waiting to see what the jaguars did next.

Demetria was ready to head back to the snowmobile rental place so they could get on the road home and stop somewhere along the way where she could make love to her big cat.

Cameron barked at his pups, and they turned to look at him. He barked again, and they dashed off to join him. The wolves headed inside, and Demetria looked at Everett, smiling at the sight of snow resting on his nose and icicles hanging off his whiskers. She licked his face.

He was smiling just as much and licked her back, and then Cameron, dressed in jeans, said to them, "Why don't you come on in and get dressed, and we'll—"

"Make a snowman?" Corey asked, half dressed in jeans and socks. "Daddy, can we? They never made a snowman before. They catch caimans in the jungle."

Cameron looked at them as if they were deadly predators. He had to know that the jaguars didn't just catch the caiman. He cleared his throat. "If they want to. I think you wore them out."

Both Demetria and Everett got up and raced each other to the cabin, wanting to show the wolf pack leader that three little wolf pups did *not* wear them out.

They returned to the guest room where they'd left their clothes.

Demetria shifted, and as soon as Everett was standing before her naked, she pulled him into her arms and kissed him. "After we make a snowman, we need to leave," she whispered. "We need to take care of some very important business."

Everett wrapped his arms around her and kissed her back, smiling down at her. "I never thought I'd see such a pretty sight—you in the snow, with it clinging to your nose and whiskers. We may have to take trips up to snow country every once in a while."

"I'd like that. It's been fun."

Once they were bundled up, they went outside. This time, the men were all helping the kids build a snowman. Faith brought out a tray of hot chocolate and cookies.

Demetria added some snow to the snowman, then joined Faith on the porch. Faith smiled at her. "Thanks for taking care of Corey. He's told me all the wonderful things you did for him. The trip to the zoo, seeing the Christmas lights, playing with the jaguar cubs at the day care, playing with Everett and Maya, and now you. The birthday party all of you had for him. He said Mary told him he had to share with his brother and sister, and we can't thank you enough that you searched for us so you could bring him home for Christmas. That couldn't have been easy when you didn't even know our kind existed."

Faith's eyes filled with tears, and Demetria hugged her. "He was so good. You've raised a great little boy. All of your children are adorable. We were proud to have him with us for the short time that we did."

Faith handed her a mug of hot chocolate. "We want

you to return again. To see the kids. They were so excited about playing with you. We don't want this to be the end."

"How about if we come up for the kids' birthdays next year? We can play in the snow again. Everett and I weren't too sure what to expect. It was the first time for both of us. But we loved it."

Faith laughed. "We have plenty of it to play in. Sure, that would be wonderful. You can tell me to mind my own business, but we wondered... Well, are you mated?"

"Everett has asked me to marry him, and I said yes." She smiled at Everett as he turned to look at her, and he smiled back.

Along with the other men, he continued to work hard on building up the base of the snowman.

"Did you know that when wolves...have intimate relations, we are mated for life?" Faith asked.

"No." Demetria drank some of her hot cocoa. "Leidolf told us a lot about wolves, but he missed telling us that part. Though he did say you were mated for life after you were committed to each other. I didn't realize that meant after you consummated the relationship. He said you don't divorce."

"True. So, are you mated jaguars?"

Demetria took another sip of her hot cocoa, feeling her face warm. "Umm, yeah, we are." She glanced in Everett's direction, and he winked at her. Her face felt even hotter.

"For life."

"Some jaguars aren't like that. But yes, we're committed to each other."

Faith let out her breath with relief.

Demetria frowned at her. "Is there a problem? Something troubling you?"

"I didn't want to lie to Corey, but he said you were sleeping in the same bed, naked."

Demetria's lower lip dropped as she recalled when Corey had walked into their bedroom wide awake and Everett had gotten up to fix him breakfast.

Faith smiled. "So no problem. You're mated jaguars, and that's all he needs to know. Though he did ask when you're going to have cubs so he can play with them."

Demetria laughed.

"Sorry. I didn't mean to get so personal, but he just assumed that since you were shifters, that meant you were like us."

Demetria smiled. "Well, we were asleep when Corey came into the bedroom. But we were covered up. I'm not used to having a little one come in to get me up to feed him breakfast."

Faith chuckled. "Believe me, with three of them, one or another of them is always coming in for some reason. That's why we have their grandparents here. They love to help out a lot."

"Leidolf mentioned them. He was concerned that they hadn't contacted him to let him know where they were. Where are they?"

"Oh, they're on a vacation. They said they'd come home for Christmas, but they needed some adult alone time. Believe me, I don't want to hear any of the details from my dad. They're going to wish they'd been here to meet you both. We'll be sure to let Leidolf know where we've finally settled down."

Demetria wished her father felt that way about her mother. "Listen, we have to run after they build the snowman. We need to get home for Christmas. You don't have any reception out here, and we need to let our families and work know Corey is safely with his family too."

"I understand."

But she thought Faith understood more than that. She and Everett needed their adult time after having babysat Corey for so long. Not that they hadn't had their moments.

"There," Cameron said, holding Angie up so she could stick the carrot into the snowman's face for a nose.

Uncle Gavin helped Nick place blueberries for the snowman's mouth, and Everett helped Corey place two black buttons for the eyes.

The kids stuck buttons on the body, Demetria tied a scarf around the snowman's neck, and Faith stuck a cap on its head.

For everyone at home, Cameron snapped pictures of the wolf family with the snowman, taking turns while Uncle David took pictures of the kids with Everett and Demetria in front.

"We should have gotten pictures of everyone in their shifter coats," Demetria said, annoyed with herself. "Everyone back home would love to see all of you and us together."

"Done," Uncle Owen said. "As soon as I saw the kids and you playing, I had to get a few shots for posterity's sake. I ran in and shifted, dressed, and returned to take pictures. I'll forward them to your emails when we're in town. Or I can send you a disk."

"Thank you," Demetria said. "We've had fun, but we

need to return home to our families for Christmas. We want to thank you for everything."

"We should be thanking you"—Cameron lifted Corey into his arms—"for everything."

"Can they stay the night again?" Corey asked.

"No, Corey, we have to get home. If we don't, Santa Claus won't know where we are," Demetria said.

That seemed to make more sense to Corey than anything. They exchanged email addresses, phone numbers, and home addresses with the family, though Demetria suspected she and Everett would be finding a house with a yard and moving soon.

They said good-bye to the Arctic wolves, knowing that one small wolf pup and four-year-old boy had brought their worlds together in an extraordinary and wonderful way. It was a bittersweet moment when Corey got out of his dad's arms to give them tearful hugs. "I don't want you to go."

"We promise to come see you on your birthdays." Demetria hugged him to her breast, tears filling her eyes. "We'll come play with you and make a snowman again. And bring presents. Okay?"

He nodded. He hugged Everett again, and Everett agreed. "You send us pictures, and my mom will want you and your family to come see us so you'll be able to play at her day care with all the other kids again."

Corey glanced back at his mom and dad.

"During the phase of the new moon," Faith agreed, smiling.

"We'll look forward to seeing you then." Demetria gave Corey one more hug, and he stood there watching them until his brother hit him with a snowball.

She and Everett laughed as Corey prepared his own snowball in retaliation.

"Oh, and we'd love to see the northern lights again. They were just spectacular," Demetria said.

"And unpredictable, but that's what makes them so magical. They say some Native Americans believed that when the northern lights danced across the sky, mystical or divine wolves came down to earth," Faith said. "We never tire of them. We never know when they'll appear, but in the dark on a night like last night, they paint the black sky in brushstrokes of extraordinary colors."

"You are like the mystical wolves, shape-shifters like us," Demetria said. "Legends in South America exist about us too. About jaguar gods and goddesses that shape-shifted."

Faith smiled. "That means we are all divine."

"I couldn't agree more."

"Let us know where you're staying tonight. The roads can be treacherous this time of year, and we'll be anxious to know you made it to a hotel," Faith said.

"We will," Demetria agreed and gave her a hug. "And when we arrive home, we'll let you know."

"Thank you."

They said their farewells one last time, then Demetria and Everett rode off to their own new adventure, a new life together, in charge of a new specialized team that would deal with all shifters, though Demetria knew Everett had to tell his boss he had decided to take the job first. She and Everett had wanted to wait until they'd officially solved a mixed shifter case. And they had, she thought with glee.

After reaching the snowmobile rental shop and turning in the snowmobiles and sled, they drove until they reached Wichita, enjoying the lights all over town. A few inches of snow covered everything, giving it that real Christmas feel. When they arrived back in Texas, Demetria would miss the snow.

Once Everett asked for the honeymoon suite, it felt good settling into the warm room together, just the two of them. No worries about a little tyke catching them together in bed.

They might not be officially married, but if they lived by the rules of the wolf shifters, they were good and mated, and that meant for life.

"We need to call everyone and tell them the good news," Demetria said as Everett turned on the fireplace, and she tossed her heavy coat, scarf, gloves, and hat onto a chair. She sat down on the mattress to take off her boots.

"I know you and your need for closure on a mission." He jerked off his coat, hat, and gloves. "So if you have to do this first, we will."

She smiled up at him and grabbed on to his belt to pull herself up. "I know that hot look in your eyes. No way do you want to get to business first."

He smiled lazily down at her, his eyes darkening with interest. "Yeah, I do." His voice was already rough with need. He kissed her slowly on the mouth, and she knew damn well he was trying to convince her *this* was the business she needed to take care of first.

And she loved him for it. Yes, she normally would have been impatient to let everyone know they'd been successful and to let Faith know where they settled for the night, but a few more minutes wouldn't matter. Connecting with Everett in this primal way did.

She kissed him right back, licking his lips, asking for an invitation, and when he smiled a little, she plunged right in and took advantage.

Their noses and cheeks were chilled, their faces a bit sunburned from the light reflecting off the snow and wind-burned from the bite of the cold. They thought they had bought enough clothes to protect themselves, but what did they know? These two jaguar cats were not used to the cold.

Everett pulled back from Demetria. "Miss him?"

"Sorry."

"Don't be. I keep thinking he's close by and we have to be careful about what we do in front of him."

"But he isn't, though he'll always have a special place in our hearts." And then she cradled Everett's face in her hands and kissed him thoroughly with no more thoughts about anything but Everett and how she wanted to make hot, passionate love with him.

He was gentle and rough and gentle again, the need evident in his compelling, darkened eyes and insistent touch. She was just as needy, wanting, reckless, yanking off his clothes, her clothes, making him smile wickedly.

He was all muscle and heat and passion, and she loved this part of their relationship. The intimacy, the touching, the kissing, melting against him before he took the plunge. She rubbed her bare body against his like a cat. She loved how she kicked his pheromones into high gear, just as he did hers. Which only strengthened the desire, the craving, the need.

He lifted her chin to kiss her mouth, his tongue

stroking hers, his hands each cupping a breast. Lowering his head, he took a nipple in his mouth and tugged gently, then swirled his tongue around it.

This was what made her melt. She gripped his hips for support. He moved to the other breast and tongued her nipple, teasing, making her moan.

She was boneless when he swept her up in his arms. He yanked the bedcovers away and laid her on her back against the cool sheets, the jaguar in him on the prowl, hungry. He settled beside her, taking charge of pleasuring her, his hand sweeping up her inner thigh, his hot mouth kissing her breast.

She tangled her fingers in his hair, tensing as his fingers caressed her leg, up higher, until he found her nub and began to stroke her.

Her need roared in her breast, her heart pounding as hard as his, like the beat of drums in the jungle, the wild calling to them both. His cock brushed her thigh as he pressed himself against her, showing her what he had for her next. *Wicked, wicked jaguar*.

She clawed at his back, making him stroke harder, faster, and she growled in big cat satisfaction.

He growled right back in a purely male jaguar way that said he loved pleasuring her. She smelled his sexy, musky arousal and her own and lifted her pelvis to connect more with his fingers when she felt the end draw near. "Ah, yes!" she groaned out as the climax crashed over her with a roar.

She felt drunk with his touches, his hand sweeping up her belly before he parted her legs with his knee, centered himself, and plunged in.

The she-cat was all his, body and soul, and he loved

making love to her on this cold winter's night in a state still far from home. He sank fully into her, his body primed, his need for release urging him on.

He wanted deeper, tugging her leg over his hip, and she quickly obliged by wrapping her legs around him. He dove deeper, pulling out and pushing back into her hot, wet sheath.

She ran her hands over his shoulders and then reached up to cup his face. He leaned down and kissed her profoundly, drank her in, savored the sweetness that was all Demetria, the taste of his mate, the love of his life.

He groaned against her mouth, so close, and then he let go, spilled his seed deep inside her, and growled her name in a rough and well-satiated jaguar way.

"God, you're good for me," he said, pulling her into his arms.

She covered them with the comforter. "I can tell you right now, you are the best Christmas present I've ever had."

"I feel the same about you, honey. A present that just keeps giving."

She laughed and kissed his chest, then yawned. "Remember that when I wake you up in the middle of the night."

"If I don't wake you first."

He was thinking that since they didn't have any other missions right now, they'd take off for a two-week vacation. As soon as they got home, he was putting in for it because, except for planning a wedding and moving in together, he wanted to enjoy Demetria just like this.

"Aww, darn," Demetria said. "I knew we should have gotten the other business over with before we got to more pleasurable business."

"I'll make the calls."

"Are you kidding? It would take you half the night. I'll start with the MacPhersons. You call your boss, and we'll go from there."

Demetria had just finished talking to her mom and Everett had ended the final call to the wolf packs when someone knocked at their hotel room door.

They both turned to look at it.

"Wrong room. Has to be," Demetria said.

"Room service!" a man called out at the door.

Demetria and Everett shared a look.

Everett threw on his jeans and went to the door.

A smiling waiter said, "Where do you want me to put this?"

Everett could smell steaks under the metal covers and spied a chilled bottle of champagne.

"Courtesy of the MacPhersons and friends," the man said.

When the waiter left, Everett smiled at Demetria. "They must have known we'd need more energy for later. Certainly is a nice payback."

"Open the bubbly. This definitely calls for a celebration." She called Faith to thank them for the thoughtful gesture. When they ended the call, Demetria said, "Now I know why she put Corey on the phone to talk to me earlier. He asked which room we were staying in, and as soon as I told him, he hung up on me."

Everett laughed. "When it's time"—he popped the cork—"I'd be happy to have a son just like him."

"Or daughter."

He laughed again. "We'll probably end up with both."

Chapter 21

"My mother wants to meet you, but she's not happy with you," Demetria said, reading her emails on her cell phone as they stopped for gas in Dallas. "So we need to go over there first thing. She wants us to have lunch with her. We'll see your mom at the day care afterward. Your dad is coming home for Christmas, isn't he?"

"Yeah, he will be. And we'll make sure we see everyone Christmas Day." Everett smiled at her, rubbing her arm. "About your mother? All mothers like me. Why wouldn't yours?" Then he frowned. "Because she feels I'm replacing Ma—"

"Shhh," Demetria said, placing a kiss on his mouth. "She knows I hoped you and I could get together. She was annoyed you waited so long. She believes I've been pining away for too long. I reminded her you were grieving too. But she just didn't buy it. She just thought you were afraid of my bite."

He laughed. "As long as you want to marry me, that's all that matters." But Everett knew it was important to win Demetria's mother over too. He understood about family, and Demetria and her mother were close.

When they arrived at the white, French country house–styled home in the suburbs, Everett meant to get Demetria's car door, but she hopped out instead.

They walked up to the front door and Demetria opened it. "Mom, we're... My dad's here," she suddenly said.

Everett smelled her father's scent but no sign of aggression.

"Mom?" Demetria called out and rushed into the house.

Hearing laughter on the back porch, they hurried that way, then saw Joel barbecuing ribs and Martha fixing vegetables.

Demetria looked shocked.

Her mother and dad were kissing. Then, as if they suddenly realized they had an audience, they turned to face Demetria and Everett.

"Food's nearly done. Just grab a drink from the fridge and come join us," her mother said.

Everett said, "Thanks. I'm Everett Anderson, by the way."

"I know who you are, young man. You waited much too long to date our Demetria. Now, go on. Get your drinks, and come out and join us," Martha said. "Joel told me all about you."

Demetria turned and went back into the house, Everett following behind her and shutting the door behind them. Tears filled her eyes.

Everett pulled her close. "Are you all right?"

"Yes. I just haven't heard Mom refer to herself and Dad as 'us' for years. And the kiss... These, these are happy tears."

Everett smiled, gave Demetria a sound hug, and kissed her. "Good. I guess I'm still on the hot seat with your mother though."

"You'd better not be. My mother might have forgiven my dad for abandoning us, but I haven't."

They grabbed a couple of bottles of water and joined Demetria's parents outside.

"We're getting married again," Martha said. "It wasn't what you and I thought at all. Your dad was Special Forces in the army, got out, and worked for a cyber warfare firm. We were fine together before he was recruited for a job that required him to give up his family to keep us safe. He's retired now, through with it. And he has come home to stay."

"Why didn't you tell us?" Demetria asked, looking totally peeved with her dad.

"I couldn't, kitten. No correspondence, no payments. I've deposited over a million dollars in your mom's bank account to prove I want to make this work. Your mom has always been the one for me. I've never looked anywhere else." He put his arm around Martha and kissed her cheek. Then he gave Everett a steely-eyed glare. "When is your wedding date?"

"First of the New Year. We didn't want to wait any longer than that," Demetria said.

"Then we need to start making wedding plans," Martha said.

The women talked about what they needed to do, and Everett spoke with Joel, who gave him all kinds of fatherly advice, despite the fact he hadn't been around much.

After visiting with her parents and having a really good time, Demetria and Everett made their excuses so they could see his mom next. She still had kids at the day care, and they'd already let her know they had returned to Dallas and were meeting her parents first, which Mary had been thrilled about.

When they reached his mother's day care, they showed her pictures on Everett's cell phone of the reunion between Corey and his family, both as wolves and as humans. And of the northern lights. Mary loved the ones that showed Everett and Demetria playing as jaguars with the wolf pups.

"Oh, oh, I have to tell you. There are two wolf pups here today." Everett's mother looked as proud as she could be.

"You're kidding. The woman we saw at the mall? A couple of her children?" Everett asked.

"No, another woman in the pack. One of Rafe Denali's PIs found the pack in Dallas when they were trying to locate the Arctic wolf pack. He shared the information with his brother, Dr. Aidan Denali, the one who is testing them for longevity issues, and he told them about us. The pack was so impressed that we had a day care for jaguar shifters and that we had accommodated Corey that they asked if they could bring their toddlers here when they needed to. This summer, we're going to have lots of pool-time fun. I'm having another mural painted in the entryway that shows some gray and red wolves playing with the jaguar cubs too."

Everett couldn't have been more pleased. "Our shifters are all right with it?"

"A couple of mothers were grumbling a little, worried about cat and dog fights. Well, wolf, as Corey would say. Wolves are *not* dogs. So I told the mothers that all the little girls and boys would learn to get along like little angels under my roof. And they have. Once they got used to the notion that wolf pups were coming to the day care, they looked forward to seeing them."

Mary sighed and gave them both a hug. "Now, tell

me about this wedding you have planned. What do I
need to do?"

———∿∿∿———

It was Christmas Eve already and tomorrow, Everett and
Demetria had plans to visit with both her family and his
after all the grown children arrived in town for lunch,
dinner, and gift giving. They also planned some private
gift giving before they headed over there.

They'd learned that Paddy and Belinda O'Leary
were released from confinement as soon as Martin had
word that Corey's family had been found. Howard had
taken leave for a week too. Everett and Demetria were
looking forward to having a relaxing time for the next
two weeks.

But tonight, they had just finished making love and
were happily snuggling, talking about the upcoming
wedding, the plans to find a home, and working as a
multi-shifter team, though they had no other cases in
the works.

Then Everett got a call and checked the ID. Leidolf.
Expecting Christmas well-wishes, Everett answered and
put the call on speaker.

"I'm so sorry to disturb you on Christmas Eve, but
I've got a situation here. Now that you've taken care of
Corey, I figured you were the ones to handle it. Here's
the deal. One of my sub-leaders called me when I was in
Dallas, saying that two men were shooting at each other
on my ranch lands. Some of our pack members tried to
track them down, but both men were wearing hunter's
spray. When I arrived home, the pack still hadn't located
either of the men. Then tonight after trying to track them

down, one of my men found one of them. The man had been shot twice and was brought to my ranch house because he had been trespassing on my lands. We were going to take him to the hospital, but he begged us not to. Said that he would heal up fine. He didn't smell like anything because he was still wearing hunter's spray. And then he must have been so out of it that he shifted. Into a jaguar. Surprised the hell out of all of us. I told him we'd get him help from his own kind, and I mentioned your name. All he said was 'That son of a bitch.' His name is Brandon Williams. Do you know him?"

Smiling, Everett cuddled with Demetria and kissed her forehead when she looked up at him questioningly. "Yeah, I know him. And despite that, I'll pick up his sorry ass. Oh, and Merry Christmas to you and yours, Leidolf."

"Merry Christmas to you and your partner. I hope it's wolf-permanent by now."

"Believe me, it is." Demetria smiled at Everett in that devilish way that meant he wasn't going to go right back to sleep anytime soon, and that suited him just fine.

"One other thing. You might need to put on your JAG agent hats for this case. The person who shot him was another JAG agent, and he tried to shoot one of my people too."

"Hell, a JAG agent? Are you sure?"

"Yeah, that's what Brandon said. A guy by the name of Herndon Walker. Brandon's one of yours too, isn't he?"

"Yeah, he is. Okay, I'll call my boss and let him know we're gathering the team and headed out there as soon as we can get a flight, though it might not be until the day

after Christmas," Everett said, hugging Demetria against
his body.

"I'll have someone bring you to my ranch as soon as
you arrive."

"I'll let you know when we're coming in." Everett
ended the call.

"Our first official case while serving in our new
office." Demetria reached over to the nightstand to grab
her phone. "I'll make reservations for the first flight out
of Dallas that I can get."

"I'll call the boss to let him know we agreed to be in
charge of this new office, and I'll give Howard a call to
see if he's ready to go. I think this time we might need to
have an Enforcer doing Enforcer-like work. Terminating
a jaguar shifter?"

"He'll love it."

Everett called his boss and said, "Sir, my team is
accepting your offer. We'll be known as the United
Shifter Force, USF. Currently, Demetria and Howard
will be on the team, at least once I contact Howard to
make sure he's agreeable. And we have our first mission in Portland, Oregon." He explained what had happened there.

Martin said, "I knew you could do it. Let me know
the details as soon as possible. I want to know why the
JAG agent was shooting one of our own and a wolf."

"Will do." Everett called Howard after that. "Hey,
ready to be on the United Shifter Force team?"

"I thought you'd never ask."

Everett told him about the case. "We'll get right back
to you with flight times."

"Okay, I'm packing up now."

"Probably be the day after Christmas, first thing."

"I'll be ready."

Everett wished Howard a Merry Christmas, then ended the call.

Demetria frowned. "How do you know this Brandon Williams?"

"He nearly killed me. And I attempted to return the favor."

She shook her head.

"Believe me, if you had to deal with him, you'd use your teeth on him, and *not* in a sweet, loving way."

"In that case, I'll be prepared. My bite is much worse than my growl."

Everett smiled. How well he knew. "Do you want to open one present tonight?" he asked, already picking out the one he wanted Demetria to open first.

She kissed him and pulled a present from under the tree for him to open too, all smiles.

They opened their presents at the same time and laughed as they each pulled out a drone with aerial recording and real-time display to help in their investigations when they needed an eye up closer to the situation. They gave each other hugs and kisses before they played with their video drones.

Life would never be the same now that some jaguar shifters were aware that wolf shifters existed and vice versa. To think that saving Lacy had meant losing Matt, but that the teen Brayden Covington had brought Everett and Demetria together. And the little wolf-shifter boy had helped to cement that relationship into something endearing and permanent.

What began as an effort to train mixed jaguar teams

had evolved into something even greater—a way to help *all* of the shifter kind.

But two jaguar shifters only needed each other at the moment. They'd take care of the rest of the world after Christmas.

Keep reading for a look at Terry Spear's

A SILVER WOLF CHRISTMAS

Available now from Sourcebooks Casablanca

CONNOR JAMES SILVER, BETTER KNOWN AS CJ, couldn't believe it had been a whole year since he and his brothers rejoined their cousin Darien Silver's wolf pack. Though his oldest brother was still butting heads with Darien at times, CJ was glad they had made amends and returned home to Silver Town, Colorado. His ancestors had built the town, which was still mostly gray wolf run, and he envisioned staying here forever.

Especially now that three lovely sister she-wolves had joined the pack and were remodeling the old Silver Town Inn. In two days' time, they would have hotel guests. CJ smiled as he strode up the covered wooden walkway in front of the tavern and glanced in the direction of what had been the haunted, neglected hotel across the street, which was now showing off its former glory. The windows were no longer boarded up, the picket fence and the fretwork had been repaired, and a fresh coat of white paint made the whole place gleam.

"CJ!" Tom Silver called out as he hurried to join him. Tom, the youngest of Darien's triplet brothers, was CJ's best friend.

He turned to watch Tom crunch through the piled-up snow, then stalk up the covered walkway. He had the same dark hair as CJ, although his eyes were a little darker brown. Tom was wearing his usual: an ecru wool sweater and blue jeans. The toes of his boots were now sporting a coating of fresh snow.

Tom pointed at the hotel, evidently having observed CJ looking that way. "Don't even *think* about going over there to help with the final preparations before their grand opening."

CJ shook his head. "I know when I'm not wanted." But he damn well wasn't giving up on seeing the women—well, one in particular.

Tom smiled a little evilly at him. "Come on. I'll buy you lunch. Darien has a job for you."

Even though CJ was a deputy sheriff and took his lead from the sheriff, everyone stopped what they were doing when the pack leader needed something done. Pack took priority.

He and Tom headed inside the tavern, where the fire was burning in a brand-new woodstove in the corner, keeping the room warm. The Christmas tree in front of one of the windows was decorated with white lights, big red bows, and hand-painted ornaments featuring wolves. The aroma of hot roast beef scented the air, making CJ's stomach rumble. Sam, the black-bearded bartender—and now sandwich maker—was serving lunch without Silva, his waitress-turned-mate. She was now down the street running her own tearoom, where the women ate when they wanted lunch out. The men all continued to congregate at Sam's.

The tavern usually looked a lot more rustic, less…

Christmasy. Sam loved Silva and tolerated her need to see that everyone enjoyed the spirit of Christmas either at her place or his, though he grumbled about it like an old grizzly bear.

CJ glanced at the red, green, and silver foil-covered chocolates in wooden Christmas-tree-shaped dishes on the center of each table. Those were new. Silva had also draped spruce garlands along the bar and over the long, rectangular mirror that had hung there since the place opened centuries earlier. She'd added lights and Christmas wreaths to the windows and had put up the tree, though Sam had helped. He looked rough and gruff, and was protective of anyone close to him, but he was a big teddy bear. Though CJ would never voice his opinion about that.

"We'll have the usual," Tom called out to Sam.

He nodded and began to fix roast beef sandwiches for them.

"Staying out of trouble?" Tom sat in his regular chair at the pack leaders' table in the corner of the tavern. This spot had a view of the whole place, except for the area by the restrooms.

"I haven't been near the hotel." CJ glanced around the room, nodding a greeting to Mason, owner of the bank; John Hastings, owner of the local hardware store and bed-and-breakfast; Jacob Summers, their local electrician; and even Mervin, the barber—all gray wolves who were sharing conversations and eating and drinking. It was an exclusive club, membership strictly reserved for wolves.

CJ looked out the new windows of the tavern—also Silva's doing, now that the hotel was quite an attraction instead of detracting from the view. The new sign proclaimed Silver Town Inn, just like in the old days, as it rocked a little in the breeze. Only this time, the sign featured a howling wolf carved into one corner. CJ loved it, just like everyone else did.

The pack members couldn't have been more pleased with the way the sisters had renovated the place, keeping the old Victorian look but adding special touches. Like the two wrought iron and wood-slat benches in a parklike setting out front, with the bench seats held up by wrought iron bears.

Tom turned back to CJ. "Darien said—"

"I know what Darien said. My brothers and I were getting under the women's feet. They didn't want or need our help. Don't tell me we can't participate in the grand opening." Even though CJ would be busy directing traffic for a little while, he intended to stop in and check on the crowd inside the hotel to ensure everyone was behaving themselves.

Sam delivered their beers in new steins, featuring wolves in a winter scene etched in the glass, along with sandwiches and chips on wooden Christmas tree plates. He gave CJ a look that told him he'd better not make a comment about the plates or steins. CJ was dying to ask Sam how domesticated life was, but he bit his tongue.

"I'll be setting up the bar for the festivities," Sam said. "Silva is bringing her special petit fours, and she's serving finger sandwiches. The hotel had better be ready to open on schedule."

"Do you think any of the guests will run out of there screaming in the middle of the night, claiming the place is haunted?" CJ asked. It was something he'd worried about. He wanted to see the sisters do well so they could stay here forever.

Sam shook his head. "Blamed foolishness, if you ask me."

Sam didn't believe in anything paranormal. Some might ask how he could feel that way when they were *lupus garous*—wolf shifters. But then again, their kind believed they were perfectly normal. Nothing paranormal about them.

Someone called for another beer, and Sam left their table to take care of it.

"When you were over there getting underfoot, did you see anything?" Tom asked, keeping his voice low.

"Nothing unusual." Even though they'd been best friends forever, the ghostly business with the hotel was one thing CJ really didn't want to discuss with Tom. Neither of them had, not once over all those years.

CJ took another bite of his sandwich, hoping now that the hotel was opening, he could finally start seeing Laurel MacTire in more of a courtship way. He would never again make the mistake of mispronouncing her name. Who would ever have thought that a name that looked like "tire" was pronounced like "tier"? He couldn't know every foreign word meaning "wolf." But he did love that she was a pretty redheaded, green-eyed lass. She had been born in America, but she still had a little Irish accent, courtesy of her Irish-born parents. He loved to listen to her talk.

The problem was that she and her sisters, Meghan and Ellie, acted wary around him and everyone else in the pack. In fact, they didn't seem like the type of proprietors that should manage a hotel, since they were more reserved than friendly or welcoming. He wasn't sure what was wrong. Maybe they'd never lived with a pack before. He had to admit that everyone had been eager to greet them, so maybe they felt a bit overwhelmed.

The pack members were so welcoming because fewer she-wolves were born among *lupus garous* than males, and many of the bachelors were interested. The women in the pack were also grateful that they had more women to visit with. Besides that, the wolf pack's collective nature was such that its members openly received new wolves.

After eating the rest of his sandwich, Tom leaned back in his chair. "The two painters working on the main lobby left prematurely yesterday after demanding their pay for what they'd finished. They said that when they returned from a lunch break, their paint cans had been moved across the room, their plastic sheeting was balled up in a corner, and an *X* was painted across the ceiling in the study."

CJ frowned. "None of the sisters saw or heard anything?"

"The sisters had returned to their house behind the hotel to have lunch."

"Could it have been kids? Vandals?" CJ figured that what had happened wasn't the result of anything supernatural.

"Who knows? If we discount the ghostly angle, could have been." Tom finished his beer.

"Did the women smell the scent of anyone who had been in there earlier?"

"Not that they could say. So many people have been traipsing through the hotel, finishing up renovations, that maybe somebody else just moved the stuff. The electrician and a plumber were in earlier."

"About that… I've seen that they've hired humans for a number of the jobs. Except for Jacob, the electrician. I would think everyone, even if they're new to the pack, would hire wolves."

Tom shrugged. "They've never been in a pack before. It'll take a little getting used to. Maybe no one gave them a list of who could do the jobs for them. We all know who does what in the vicinity. The sisters wouldn't have a clue."

CJ nodded, but he was already thinking about how the painters had left the work unfinished. Maybe the women could use his help in painting the rest of the place. As long as the town or surrounding area didn't require him to get involved in any law enforcement business, he was free to help out. And eager to do so.

"Of course, that doesn't explain the *X* on the ceiling," Tom said.

"Most likely vandals."

CJ wasn't afraid of any old ghost in the hotel. He hadn't been since that day when Darien and Jake had tried to scare him and Tom when they were all kids. CJ told himself it had just been them. But neither of the Silver brothers had said anything about what CJ had witnessed, confirming or denying it. He was still telling himself the apparition he'd seen was only a figment of his imagination. That, as a kid, he'd been so scared, he could have imagined anything. That the darkened shadow of a woman was nothing more than dust particles highlighted by moonlight shining through the basement door's window.

Tom sat taller in his chair. "If visitors ask about the hauntings, Darien wants everyone in the pack to tell them the stories are just rumors."

"Right. Ghosts don't exist."

Tom let out his breath. "But you know differently. We both know differently."

That made CJ wonder what Tom had experienced. But if CJ admitted to even one soul that he believed the hotel was haunted, there would go his best-kept secret of all time. Besides, Tom had never shared what he'd experienced either.

Tom straightened a bit. "Okay. Well, as I said, Darien has a job for you."

If it had to do with helping Laurel MacTire, CJ would jump right on it. He was certain that she *really* didn't mind that he'd been so in the way when she was trying to get the place fixed up. She was just overcautious about everyone in the wolf pack.

"Hang some Christmas lights on the hotel?" Then again, the job could have nothing to do with Laurel, her sisters, or the hotel. CJ finished the last of his beer.

Tom tilted his chin down. "*No* helping the women with the hotel. Unless they change their minds and ask you to."

"All right," CJ said. "What then?"

"We have some ghost busters in town."

"That's just what we need." CJ was ready to protect the three sisters from anyone who might try to ruin things for them.

"For now, they're staying in the Hastingses' bed and breakfast, both tonight and tomorrow. But they have reservations at the hotel, and they will be moving over there as soon as it opens. They've been grilling Bertha Hastings and everyone else about the hauntings."

"That's not good."

"Of course, we're worried they might stir up trouble for the ladies by reporting the place is haunted to discourage people from staying there. But what we're really concerned about is that they'll learn that something a lot more serious than ghosts exists in the area."

"*Lupus garous.*"

"Yes. Us."

"You want me to get rid of them?" CJ asked, surprised. Not that he thought Darien wanted him to kill anyone, but keeping their wolf halves secret was paramount to their well-being.

Tom chuckled. "No. But you're assigned to watch over them. If they see anyone shift when they shouldn't, then we'll have to take care of it."

CJ's whole outlook brightened. "Right. They're staying at the hotel." And if he had to really watch them, he'd have to stay there too! That meant he could see Laurel more.

"Can you handle it?"

"Hell yeah."

"I mean…" Tom glanced around the tavern where pack members filled nearly every chair at the wooden tables. The room was humming with conversation. He leaned forward. "Because of the ghosts."

"That don't exist."

"Right."

"Yeah, I can handle it." CJ smiled. He would do anything to be able to spend more time with that wickedly intriguing she-wolf. Though he hoped he wouldn't be

running out of the hotel and breaking out into a cold
sweat—again.

More than that, he knew something else was going
on. The women didn't just buy the hotel because it was
a beautiful building or a great investment opportunity,
or because they desperately wanted to join a pack.
They'd been reservedly friendly. Like they didn't trust
anyone. And they hadn't joined in any pack functions
during the six months they'd been renovating the hotel.
Not once.

Of course, they said it all had to do with getting the
place ready, and they were too busy or too tired afterward to participate. But he'd noticed the looks between
the three sisters when he'd asked them why they had
chosen this hotel to buy. It was as if they had some deep,
dark secret, and they had to keep it that way.

So yeah, he was definitely interested in Laurel, but
not just because she was a hot she-wolf. He wanted to
know what she and her sisters were *really* doing here.

*The adventure continues with the first in
the Silver Town Wolf Untamed series*

*Between a Wolf
and a Hard Place*

WOLF SHIFTER BRETT SILVER HAS AN ULTERIOR
motive when he donates a grand piano to the newly
remodeled Silver Town Hotel—to get closer to the
owner, beautiful she-wolf Ellie MacTire. But Ellie's
frustrated by Brett's refusal to believe in her unique
ability to commune with the dead. As they wrangle
over the piano, and mysterious guests who are causing
trouble throughout the town, Brett questions how one
gift could turn so complicated—when what he wants is
to win Ellie over for good.

Coming soon from Sourcebooks Casablanca

Acknowledgments

Thanks to Donna Fournier, who always helps me so much with brainstorming and catching mistakes. And thanks to my editor, Deb Werksman; the cover artists; Amelia Narigon, who helps with promotion; and Sara Hartman-Seeskin, who is helping to bring the books to life in audiobook form.

About the Author

Bestselling and award-winning author Terry Spear has written over sixty paranormal romance novels and several medieval Highland historical romances. Her first werewolf romance, *Heart of the Wolf*, was named a 2008 *Publishers Weekly* Best Book of the Year, and her subsequent titles have garnered high praise and hit the *USA Today* bestseller list. A retired officer of the U.S. Army Reserves, Terry lives in Spring, Texas, where she is working on her next werewolf romance; continuing her series about shape-shifting jaguars and cougars and starting a new bear shifter series; having fun with her young adult novels; and playing with her two Havanese puppies, Max and Tanner. For more information, please visit www.terryspear.com or follow her on Twitter @TerrySpear. She is also on Facebook at www.facebook.com/terry.spear. And on Wordpress at http://terryspear.wordpress.com.